Holding tightly to Damon's hand, Jenna pushed forward through the crowd, past the podium and down Memorial Steps.

She caught a glimpse of Detectives Mariano and Gaines as they rushed over to the scene of the disturbance. "I want to see what's up."

It took her and Damon a while to get through the sudden crush of onlookers, and when they finally did, what she saw made her heart flutter in her chest. A thick, sour sensation filled her stomach.

Sitting on the ground was a black girl. Her legs were splayed out awkwardly in front of her, and she was rocking back and forth, holding both hands to the side of her head where blood seeped out from between her fingers.

Jenna pushed up beside Danny Mariano. "What happened?"

Danny gestured vaguely. "Looks like he jumped her. Even with a big crowd like this around." He shook his head. "I just don't—"

D0836238

christopher golden
SKIN DEEP

A *Body of Evidence*
thriller starring Jenna Blake

POCKET PULSE
New York London Toronto Sydney Singapore

This book is a work of fiction. Names, characters, places and incidents are products of the author's imagination or are used fictitiously. Any resemblance to actual events or locales or persons, living or dead, is entirely coincidental.

An *Original* Publication of POCKET BOOKS

 POCKET PULSE published by
Pocket Books, a division of Simon & Schuster, Inc.
1230 Avenue of the Americas, New York, NY 10020

ISBN: 0-671-77583-9

First Pocket Pulse printing October 2000

10 9 8 7 6 5 4 3 2

POCKET PULSE and colophon are trademarks of Simon & Schuster, Inc.

Front cover illustration by Kamil Vojnar

Printed in the U.S.A.

for Lisa Delissio

acknowledgments

Special thanks to Rick Hautala, whose contributions to this book were invaluable. Welcome aboard. Thanks also to Connie and the boys; my agent, Lori Perkins; my editor, Lisa Clancy; and her team, Liz Shiflett (keeper of the map!) and Micol Ostow. Thanks to Dr. Jennifer Keates and Dr. Carlos Baleeir.

SKIN DEEP

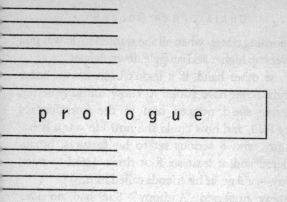

prologue

Brittany felt lucky.

It was the dead of winter in New England, the end of January, the time of year when a long romantic stroll is usually out of the question. After Christmas break she had returned to the Somerset University campus from her home in West Virginia to find a barren, frigid wasteland. According to some of her friends who lived locally, there had been snow in the Boston area for Christmas, and then off and on for a week or so. It warmed up enough the Wednesday after New Year's to melt what was there. From that day on, there had been nothing but cold.

When classes resumed almost two weeks ago, Brittany and her friends spent most of their time indoors, studying or watching movies. There were no snowball fights, no sledding, no snowmen. It seemed too cold even to snow. The campus lawns were frozen and brittle, and it was harder than ever to make it to those early morning classes when all she wanted to do was pull her covers up higher and snuggle down deeper.

On the other hand, if it hadn't been for the snow she might never have gotten to know Anthony better. Of course she'd noticed him in the corridors of Bentley Hall, and how could she not? He was a handsome guy with a serious set to his features, broad-shouldered and at least six foot three. Hard to miss, Anthony—or Ant, as his friends called him.

Brittany preferred "Anthony." She had no idea where "Ant" had come from, but she suspected it was a football thing. Anthony Williams played for the Somerset Colts. Though he was a freshman, she'd been told he had done very well that first year. Not that Brittany paid any attention to sports, but she had friends who did.

So she'd noticed him, sure. But she was a junior, two years older than Anthony. He spent a lot of his time either out of the dorm or hanging around with his crew. When she did see him on his own, studying in the common area or walking to class, he always seemed grim and silent. So quiet.

But in the first week of second semester, that had changed. Anthony was still far from talkative, but he *did* talk to her. Brittany had been curled up in an uncomfortable lime green chair in the common area reading *R. L.'s Dream* by Walter Mosley when Anthony came back from a class. She looked up, smiled, and he nodded and continued toward his room.

He came back.

In a shy, tentative way, he struck up a conversation

about Mosley, and she discovered there was more to
Anthony Williams than football and broad shoulders.
Though he was a freshman, she felt in some ways that
he was much older.

Since then a week had passed, a span of days in
which nearly every moment she was not in class had
been spent with Anthony. Nights out in Cambridge or
in Lafford Square and a party at the Arts House put
them in public together, and some of her friends were
a bit surprised that Brittany would date a freshman.
But they didn't know him. Anthony didn't say much,
but he had romance in his soul. They sat in Brittany's
dorm room—a single, the benefit of being an upperclassman—and listened to music and talked only a
little.

It was nice.

Over the weekend, the temperatures had dipped so
low that the campus was like a ghost town. Though
January was supposed to be a new beginning, Brittany
found that in New England it was a depressing time of
year. The winter blues came down hard on her. Or
they usually did. The stretch between New Year's Day
and Valentine's normally seemed eternal, and this cold
would only have made it that much worse. But
Anthony changed that.

Calm down, she had told herself a dozen times. *It's
only a little more than a week. They're all dogs inside. Not
all the same kind of dog, but all dogs. Give him time to show
it before you get silly over him.*

On Monday the weather had changed abruptly. From
eighteen degrees the day before—and much colder with

the wind-chill—it surged to nearly fifty by eleven in the morning. Overnight it only dropped to thirty. Then, this morning, Brittany had woken up to snow.

Thirty-two degrees, according to the blond on the morning news, just cold enough for snow. It came down all day, fat and lazy, and by dinnertime seven inches of white had blanketed the campus. They had eaten fried scrod at Nadel Dining Hall, and then Anthony had suggested they walk. She had gazed up into his eyes and seen something simple and wonderful there. And he had smiled sweetly, knowingly.

Now, hand in hand, they weaved through campus on freshly shoveled paths. Brittany shivered and Anthony put an arm around her and pulled her tightly to him. She had been all but buried in her winter coat, but tonight she wore only a black leather jacket her parents had given her for Christmas, as well as gloves and a scarf. Anthony had his Somerset Colts football jacket on, the nickname Ant sewn onto the breast.

Together, they were warm. The snow had all but ended, save for a few fat flakes that still twirled slowly to the ground. There was very little wind. The sky had begun to clear and stars were peeking through. The evergreens and bare oaks that dotted the campus lawns were heavy with the fresh snow, which glistened in the light thrown by streetlamps.

Wandering along the paved paths, they passed several other couples who had apparently had the same idea, and two groups of guys whose cabin fever had resulted in their getting very drunk the first day out of the cold snap. And the second. As they walked up the stairs cut into the hill that stretched between the President's House to the left and Mayer Library to the right, they heard wild laughter, cursing, and even a little shriek of pleasure.

"What are they doing over there?" Anthony asked.

"Traying."

"Traying?"

"They steal trays from one of the dining halls and sled on them."

Anthony frowned and tilted his head doubtfully to one side. Then he shook it slowly, as if to say *damn fools, that's not sledding*. Which was almost exactly what Brittany said the first time she had seen students traying on the hill.

Under her breath, barely loud enough for Anthony to hear, she sang a verse of "Winter Wonderland," snatched from the ether to appear on her lips almost before her brain was aware. It was long past Christmas, but everything around them evoked the feeling of the holiday—or at least that archetypal holiday everyone wished it could be. The mythical Christmas, the winter wonderland.

She was astonished when Anthony began to sing the next verse. Though low, his voice was smooth and clear as crystal, a gospel voice, though she doubted he spent much time in church.

"What?" he asked when he caught her staring.

But Brittany could see a mischievous twinkle in his eye she had never noticed there before. Beneath the silence and the brooding and the thoughtful remarks, this was Anthony.

"You sing beautifully. Have you ever done anything with it? Choir or theater, anything?"

He shook his head. "That's all Brick's thing."

"Brick" was his roommate, James Bricker. Another one of those nicknames, like Ant. Brittany understood what Anthony meant. Brick was into theater. Not necessarily musical theater, either. First semester, he'd been in a Somerset production of *A Soldier's Story*, and by all reports, he'd been excellent.

"Just because Brick does theater, that doesn't mean you can't do some singing yourself. You guys would probably have fun if you did it together some time."

"More likely I'd kill him, spending that much time together."

Brittany laughed, but she could see it was not just a joke. The roommates spent a lot of time in each other's company as it was; Anthony loved Brick, but maybe they spent *enough* time together. She thought it was a shame. Anthony had a nice singing voice, but it was obvious he had no real interest in doing anything with it.

"Well, maybe you can just sing to me," she suggested.

Without cracking a smile, or even glancing at her, his low voice, almost a whisper, went into Louis Armstrong's "What a Wonderful World." Brittany laughed and clung more tightly to him as they passed the library. It was built into the side of the earth, so that downhill, students could enter on the ground floor, but uphill, they could walk up three concrete steps and be on the roof.

At the top of the stairs, with the darkened facade of Brunswick Chapel looming over them, Brittany and Anthony paused. He stopped singing when their lips met. She felt a chill run through her that had nothing to do with winter, and then it turned to heat. When their lips parted, she lay her head on his chest.

"Let's go on the roof," she said.

He laughed and his chest rumbled against her cheek. "They haven't shoveled up there yet."

Brittany saw that he was right. Half a foot of snow draped the library roof in a shapeless white cover. Laughing, she held his hand tightly and pulled him toward it. With an indulgent shake of his head, he allowed her to lead him into the snow and up the steps to the roof.

The view was incredible. The snow had stopped completely now, and from the roof they could see the Boston skyline.

"It's beautiful," Brittany whispered.

Rather than respond with words, Anthony approached her from behind, encircled her with his arms. He kissed the top of her head, then bent to let his lips touch gently upon the goose-pimpled flesh of her neck.

She turned, rose up on the tips of her toes, and kissed him more deeply. Minutes passed. She took her gloves off so she could feel the heat of his hands, touch his face, reach inside his jacket for his warmth. His fingers twined in her hair, caressed her face, and as she studied his eyes, she saw—felt—him opening up to her. Beneath that quiet air, she knew there was something very special. She'd been allowed glimpses of it, but Brittany was starting to think she wanted it all. It worried her. She wasn't used to needing anybody, and she didn't think they'd been together long enough for her to need Anthony.

"You're something," she whispered to him.

He only smiled and kissed her again.

"Maybe we should pick this up back at the dorm?" she suggested.

"Wherever you go, I'll follow," he told her.

God, does that sound like a line. But somehow she knew it wasn't. She gazed up into his eyes for several heartbeats, then sighed, smiled softly, and kissed him again.

"Animals."

With the snow so thick, neither of them had heard anyone approaching. When he spoke, they both turned instantly, alarmed not by his mere presence but by the tone of his voice. So angry. So hostile. So filled with . . . what?

Disgust.

Anthony didn't have a chance to speak. Even as they turned, the shovel cut across the space between them. It was an old-fashioned wood-and-iron tool with a square blade, more appropriate for digging earth than snow. The flat of the blade slammed into Anthony's face with a sickening crack, splaying his shattered nose and spattering blood into the air.

Crimson spattered snow.

Anthony went down, groaning.

It was a white guy, a student, if his Somerset jacket was any indication. A black watch cap was pulled down on his head, but other than that, there was nothing remarkable about him. Except for the shovel in his hands.

Brittany screamed for Anthony to get up, screamed at the son of a bitch who had just attacked him. Screamed for help.

She heard someone respond, not far off. People calling out. Help on the way.

"Your kind just can't keep your hands off each other, can you?" the guy with the shovel said. "Animals, I swear."

Anthony roared, started to lunge at him from the snow. The shovel came down again, striking his skull with a dull thud. Brittany screamed for help and once again someone called a reply. They were coming. They were close.

He went at Anthony again, but she wouldn't let him. Brittany grabbed him from behind, her hands tight on his throat, trying to choke him. Her fingernails dug into his flesh, drawing blood, and he cried out in anger and pain. An elbow rammed into her stomach and she almost threw up, tumbling into the snow.

She stood quickly. He had forgotten about Anthony and was focused only on her now. "Don't come near me," she snarled, backing away, hands in front of her.

He broke her hands with the shovel. As she cried out in pain, he drove it blade first into her gut. Her leather jacket saved her from being cut open, but the wind was forced from her lungs.

Help's on the way, she told herself again. She heard them, so close.

Not close enough.

The shovel fell silently into the powdery snow as he rushed at her. He drove her backward and she slammed her spine against the waist-high concrete retaining wall that ran around the edges of the roof. One more shove, and she was over.

For a single eyeblink, she held on with the tips of the fingers of her left hand. Below, the newly shoveled courtyard in front of the library's entrance had just a dusting of snow covering it.

Brittany didn't scream. The drop from the library's roof to the courtyard was more than thirty feet. Even as she fell, the powdered concrete rushing up to shatter her bones, she could hear the shouts of people who were coming to try to save her. Her sorrow welled up in her, the knowledge that they had been so close bringing a tear to her eye.

It never fell.

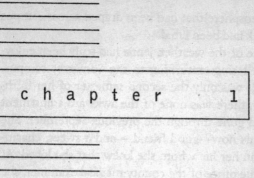

c h a p t e r · 1

There was magic in the world again. Hope. Bright smiles and laughter. That was how Jenna Blake felt on Wednesday morning, walking across the academic quad at Somerset University. A little voice at the back of her head told her she was overdoing it, but she shut the voice out. The week or so since classes had started up again had been bleak and gray and unforgiving, with the wind cold enough to chill the bone, no matter how many layers she wore.

When the snow had come the day before, and it warmed up a little, she was relieved. Even pleased.

But this was another thing entirely. Wednesday morning dawned blue and clear. The sun shone down upon the newfallen snow and glistened, refracting into a million tiny jewels of light. Heavy, wet snow slid off branches as she passed the trees. Students on their way to early classes threw snowballs at one another. The

11

grim atmosphere that had been draped across campus for a week had been lifted.

In spite of the weather, Jenna had truly been enjoying herself since returning to the Somerset campus. Though it was only the second semester of her freshman year, there was none of the awkward adjustment that she'd gone through the previous September. She had friends now—good friends—and a sweet, charming man in her life whom she knew that she loved. At work in the office of the county medical examiner, she felt like part of a team, a vital element of their process.

The first day back, she'd felt some trepidation about her class load. In addition to her history, English, and language courses, all of which fulfilled parts of the university's core curriculum, she was taking both gross anatomy and medical anthropology. Her adviser, Professor Schaeffer, had thought the combination a bit much, even for a premed student. If he was worried, then so was she.

Soon enough, though, she realized she had no reason to be. After the first two gross anatomy classes, she realized that working in the M.E.'s office, transcribing records, sitting in on autopsies, and even participating in a few had given her a huge head start over the other students. Medical anthropology wasn't going to be as easy, but it was fascinating.

All in all, coming back to campus felt a lot like resuming adult life. This was home for her, at least for a while. The colonial forty minutes away in Natick, Massachusetts, was just her mother's house now.

Still, cheery as she'd been since coming back to

Somerset, Jenna had sensed how grumpy the weather had made everyone and toned down her own attitude accordingly. When one was aggravated, there was nothing worse than being around an incessantly happy person. She remembered wanting to whack her roommate, Yoshiko, a couple of times for just that little crime last semester.

Now that the weather had broken, however, and particularly with the beautiful cover of snow, she figured everyone could get back to the business of enjoying the college adventure.

Of course, that was before she saw the yellow police tape that declared the library roof off-limits. A pair of police cars were parked half on the grass in front of Brunswick Chapel. An officer stood talking to a couple of plainclothes cops Jenna didn't recognize, and a second uniform was holding back half a dozen inquisitive students, giving them what little information he could.

"What now?" she whispered to herself.

A small fire burned in her gut like a white-hot coal. She shook it off. Police cars did not automatically mean she had to investigate. It was none of her business. Right now, getting an education was her only business. Gross anatomy was waiting. Normally she might have been more actively curious, tried to find out what was going on. But at that moment, she really didn't want to know.

Things had been floating along pretty nicely. But now, as she went on her way to class and passed more yellow tape that cordoned off a part of the courtyard in front of the entrance to the library, the contentment she had felt began to dissipate quickly.

This semester was supposed to be different, she reminded herself. *How much can happen on one campus?*

Jenna realized she didn't have an informed answer to that question and tried to let it go. It wasn't going to be that easy, though. She knew that. By the time morning classes were over and she went to lunch, the story—whatever it was—would have begun to make the rounds. And if she didn't hear it there, well, she had work at Dr. Slikowski's that afternoon. If someone had been killed, whether by murder or accident, she'd find out about it then.

For the rest of the morning, she just wanted to enjoy herself, and the superior feeling she had in gross anatomy. She tried, but in that class and in Europe from 1815, which came right after it, her mind kept drifting back to the ominous yellow tape stenciled with the words Police Line Do Not Cross over and over.

Keates Dining Hall was loud and busy that day. Jenna was a little startled by that. The positive energy that had been crackling all morning still seemed in effect, despite whatever business the police had had on campus. *Maybe it wasn't anything too serious after all*, she told herself. *Maybe your intuition is on the fritz.*

That would be nice.

She passed on the meal that vaguely resembled some kind of meat and went with what was quickly becoming her usual campus food safety: tuna sandwich and nachos. In line, she ran into Roseanne Kerner, a girl who was in her medical anthropology class, and they sat down together in front of the long row of windows at the back of the dining hall. Outside they could see Carpenter Street, and Jenna imagined she could hear the shush of tires in melting snow as the cars sped by.

Roseanne got her mind off things. She was from Weston, a wealthy community not far from where Jenna had grown up, and they found that they knew a few people in common. Her straight blond hair was shoulder length, her features so thin and pixieish she didn't look much older than thirteen. Jenna wondered if Roseanne ever had trouble being taken seriously because she looked so young.

"So what do you think of class so far?" Roseanne asked.

"Very cool," Jenna enthused. "I actually look forward to doing the readings."

The other girl stared at her in horror.

Jenna shrugged awkwardly. "But not in a really geeky, teacher's pet kind of way."

They both laughed at that. Roseanne shook her head in amazement.

"I wish I could be that enthusiastic. Maybe we could study together when the tests come up. I have a feeling I'm going to be lost in the shuffle in there. I'm interested in medicine, but pretty much from the organizational end of things. The health care system, pharmaceutical companies, all of that. The rise of evil HMOs."

"Okay, now who's geeky?" Jenna teased.

Roseanne shot her a withering look, but couldn't hide a smirk. Jenna knew then that she'd found a new friend.

"So do you want to be a doctor?" the other girl asked.

The answer to that was very complicated, and Jenna didn't really have the time to get into it. She had to work that afternoon, which meant rushing back to the dorm to change into something more office-appropriate than blue jeans and a sweatshirt. Plus some people thought that it was weird for a person her age to be working with dead bodies every day.

"Something like that," she replied, and let it stand at that for the moment.

Vowing to get together again, the girls said their good-byes and Jenna hustled the short distance across campus to her dormitory, Sparrow Hall. It was a beautiful old stone building with Gothic peaks and ledges that sat at about the midpoint of the uphill part of the campus, between a quad surrounded by dormitories and one surrounded by academic buildings.

Jenna went up the stairs to the third floor, which was split between male and female students. The guys were all on one end, and the girls on the other, with a carpeted common area in between. Jenna lived in Room 311 with Yoshiko Kitsuta, who had quickly become one of her best friends. She'd heard a lot of roommate horror stories and felt lucky to have Yoshiko.

On the door to 311, a note was scrawled on the message board. "Dinner at Nadel tonight?" it read. It was signed "Y & H." Yoshiko's boyfriend, Hunter, lived just down the hall, only a few rooms away from Jenna's boyfriend, Damon Harris. It had seemed weird at first, too convenient, having them both so close by. What were the odds of that? But Jenna decided just to appreciate the confluence of destiny instead of questioning it.

Thoughts of Damon tempted her to head down the hall to see if he was in. They hadn't been back long enough for her to memorize his schedule as well as her own. But a quick glance at her watch told her she didn't have time to snuggle with her guy, not even briefly. She felt a pang of regret about that.

Then another, when she remembered the police presence on campus that morning. *Why are you in such a rush?* she asked herself. There was no answer. *'Cause if there was an answer, that would mean I'm insane, so it's for the best.*

Jenna enjoyed her job. Didn't mind working with the dead at all—or not much at least—not even the particularly gruesome murder and accident victims they'd worked on. The one thing she didn't like was working on cadavers her own age. Worse yet, Somerset students. There'd been a few of those and that was too many. During first semester Jenna's best friend, Melody—Hunter's sister—had been one of them, and she had found out the hard way, by walking in on the autopsy.

She shook the memory off.

Five minutes later, she was ready to go. That morning she'd been in the comfort zone, jeans and sneakers

17

and a Somerset sweatshirt. Since she spent most of her time at work in the office, she needed to look more professional than that, so she'd made a quick change into black Banana Republic pants, an ivory turtleneck, and ankle-high black boots that were, as she'd told her mother, sort of for snow and sort of for show.

As she pulled on her leather jacket, someone knocked on the door.

"Who is it?"

"Jenna, it's me."

Damon.

She wore a grin as she opened the door, but it disappeared the moment she saw the expression on her boyfriend's face. Damon was very handsome, with a maturity to his dark features that made him even better looking. Jenna had never seen him look so grim. Behind him stood Brick, one of his best friends. Brick was almost always joking around, giving her a hard time. Whatever was on his mind now, it wasn't a joke.

"God, what's wrong?" Jenna asked.

Who died? The words almost made it to her lips, not an honest inquiry, but the kind of joke people always made when someone was behaving a bit too seriously.

Damon's frown deepened. "You haven't heard about last night?"

Jenna shook her head. She stood aside to let them in, and they entered in silence. Brick was fidgety, rubbing his hands together, then scratching at the back of his neck. After a moment, he leaned against Yoshiko's desk, his foot tapping with nervous energy.

Once the door was shut, Damon started to speak

and faltered. His face twisted up with emotion, and Jenna went to him.

"Hey," she said, her voice soothing.

"Brittany's dead."

"The girl Ant was dating?"

He nodded. There it was. Her intuition had been right all along. *And hadn't you known it would be?* she thought. Ever since she'd seen the police tape that morning she was dreading news like this, but now that it was here, she felt almost relieved. *If this is what it is, I can handle it. Maybe even do something about it.* It was awful. But in her job, there was a great deal of awful. Dr. Slikowski, the M.E., had told her she'd get used to it. She figured maybe he was right, but she wasn't there yet. Wasn't sure she ever wanted to be.

"She was murdered?" Jenna asked.

"Last night," Damon confirmed.

Jenna went to her own desk and picked up a snake-like plastic puzzle, fiddled with it as she went over in her mind the things she had seen that morning.

"Someone threw her off the library roof," she said.

Damon blinked in surprise. But at the other desk across the room, Brick's expression was almost angry.

"How did you know that?" he demanded.

Jenna explained about the tape and the police. Damon nodded as he took that in, but Brick just shook his head.

"It wasn't just Brittany," Damon explained, gesturing almost imperceptibly toward Brick, as if to offer an apology for his surliness. "We didn't know her that well, but Ant was with her. Whoever killed her beat him something fierce with a shovel, busted up his head. He's over at the medical center now."

Jenna felt a little pain in her gut, like her stomach had made a fist. "He's going to be all right, though. Isn't he?"

"He should be."

She went to him then. The pain in his eyes tore at her own heart. Jenna didn't know Brittany at all, but she certainly knew Anthony and liked him quite a bit, though he didn't have a tenth of Damon's charisma or Brick's flamboyance. The girl was dead, and that was horrible enough. Thoughts of her parents and what they must be going through made Jenna wince. But Anthony was a friend.

"Damon, I'm sorry," she whispered.

She hugged him tight and he held on like he was afraid he might float away if he let go. Jenna was relatively tall, but she had to rise up a little on her toes to kiss him properly. For the moment, she pressed her lips to his stubbly cheek and then his throat, and just held on.

After a moment, she remembered Brick and broke away from Damon. Anthony was Brick's roommate, probably his best friend. No wonder he was behaving so oddly. She knew it must be tearing him apart.

"Hey," she said as she went to take Brick's hand. "He'll be okay."

"Yeah," Brick replied, but it was noncommittal. Almost a grunt.

"Really," she insisted. "Somerset Medical Center has some of the best doctors in New England, and that's really saying something. He'll be okay."

He almost scowled when he looked at her, and Jenna flinched, surprised by the anger on his features.

"He might get better, Jenna. You're right about that. He's a tough one, so yeah, okay, he'll probably heal up pretty good. But some nasty, sneaky white boy beat the crap out of him with a shovel and murdered his girlfriend, all 'cause they're black. I think it's a little premature to say he's gonna be okay, don't you?"

"Brick," Damon said sternly.

Jenna's gaze darted from one to the other, mind racing, heart pumping. What had she said? All she had wanted was to comfort him somehow.

Nasty, sneaky white boy. The words reverberated in her mind.

The last thing she wanted was to believe that Brick didn't want her comfort because she was white, but once the thought entered her mind, she couldn't rid herself of it.

She swallowed, glanced quickly at Brick and then back at Damon, shaking her head. "They know it was a racial crime?"

"Ant came around long enough to tell them that much," Damon said, eyes roving around the room, uncomfortable with the tension Brick's outburst had created. "Guy said some things. And no question he's white. There were four witnesses."

"Witnesses?" Jenna repeated brightly. "But that's great. The cops should have no trouble finding him."

"You'd think," Damon agreed. "Problem is, from

what I hear not one of the descriptions matches up to another. The clothes, yeah, but they don't have much more that's solid."

"The witnesses were all white, too," Brick added.

Jenna looked at him, a pain she could not explain spiking through her, making her feel nauseous and angry and unclean all at the same time.

"Brick," she pleaded.

Maybe he saw some of that pain in her eyes, because he softened a bit. Through what Jenna knew must be the haze of his own pain, Brick seemed to really see her for the first time.

He stepped away from the desk. "I'm sorry, J. It's just . . . the guy *killed* her. Ant was falling hard for this girl, and that guy killed her. Never mind what they did to him. You should see him."

"I will. I have to work this afternoon. I'll go up and see him when I'm off."

Damon reached out and massaged her shoulder gently, almost absentmindedly. "You're working. Think they'll do Brittany's autopsy over there?"

She nodded slowly.

Damon's expression was intense. "I know you're not supposed to talk about stuff when there's an investigation going on—"

"If I find anything out, I'll let you know," she promised. Jenna reached to her shoulder and took his hand, then kissed it. Then she put a hand behind his head and pulled him down for a real kiss.

"I love you," she whispered.

She shot a glance at Brick. "You too."

A pained smile flickered across Brick's features. He nodded.

Damon pulled her close again, and they stood that way for a minute. He was in such pain, yet holding it so tightly to him, that in a way she felt closer to him than ever before.

But the tension that had been in the room only minutes before lingered with her, like a specter, for the rest of the day.

Somerset Medical Center (SMC)—a teaching hospital affiliated with the university's medical school right next door—was across Carpenter Street from the main campus. It sat upon the tree-lined hill overlooking Somerset and Medford. The emergency entrance and parking lot were on the opposite side, but the main entrance was there among the trees, beautified so that it looked very little like a hospital.

Jenna's mind was clear as she went in, past the patient check-in and visitor information desks, and then by elevator up to the second-floor administrative wing. At a T-junction, she turned down a short corridor and was not at all surprised to find the door to the medical examiner's office locked.

Grimly, she removed her key card and used it to gain entry, then went in and put her jacket over the back of the chair at her cubicle. No sign of Dr. Slikowski, or of Al Dyson, the pathology resident who was the primary member of Dr. Slikowski's support staff.

Jenna sat behind her desk and stared at the phone. No messages. No notes from either of the doctors. Just a couple of audiotapes, verbal autopsy records that needed to be transcribed, along with the charts that went with the cadavers.

The office was one medium-size room with three cubicles, one each for Jenna and Dyson, and a third for whatever resident or student might be helping out or doing a minirotation through the office. Most of them didn't even bother to tell Jenna their names. There was an interior office as well, where Slick—Dr. Slikowski— did most of his paperwork, prepared for the lectures he gave at the medical school, and often met with representatives from a number of local police departments who consulted with him on various cases.

It was too quiet in there. When Slick was around, jazz music always filtered out into the main office area. The phone was unusually silent as well. No transcription tapes playing, no printers humming, and no Al Dyson shooting the breeze. Normally it would have been a great work environment. Jenna might have gotten a lot done.

She picked up the phone and dialed the extension for the autopsy room. It took Dyson four rings to pick it up.

"Autopsy."

"Dyson, it's Jenna."

He didn't say anything at first. His silence told her all she needed to know.

"You've got a subject down there, Brittany Forrester? Somerset student."

"That's right," he said cautiously.

"I'd like to come down. Assist, if you could use the help."

"Hang on, Jenna."

He put Slick on. The M.E. didn't waste any time getting to the point.

"Maybe you should sit this one out, Jenna. It's fairly brutal, and I know it bothers you when the victim is—"

"I'd like to help," she interrupted.

He paused, but only for a moment. "By all means. We were actually just beginning. I'll wait for you."

The autopsy room was in the basement, next door to the morgue. Oddly enough, despite all the things Jenna had seen in the autopsy room, it was the morgue that bothered her. She'd never quite understood why. When she thought about it—which wasn't much; she preferred not to let her mind wander in that direction—she thought it might have to do with how quiet the morgue always was. And how *outnumbered* she always felt in there. The autopsy room had a medical purpose, but the morgue, that was *their* place.

The dead ones.

Dyson had white scrubs ready for her when she walked into the autopsy room. She was surprised to note that Brittany's corpse was covered. That was unusual. What it indicated was that the body was in such bad condition that one or both of the doctors didn't want to have to look at it.

Jenna wondered if she had made the right decision, coming down here.

And why had she? What had made her feel so determined to involve herself in the girl's murder? She had a habit of becoming too involved in the cases they

worked on; it was one of the traits she shared with
Slick, and it had put her in danger a number of times.
The more mysterious the death, the more it got under
her skin. Every cadaver that came across that table had
left loved ones behind, survivors who needed answers
to the puzzle of sudden death. Helping to provide
those answers, to allow those people to rest easier,
made Jenna feel wonderful. The grim reality of the job
was a necessity to achieve that end result.

But there was more to this one. The girl was a
Somerset student, two years older than she was. It was
the sort of thing that normally unnerved her even
more than usual. And it did this time as well, she
couldn't deny that. So why?

Simple enough: Damon. Damon and Brick; and the
expression on Brick's face when he'd snapped at her.
She wanted to see this one wrapped up as quickly as
possible and was willing to do whatever it took to help
make that happen.

When she had her scrubs on, Jenna went to join
Dyson and Slick at the autopsy table. The M.E. sat in his
wheelchair at the stainless steel table, white mask covering his features, save for the eyes with which he regarded
her closely from behind wire-rimmed spectacles.

"You don't really need to be here, you know," he
told her. "It might take some time, and I don't want to
keep you too long."

With her own mask on, he couldn't see the small
smile on Jenna's face. Though only in his mid-forties,
Walter Slikowski often spoke with the primness and air
of propriety more commonly found in a very old man.

"I'm good. Let's get to work."

Slick glanced at Dyson, who raised an eyebrow as he in turn regarded Jenna. She sighed. They both got the message. These two men wanted to protect her, and she loved them for it. But she also wished they would realize that when she needed protection, she would be more than happy to ask for it.

The M.E. used controls on the side of the table to lower it so that it leveled just above his knees. It was an unusual setup, rigged so that he could perform autopsies despite his disability. While the table went down, Jenna moved behind him and began to pull gleaming steel instruments from a drawer and place them on a metal tray.

"Did you know her?" Dyson asked.

Jenna shook her head. She looked at him, or what she could see of him, kind eyes and olive skin. He was a good friend. Slick was her mentor, yes, but Dyson was like a big brother, always watching out for her.

"She was the girlfriend of a friend. I only met her once, and then only in passing in the dining hall."

They turned together to see that Slick was ready. He nodded, and Dyson peeled the sheet down off the corpse, letting it drop to pool on the floor at the far end of the table.

Jenna said nothing. She sucked in a quick breath through her nose, the smell of formaldehyde that saturated the room burning her nostrils, and then she shuddered. Brittany's arms and legs were broken and misshapen. Most of the breaks were beneath the skin, but her right forearm and left femur had been shattered so violently that the jagged edges of bone had torn through.

Her face was a wreck, mainly because her skull had been splintered upon impact. It wasn't the first fall victim Jenna had seen, but it was equally repulsive the second time. In a couple of places, her scalp had ripped open, showing bloodstained bone and gray matter inside.

Despite her horror, Jenna kept her revulsion to herself.

The autopsy had begun, and any speculation, even to the most obvious aspects of the subject's death, were unwelcome outside of procedure. Dyson handed her the controls for the enormous X-ray camera setup above the table, and Jenna used it to take half a dozen shots of the corpse from various distances. With all the broken bones, they'd want a clearer picture of her skeleton than they'd get from needlessly cutting her up. If there was anything odd about the breaks, the M.E. could always investigate further.

Slick clicked on the recorder.

"Autopsy 023-472-03; subject Brittany Forrester; African-American female; age twenty; height five feet five inches; weight one hundred thirty five pounds; surgical scar on right knee; otherwise no visible birthmarks, tattoos, or other distinguishing marks. Navel and eyebrow piercings indicated."

From that point, it was pretty much by the numbers. As he talked, Jenna logged the markings and wounds—such as the girl's broken fingers—on a sheet. Then Slick used a scalpel to make a huge Y-shaped incision in Brittany's chest, and peeled back the skin. A bone saw was used to remove segments of the ribs and sternum to give them access to the internal organs.

Jenna knew that none of them expected to find anything out of the ordinary in there; but they never knew. Slick had been firm about teaching her that. There was no way to know until you looked. Organs were removed, and Jenna took tissue samples of them while Dyson helped Slick check the body cavities for fluids. There were urinary samples and a check of her stomach contents, and a million other little details, all of which Jenna had observed dozens of times, and assisted with on a number of occasions.

The examination of the skull and brain were far more difficult than usual.

In the end, of course, Slick would rule the cause of death to be massive bodily trauma caused by the fall. His report would also note that broken fingers and bruises indicated that she had been attacked immediately before her fall and was therefore likely pushed or thrown from the roof.

Simple.

But hours after they had begun, as Jenna was scraping beneath the dead girl's fingernails for samples of her killer's flesh—from which she hoped the police might get a useful DNA sample—she knew that there was going to be nothing simple about this case.

Murder was never simple.

Add race to the mix, and what one had was a powder keg, waiting to explode.

c h a p t e r 2

Beneath flannel sheets and a thick comforter stitched with a floral pattern, Jenna drifted in and out of sleep, burrowing contentedly. Twice she had woken almost completely, glanced at the sun streaming through the window and at the alarm clock on her desk, and realized that it was Thursday morning and she had Spanish in half an hour. If she wanted to make it to class, she knew she should get up. It was too early in the semester to start skipping classes.

The window was open a crack—the dormitory heat made the room terribly dry and sleep not very comfortable, so fresh air was a necessity. Earlier in the week, it had simply been too cold to leave the window open even a little. But that morning the brisk air felt wonderful.

At eight-thirty, Jenna stretched, appreciating the warmth of her bed for a last moment before throwing back the covers and sitting up. Her stomach rumbled. Soundlessly, she padded barefoot across the room to the small refrigerator and took out a cherry vanilla yogurt. Digging around in the plastic milk crate that passed for a cupboard, she found some granola and sprinkled it into the yogurt.

She sat down at her desk to eat, humming to herself softly. On the desk lay her copy of Peter Straub's novel *Mr. X*, her leather Somerset University bookmark jutting from its pages. An excellent book, but it was creeping her out.

"You're happy this morning."

"Yaaah!" Jenna shouted.

She nearly knocked the yogurt off her desk as she turned around, startled, heart thudding in her chest, to see her roommate, Yoshiko Kitsuta, sitting up in the top bunk across the room.

"You scared the hell out of me."

"Sorry," Yoshiko said, coughing a bit. "You woke me up."

"Sick?"

"I feel awful." Yoshiko sniffled a bit. Her voice sounded hoarse.

"Yeah? You should see how you look," Jenna teased. "I thought you went to class. You were so quiet I had no idea you were still here."

"It's called sleeping," Yoshiko said drily, a bit more sarcastic than usual.

Jenna chalked it up to her cold. "Sorry I woke you," she said.

"Nah. I have to get up anyway. If I'm going to be in bed all day, I should at least try to get some studying done."

31

"Or you could sit around reading and watching TV. Not that I would ever do such a thing, of course."

Yoshiko smiled at last. "Of course," she said, adding another cough for punctuation. "Not you. The girl who has class in, what, seventeen minutes?"

When Jenna was sick, she had a tendency to become a big baby about it. Soup. Hot chocolate. Old movies on TV. Those were the cure-alls as far as she was concerned. A good book helped, too.

"Just laying out your options for you, and never mind about me," she told Yoshiko. "See, now aren't you glad you gave up the paradise of Hawaii to go to college in New England?"

"You're a cruel person, Jenna," Yoshiko muttered, burying her face in her pillow.

"Yep," she agreed. "That's what they tell me."

On the brick wall behind Jenna hung a huge poster of Hawaii that Yoshiko had hung on their first day in the dorm. Jenna glanced longingly at it and wished that they were all in Hawaii.

"So why so happy, anyway?" Yoshiko asked, on her side now, peeking down from the top bunk.

Jenna shrugged. "The weather, I guess. Plus I got to sleep, which is nice. Am I not supposed to be in a good mood?"

Yoshiko grumbled. "Not when I'm sick."

"Oh, right, I'll see what I can do. Go back to sleep, grumpy. Studying will wait."

"Maybe just a few minutes," Yoshiko suggested, almost as though she were asking for permission.

"I'll wake you before I leave for class," Jenna promised.

Nodding, already surrendering to her pillow, Yoshiko put her head back down and closed her eyes. Jenna was jealous. She doubted it would be worth a cold, but she would not mind staying in bed all day with a good book.

Or her boyfriend.

A secret smile played at the corners of her mouth, then disappeared into a frown. Thoughts of Damon, even the nicest ones, invariably led to thoughts of Brittany's murder and Ant's hospitalization. Jenna had visited him the previous afternoon before coming home from work, but he had been sleeping, and she had not wanted to wake him. She planned to try again.

The killer was still out there, but the Somerset cops were on the case. Jenna had faith in them. From the sound of it, they could not even be certain that the attacker meant to kill Brittany rather than simply beating them both. Jenna hoped that was the case and that he would either reveal himself and be caught or had taken off to avoid capture.

One way or another, it would be better all around if there was a quick end to things.

With Yoshiko sleeping once again, Jenna pulled a robe over the flannel pajama top she wore and went down the hall to take a shower. Her auburn hair had grown longer, and she had decided to let it continue for a while. It took more time to deal with in the morning, unless she wanted a ponytail, but that was okay. It was nice to have a change.

When Jenna returned to her room, her hair wrapped in a towel on top of her head, Yoshiko was not alone.

Hunter LaChance was also a freshman, and he lived down on the guys' end of Sparrow's third floor. The three of them had been friends since the first week of school, and the tall, thin, blond southerner was also Yoshiko's boyfriend. His older sister, Melody, to whom Jenna had been quite close, had been murdered the previous semester. None of them had quite gotten over it, but in some ways, it made Hunter and Jenna closer than before.

"Hey, Hunter," Jenna said as she entered. "What are you doing? We're quarantined. Didn't you know?"

"Mornin,' Jenna," Hunter replied, New Orleans accent kicking in. "That's a nice look for you."

"Isn't it, though?" she replied. Then she held the door open for him. "Step out a minute, will you, Mr. Smartass?"

Hunter feigned a hurt expression and Jenna laughed as he walked dejectedly from the room. She dressed as quickly as she could. While she was pulling her jeans on, Yoshiko got out of bed and plugged in the hot plate.

Jenna watched her roommate as she prepared to heat a small pot of water. "Soup?"

"Tea."

"Should I let him back in?" Jenna asked, a little too loudly.

Yoshiko smiled. "I suppose so."

"I heard that!" Hunter shouted from outside the door.

Jenna let him in and he grumbled good-naturedly at both of them. He went to sit on the floor, leaning against the wall between Jenna's bed and the radiator.

Yoshiko sat at Jenna's desk while the water heated up for her tea.

"You guys see the news?" Hunter asked. When both girls looked at him blankly, he shook his head in dismay. "That girl's murder is a major story. Press is playing it as a racial thing, though the police are trying to downplay that. They talked about how this was the third student murdered on campus since the beginning of the school year."

Jenna's heart sank.

"Oh, Hunter," Yoshiko said, her voice low.

"They showed Melody's picture," he added. With a sigh, he shook his head. "I hope they get this guy. A mess like this . . . it's all we need around here."

Jenna thought it likely that Hunter was thinking a lot less about the campus in general than about himself, and her, and Yoshiko. None of them needed to be reminded about what they had lost when Melody was murdered.

Yoshiko went to her boyfriend and held him a long moment. When she broke the embrace and looked up at him, Hunter smiled.

"I'm good," he said.

"You guys have class together today, right?" Yoshiko asked.

"Shakespeare," Jenna confirmed. "After Spanish."

"With Professor Fournier," Hunter added, his voice tinged with loathing.

The teakettle whistled and Yoshiko fished a tea bag out of a box of them. "That's the one you hated, right? The new guy?"

Hunter scowled. "What a jerk."

"He really is," Jenna said. "I've never met anybody so arrogant. A couple of people tried to bring up other playwrights in class, but Fournier didn't want to hear it. As far as he's concerned, Shakespeare is it and just about everything else is crap."

Yoshiko frowned. "Sounds like a fun guy."

"I don't know why he would want to teach anyway," Hunter went on. "He treats us all like we're morons. Called the whole class ignorant savages. He's enlightening us or something."

"Why don't you drop the class?" Yoshiko asked.

Jenna and Hunter glanced at each other and shrugged.

"He's annoying, but kind of a blowhard. Not intimidating, really. I need an English credit and I like Shakespeare," Jenna explained.

"Pretty much my position on the subject," Hunter agreed. "As homework goes, I can think of worse things than reading plays. Speaking of which, Jenna, you know they're doing *Little Shop of Horrors* this semester."

The previous semester the school's musical theater group had been prepared to put on *The Sound of Music*. Melody had been given the role of Maria, but had been killed before the show could be performed. It was canceled. Hunter had also been in the cast, and she knew it was a sensitive topic for him.

"Are you going to audition?" Jenna asked.

"I think I might," he confirmed. "I'd be more inclined to do it if you'd come along."

Her immediate response was to say no. But Jenna

hesitated. After a moment, she nodded slightly, thinking of Melody. "Let me think about it," she said.

Hunter smiled. "Great."

"What's great?" Jenna asked defensively.

"He's excited 'cause you're going to audition," Yoshiko explained.

"I didn't say that."

"But you didn't say no," her roommate said patiently. "Which he figures means yes. And he's probably right."

"You've got a couple of weeks to decide," Hunter said expectantly.

Jenna glared at them both, but not with any real malice. They were her closest friends at Somerset, and they knew her very well. Though she was truly not certain whether or not she would audition—she had always wanted to but been too afraid of embarrassing herself—Jenna knew that they were probably right. Annoying as it was in certain respects, it was also very nice to have friends who knew her that well.

Hunter and Yoshiko talked quietly while Jenna finished getting ready. She wore very little makeup, so her hair was the only time-consuming part of her morning ritual. Even that did not take very long. Soon enough, she was ready to go.

"So you want us to bring you anything from the dining hall after lunch?" Hunter asked Yoshiko.

"A couple of oranges, if you can get them. Vitamin C to fight my cold."

"You've got it," he replied, and kissed her on the forehead before following Jenna out of the room.

* * *

After their Shakespeare class, Jenna and Hunter walked across the academic quad to get lunch. The sun and the warmth of the day were melting what little remained of the snow, and it dripped chilly drizzle from the trees and the cornices of buildings. There was half-melted ice on some of the footpaths, but Jenna had worn her boots and did not mind. The day sparkled.

"Too bad Yoshiko's sick," Hunter said sadly. "What a nice day."

"She's from Hawaii," Jenna reminded him. "This probably wouldn't rate all that high on her nice-o-meter."

"Still," he protested.

"So Professor Fournier didn't seem as bad today," she noted.

"I guess," Hunter said hesitantly. "I still say he's a jerk, though. I never met anyone who looked down on other people so much."

Jenna started to reply but stopped herself. She was distracted by the sound of voices, some shouting, nearby. "Do you hear something?"

Hunter did. They hurried along the path until they could see the residential quad up ahead. On the snow-covered grass in front of Keates Hall, dozens of students were gathered; maybe more than a hundred. So many students. And from what she could see from where she stood, the large majority of them were black. Jenna saw several police cars and at least two news vans, one from Fox and another from Channel 7.

"What's going on?" Hunter asked, to no one in particular, as they walked along the edge of the quad, aiming to circumvent the crowd.

Almost in answer, one of the students in the midst of the crowd pushed forward. He had a bullhorn, and there were several very grave looking guys surrounding him, all of them black.

"Where is justice?" the guy shouted over the bullhorn, his voice deep and booming, perfect for the news cameras that were recording his every word. "It has been a long and violent year on this campus. In this city. In this nation. The local authorities have more than proven themselves capable of doing their job in recent months. Something nasty happens, we see them on television. Read about their efforts in the newspaper.

"But where are they now? Now that a black woman has been brutally slaughtered and a black man sent to the hospital by a white man, where are the boys in blue? Have you seen them on the news? Have you read about them in the newspapers? Yes, indeed. But have they talked about what they are doing to find this killer? Not once. Instead, they tell us that there is no reason to believe that race was the reason for this horrifying incident.

"You know as well as I do, my friends, that they say this because they want us to keep calm. They want us to keep silent. They want us to forget what has happened and pay no attention to the fact that they're not really going to expend much energy searching for a white man who murdered a black woman.

"They'll tell us it isn't true," he said, voice lowering. "I would dearly love to believe that. But where is the proof? Where is the justice? Where is the killer? Our

Muslim friends would tell you that we have to embrace our destiny as the chosen race upon this earth. That's not why I'm here.

"I'm here for justice. I'm here because in this nation and in this city and on this campus, black faces are the exception, and not the rule. The mechanism that runs it all is in the hands of white people, and when it comes to the list of priorities, the problems of black people are nowhere near the top of that list.

"That means if we want justice, we have to demand it! We have to scream for it! Cry for it! Roar our fury at the inequity of it all, and show them that the only acceptable outcome is justice!

"Now what do we want?" he screamed.

"Justice!" the crowd shouted back.

"When do we want it?"

"Now!"

The chant took on a life of its own.

Jenna thought that the handful of uniformed police officers and campus security personnel looked very nervous. Several moved closer to the front of the crowd, flanking the guy with the bullhorn. Jenna recognized him from campus but did not know his name.

"This cannot be good," Hunter muttered to her as they moved onto the snow in front of Brackett Hall and toward Keates.

In order to get to the dining hall, they would have to go through the outer edges of the cluster of protesting students. Jenna was certainly not a racist, but she knew she would be a fool to ignore the race-based tension of the people milling about in the snow on the quad.

Though there were a handful of white students among them, most of the protesters were black. They were angry at the way the authorities were handling the investigation into Brittany's murder and had obviously decided to ignore the fact that the state legislature and local law enforcement were hardly all-white.

As they walked up toward the edge of the crowd, Jenna grew nervous.

"Maybe we should go out for lunch?" she suggested, trying to keep her tone light.

"Just walk," Hunter said, his voice low. "It will be okay."

He took the lead, and Jenna followed. The protesters moved aside to let people leaving Keates pass, and Hunter aimed for that same break in the crowd. Others fell in behind them, also headed for lunch.

A pair of grim-faced students were chanting loudly, but as Hunter and Jenna approached, they quieted.

"Could we get by?" Hunter asked.

The two guys just glared at him.

"Oh, this is just ridiculous," Jenna huffed, covering up her anxiety. She pushed past him and went right up to the guys. "Come on, you guys. We're going to lunch. Do you mind?"

They moved out of the way, looking a little embarrassed. When Jenna was through the crowd, moving up the steps to Keates with Hunter and several other students behind her, she looked up to see Olivia Adams watching her from the top of the stairs. She was a friend, but also a member of the Somerset African-American League, a very vocal group on campus.

Jenna realized that SAAL had more than likely put together the protest.

"Hey Olivia," she said. "Who *is* that guy?"

Olivia seemed surprised by the question. "Darnell Thomas. He's a senior. Prelaw."

Jenna stood beside her at the top of the stairs. "He's with SAAL?"

"He is now," Olivia said. "He's been sort of off our radar for a long time. But this murder just got under his skin, I guess. Like it did the rest of us."

Under his skin, Jenna thought. She had no idea if Olivia was being purposely ironic in her choice of words and decided not to mention it. The other girl was a friend, but she had always made it very clear that she did not think Jenna and Damon should be dating. Olivia seemed to believe that black men—particularly educated, successful black men—owed it to the African-American community to strengthen the race by marrying within the color boundaries.

Jenna could not possibly understand that position for a number of reasons, her own race primarily among them. But she also knew that as a white female she did not have the experience to judge Olivia's beliefs.

She was only grateful that Damon did not agree.

"You're lucky those two guys let you by," Olivia said, almost as an afterthought, just before Jenna and Hunter were about to go in.

"Nah, they're okay," Hunter replied. "They're upset about the attack and that girl's murder. And they're angry 'cause they think not enough is being done. But it isn't like they would just start something for no reason."

"You think?" Olivia asked, smirking. "Maybe you're right. And maybe they're even angrier than you think. They probably only let you by because Jenna was with you."

Jenna frowned. "What? I don't know those guys."

"They know *you*," Olivia told her, all traces of friendliness gone from her features. "How many black students are there on this campus, Jenna? Less than four hundred. Half of them are guys. How many of them are dating white girls? Less than ten. They may not know your name, but they know your face."

Dave Berman was bummed. The party at the Arts House had pretty much sucked. The climate on campus had everybody talking, and in the creative community—which included most of the people at the party—it was a particularly hot topic of conversation.

The music had been plenty loud. An early nineties retro theme night. And there had been a very large supply of fuzzy navels in a seemingly bottomless punch bowl. Come to think of it, there had also been plenty of dancing. But Dave's buddy Mateo had taken off with a girl he knew from his drama class. Half the reason he'd even gone to the party was to hang with Mateo. The other half was to try to get up the guts to finally ask out Elena Davidoff, subject of a three-year crush that had begun halfway through their freshman year. They were friendly. They talked. They had even gone out . . . in groups.

Tonight should have been the night. Mateo was supposed to be there for moral support. But then he had bailed. Elena was locked in conversation with a couple of underclassmen Dave did not recognize; they were talking about the junior who had been murdered on campus.

So there was music. There was booze. There was dancing. But not for Elena, and therefore, by extension, not for Dave. He danced and drank, but they were empty things. When he left, the clock had not even struck eleven. Early for him to exit a party, that was for sure.

The fuzzy navels were misnamed, he thought. It was his brain that was fuzzy as he walked across campus headed for his apartment. As a senior, it was considered a luxury to live off campus. Dave had thought it would be cooler; that it would add an upperclassman mystique and coolness that would be tangible to him. He was surprised to find that he hated it. It was a long walk that took him away from all the action on campus.

He swayed only slightly as he went through the open gate and started across the field where the Somerset Colts played football. An eight-lane, oval track went around the field and the bleachers. At the opposite end of the field, Dave felt a twinge in his gut and wondered if he had had one too many fuzzy navels after all. The last thing he wanted was to throw up.

He moaned, swayed a bit more. The twinge of nausea grew stronger. Filled with dread, he staggered to the edge of the bleachers and put his hand on the metal to hold himself up.

Dave never saw the man who stepped out from

behind the bleachers and shattered his skull with a baseball bat. He let out one yell, a kind of primal cry for help, even as he crumbled to the ground. The weapon fell again. And again.

In the bleachers, Annie stiffened and looked up at Todd.

"What?" he asked, a bit annoyed.

"You didn't hear that?"

"I didn't hear anything."

"Get up."

"What?"

"Get. Up."

He did as she asked, and the two of them arranged their disheveled clothes even as they sat up to look out across the football field. They saw the guy with the bat right away. Then the bat came down, and they saw the other . . . the guy on the ground.

"Hey!" Todd shouted.

"Oh, my God!" Annie whispered, terrified.

He looked up at them, face bathed in dim illumination from the streetlights beyond the field. Then he brought the bat down again and it splintered with a loud crack. He dropped it there, turned, and disappeared behind the bleachers on the far side of the field.

They ran down to the field. The guy was dead. Annie and Todd went together to call the police, and lied, saying they were out for a walk and just happened to wander onto the field. Of the killer, they could offer only one observation.

He was black.

c h a p t e r   3

On Friday afternoon, after lunch, Jenna met Damon back at Sparrow Hall. Together they walked to Somerset Medical Center to see Ant. She and Damon talked about the news coverage of the rally the day before, but she did not mention her conversation with Olivia. It had disturbed her in a way that she could not put into words, nor even organize into coherent thoughts, and she felt it better to remain silent for the time being.

Jenna waited outside Anthony's room while Damon went in first. She checked her watch several times. Dr. Slikowski was expecting her for a two-to-five shift. A few minutes after he had gone in, Damon poked his head out.

"You want to come in?"

"If he's up to it," Jenna replied.

Damon nodded. She went in, feeling a bit awkward after the way Brick acted the last time she had seen him. Brick chilled out after that, but Jenna had never been as close to Ant. She didn't know him as well, nor did she know what to expect.

The room faced west, and the late afternoon sun streamed in through the windows, providing a comfortable warmth. There were flowers and cards on a nightstand. Anthony smiled weakly as Jenna entered. Half his face was hidden behind bandages, and his tall form looked gawky in the hospital pajamas he wore as he lay in bed.

"Hey, Jenna," Ant said. His voice was normal, but tired. "Thanks for coming down."

"Not at all. I stopped by yesterday, but you were sleeping."

He looked surprised, and then a little touched. "I'm glad you're here."

"I'm so sorry about Brittany, Ant."

He nodded. "She's in God's hands now. Nothing to be done for her now, except to find the one responsible." He paused. "D tells me it's getting pretty bad out there."

She swallowed, tempted to play dumb. But she knew exactly what he was talking about. "Yeah."

"He also told me Brick kinda gave you a hard time."

Jenna reddened a little, glanced at Damon uncomfortably. His expression was neutral.

"It wasn't a big deal. He's upset. We all are." She met Anthony's gaze.

"C'mere, Jenna."

Curious, a bit self-conscious, she went over to sit beside Anthony on the bed. He smiled at her, meeting her gaze more directly than he ever had before. Noticing her, she would later think, in a way he never had before.

"The guy who killed her and beat on me? It was about us being black for him. I can't get away from that, you understand? Not ever. That's part of this story."

Jenna nodded.

"But only a part," Ant went on. "Brick oughta know better, and I think he does. You're right—he was just upset. We all know better. It's about color for me and the guy who did this. But it doesn't have to be about that for everyone."

Jenna had no idea what to say.

Ant smiled. "I know what you're thinking. Getting cracked in the head made Ant one talkative SOB, right? I don't have much to say as a rule. Unless it needs saying, and this does. We don't have much in common, you and me, except Damon. You can't understand me, and I sure can't understand you. But I don't need to. We're solid, Jenna. Meanwhile, the shit's gonna hit the fan. You oughta stay out of the way."

She stared at him, astonished. He had spoken more in a handful of minutes than in the entire time she had known him. Here a girl he had been involved with, maybe starting to fall for, had been murdered and he had been beaten, and Anthony was worrying about *her* instead of himself.

On impulse, she bent down and hugged him. Ant grimaced with a bit of pain, but chuckled.

"Thank you," she told him. "I hope you get out of here soon."

"You should. Somebody's got to keep Brick and your little sweetheart there out of trouble."

Damon laughed, came up beside the bed and held out a hand to his friend. Ant took it, clutched it tight before letting go.

"It's gonna get ugly, D. Don't let it get ugly for you. Stay away from it, you hear?"

"Working on it," Damon promised.

Jenna stood and Damon slipped an arm around her. She glanced up at him and he kissed her softly.

"Know what?" she said. "I'm just going to see if Dr. Slikowski really needs me today."

"I think that's an excellent idea," he said, with a grin that melted her. "Why don't we get out of here for a while? We can go into Harvard Square, have dinner at the Border."

The M.E. did not balk at Jenna's request, particularly after she promised to go in the following day, Saturday, to do several hours of transcription. That would go a long way to getting them caught up for Monday.

Jenna was thrilled to have some time with Damon, just the two of them. She had been badly unnerved by the week's events, and though he seemed to be holding together perfectly well, she knew it had to be getting to him also. Still, she preferred not to bring it up as long as he did not.

At the dimming of the day, just after four o'clock, they walked back along the path from SMC and across Carpenter Street to the campus. Damon's arm was around her, and Jenna huddled close to him, though not because of the cold. He was good and kind and strong of character, and she was in love with him. A surge of that love swept through her, and she held on extra tight. But she had to wonder if it was merely love that inspired her or fear of the forces at work around and against them.

It isn't fair, she wanted to shout.

But she knew no one would listen. Life was not fair, and nobody had ever pretended otherwise. People were prejudiced, and violence was ugly, yet ordinary. All she could do was make sure that it did not touch her or Damon or their love any more than it already had.

Secretly, though, she worried that she might not be able to do that.

When they reached the third floor of Sparrow, they went up the stairs on the girls' side of the dorm.

"I just want to change into something more comfortable—get your mind out of the gutter—and a bit warmer if we're going to be walking around Harvard Square," Jenna said.

Damon shrugged and offered a sly smile. "I'm good."

Jenna rolled her eyes. She knew enough to recognize that smile; the one that said, *you want to change your clothes and you think I'm going to go away while you do it?*

"Yoshiko's sick in bed," she told him.

"Maybe you should come to *my* room, then." His voice had altered. No longer playful, it had dropped to a suggestive whisper.

They reached her room, and Jenna turned to pull him close. She gave him a kiss that held promise. "Later. Let's get out of here and have some fun first, okay?"

"Yeah," he agreed. "Can't blame a guy for trying."

"Most guys I certainly *could* blame," she told him, running her right hand down his chest. "But not you."

When they had first entered the hallway, Jenna had heard voices coming from the common area. Now they grew louder. In the midst of the conversation, one word echoed very clearly down the corridor.

Jenna paused with her key in the lock. She felt Damon stiffen beside her, and glanced up at him. His eyes were closed, and he swallowed hard.

"That's Olivia," she said.

He nodded. Together they walked toward the common area. Olivia was not alone. Hunter was there, sitting intensely forward in an ugly orange chair. Yoshiko was slumped in another with a box of tissues on the floor beside her, one crumpled in her hand. Caitlin Janssen—a sorority sister of Olivia's with whom the girl had formed an unlikely friendship—was on the floor next to Olivia. They both sat on the carpet leaning against the wall.

Olivia was glaring at Hunter as Damon and Jenna approached.

"Of course nobody's ever called me that," Hunter told her angrily. "But I've been called an ignorant cracker a few times in my life."

"Oh, yeah, I'm sure that cut you deep," Olivia said. She snorted derisively. "You don't even know what you're talking about, Hunter, so maybe you should keep your mouth shut."

"Hey," Damon said, as he and Jenna joined the group. "There's no call for that."

"No kidding," Hunter added. "Nobody's defending the killer here. Or bigotry, for that matter. All I'm saying is there are more constructive ways to get things done than to light a fire over race and then start fanning the flames."

But Olivia was no longer paying attention to Hunter. Her eyes were on Damon. She stood up to address him. "Come on, D. You know you don't see clearly on this subject anyway."

Jenna grew angry. "What does that mean?"

"You know what it means, Jenna. No offense to you. But really, how often have you felt hated because of the color of your skin? Have you ever gone anywhere that people sneered at you like you didn't belong or said that your race was inferior, your people were *animals?* I have."

In her chair, Yoshiko sat up a little straighter. "So have I. That doesn't mean I'm going on the offensive, or that I think every white person is involved in some conspiracy to destroy my race."

Jenna was surprised. She and Yoshiko had never talked about race before. It just had not been an issue. Hunter was staring at her with equal astonishment, and he looked a bit foolish. Jenna realized that he should feel foolish and so should she. How easy it was, she thought, for the two of them to take social acceptance for granted.

"It's not the same thing," Olivia snapped, turning on Yoshiko now. "Okay, maybe we've got some things in common. When Jenna or Caitlin misses class"— Caitlin flinched at the mention of her name, obviously very uncomfortable with the whole conversation— "the professor doesn't even notice. But I'm the one black face, or maybe one of a few, in a class. If I'm not there, he *knows*. Same for you, Yoshiko. But the stereotypes aren't the same. Asians are stereotyped as being smart, blacks are stereotyped as being lazy, ignorant criminals."

She turned to Damon. "You dress nice, D. Can you go into a store without the staff watching you extra close?"

"You know I can't," he replied.

"When you take your little white girlfriend out on the town, don't even tell me that white men don't glare at you with murder in their eyes, 'cause I have seen it."

Jenna's heart sank. She turned to him, watching his eyes, hoping for an answer she knew would not come.

"Some do," Damon agreed.

Jenna flinched, but she could feel the truth of it and see it in Damon's eyes.

"Caitlin," Olivia went on, turning to her friend, "when we're hanging out, people look at us strangely. Haven't you ever noticed?"

"I guess," Caitlin replied tentatively.

"You guess. So you have noticed, and you aren't even sensitized to it." Then Olivia went back to Jenna, eyeing her intensely. "I don't want to bring you down, Jenna. You're a friend. But get a clue." She grabbed up a copy of the *Somerset Daily* from a chair, folded it open to page three, and pointed at a column in the paper. "Here. This is what I'm talking about."

Jenna frowned down at the paper now in her hands. The column was next to a story about the school administration's response to Brittany's murder, how they were adding additional safety shuttle service and new lampposts along the paths through the campus. But that was not at all what Olivia wanted her to see.

The column was by Darnell Thomas. It was called Natural Born Suspects. A few lines from the top, she read:

> There are people, more than you can possibly imagine, who will not sit next to me in a restaurant, who will cross the street if they see me coming down the sidewalk, who will not get on an elevator with me. For a lot of them, it is not because they don't like black people. Hell, some of their best friends are black!
>
> It's because they are afraid of us. If they know us, fine. But otherwise, all they know of blacks is what they see in the media. Some of it's true, sure enough. But that's all they see. They don't get to see anything else. I may dress nice, and go to a good college, but I am still a black man. How many times more likely to be accused of a crime? How much harder to get ahead in my career? You can't imagine.
>
> So when a black girl is killed, and I get the idea maybe her death isn't getting much attention or that the cops are trying to downplay the fact that it was a hate crime, I get angry.

While Jenna read, the conversation went on. When Olivia snapped at Hunter for something, she looked up.

"Look, I'm sorry if I'm on a soapbox here," Olivia said, glaring at Hunter. "I didn't mean to get started. But you're trying to tell me how black students on this campus should be behaving, and I say keep it to yourself. None of you can even begin to imagine what life is like for me and mine."

Hunter bristled at that. Jenna saw the anger rising in him and wanted to tell him to be calm, not to say something he might regret. But he was already speaking.

"Maybe you're right. I can't imagine what it's like. True enough. But I know it sucks. And I know something else, too. Most people just want to get along, Olivia. Look around out there and you will find that most people are not the cruel, violent bigots you seem to expect to jump out at you from every shadow. This is the twenty-first century. There's no big bad conspiracy to keep black people or any other race down.

"But you walk around pissed off at the world, taking your anger out on people who are on your side but don't happen to share your race. You think that's helping your cause?"

With a scowl of disgust, Hunter slid back into the chair, his face red with emotion. They all stared at him in surprise. The outburst was unlike him, but it was obvious that he felt very strongly about the issue. Jenna thought that Hunter had oversimplified things some, but she could not really disagree.

"We don't need your help," Olivia snapped angrily.

Damon cleared his throat. He had been unusually silent throughout their debate, and now everyone turned to him.

"I think we do," he said simply.

"You would." Olivia rolled her eyes as she said it.

Damon crossed the room to stand between her and Hunter. But when he spoke, his eyes were on Olivia.

"We're all friends here, aren't we? Everyone here?"

Olivia shrugged. "Yeah. I'm just—"

"Making enemies out of friends," Damon said softly. "I'm a black man. I'm not stupid, Olivia. I don't need you *or* Darnell Thomas to tell me what that means on the streets or in a store or in an office. I'm proud of my people, and the hell we've been through, and overcome. We've done it largely on our own. That was the only way it could be done."

He glanced around at the others now. Jenna saw an intensity in his eyes she had never seen there before, and pain and confusion entered her heart.

"Jenna," he said, "does race matter to you?"

"Of course not," she said, a little hurt by the question.

"Hunter?"

"Not at all. You know that."

"Caitlin?"

"No."

"Yoshiko?"

"You know better, Damon."

He nodded, took a moment to glance pointedly at Olivia, and then spoke to all of them again.

"It matters to me," Damon said. "I can't escape it." He turned to study Olivia again. "Race is a factor in our lives in a way nobody else can understand. How could they? You can't blame them for that. It's the ones who think it *does* matter that we need to look out for. We try and we try, we get up on our soapboxes and celebrate Black History Month and become senators and CEOs, and hand Darnell a megaphone. And we should. We have to. But there's something you're missing."

"Which is?" Olivia's expression was skeptical.

Damon swept an arm around to indicate all those gathered. "These are the only people listening!" he said. "The bigots and the silent racists, the brutalizers out there, are not paying attention. They will not listen. The only way we can reach them, and change them, and make them pay for what they do, is with the help of the rest of this society, the people who listen, the people who care."

His voice had risen in volume and intensity, but now it dropped low as he stared sternly at Olivia.

"That's impossible if, in trying to change things, we alienate the people who have to change right along with us."

Jenna was stunned to find herself holding her breath. She had never seen Damon so impassioned and eloquent. In a way, she felt closer to him than ever before. But in another, her new awareness of his feelings showed her that there was a gulf between them she had never envisioned; one she did not know if she could ever cross.

Olivia glared at Damon. "That's all nice in theory. Maybe you forgot that a girl is dead, and one of your best friends got his head cracked with a shovel, because some white guy didn't want to see them kiss. Now it seems to me, and a whole lot of other people, that the cops are spending more time telling us it wasn't about race than they are actually investigating the crime."

"You don't know that," Yoshiko argued.

"Then why haven't they bothered to deny it? And where are the cops that should be combing the campus looking for the guy? They should be doing a room-by-room search, and—"

"Like they did when my sister was killed?" Hunter demanded.

Olivia flinched at that.

"Hunter's right," Jenna added. "This isn't a dictatorship. The cops can't just storm every room on campus, disrupting everything. They didn't do it when Melody was murdered, and they can't do it now. They're doing their best."

"I'm sorry. I just don't believe that," Olivia said flatly.

"Maybe that's your problem, not theirs," Jenna said.

Without another word, Olivia turned to go. Jenna was about to call after her when Damon placed a hand on her arm and shook his head. She kept silent.

Caitlin was not willing to do that. She got up quickly and started down the hall after her friend.

"Olivia, come on!" she called.

Furiously, Olivia turned and glared at her. "Don't even start," she snapped. "Just back off."

Caitlin froze in the middle of the corridor. After

Olivia was gone, she glanced back toward the common area where they were all waiting for her, then looked back at the stairwell door on the other end. Back and forth. At length, she shook her head and slowly walked out the way Olivia had gone, but making no effort to catch up to her friend.

Hunter, Yoshiko, Jenna, and Damon fidgeted uncomfortably. They spoke to one another tentatively, nobody quite sure what to say after all of that. Eventually, Jenna and Damon did go into Harvard Square and have dinner, but the debate, the anger, and the issue of race hung over them like an ominously dark thunder cloud, promising a storm to come.

On Saturday morning Jenna went in to work as promised. More than likely she would be on her own and have quiet time to just sit and do transcription. It would be a nice change of pace, a kind of escape from the pall that had fallen over the campus. Or so she had imagined.

When she arrived at the medical examiner's office, it was neither empty nor quiet. Slick sat in his wheelchair just outside his inner office. Dyson leaned against the wall of one cubicle. They were talking to Danny Mariano and Audrey Gaines, Somerset homicide detectives with whom they had all worked before. The previous semester, Jenna had had a crush on Danny—and maybe it was more than that—but the difference in their ages made anything more impossible. Now she was in love with Damon, but there would always be a little secret place in her heart for Danny. Maybe not so little.

Audrey was the senior partner and the far more serious of the two. That morning, though, Jenna thought they both appeared very grave.

"It was a very simple murder," Slick was saying as Jenna entered the room.

He glanced up at her as she came in, and the others all turned around.

"Morning," Jenna said, a bit uncomfortably. "What's happening?"

Dyson glanced at Slick, who nodded almost imperceptibly.

"You didn't watch the news last night or this morning?" Dyson asked.

"No," Jenna said slowly. "What did I miss?"

"According to Dr. Slikowski, a very simple murder," Audrey replied, expressionless.

Slick bristled a bit. "You know what I meant. The killer surprised the victim from behind and beat him to death with a baseball bat. Very direct. Nothing complex or bizarre about it."

Jenna's heart sank. "Please tell me it wasn't another race crime."

Danny glanced at Audrey, scratched distractedly at his ear. When he spoke again, it was to all of them.

"Witnesses say the suspect is black. The victim was white. A Somerset senior named David Berman," he said.

"So it wasn't the same guy. Thank God for that." Dyson sighed. "The last thing we need is more tension in this city."

Jenna was not listening. Something was bothering

her. "If it happened the night before last, why didn't it make the news until last night?"

She was looking at Danny when she asked the question, but he did not seem at all interested in answering. He looked at the ground.

"Spin," Audrey put in bluntly. "That's all it is. It wasn't the same perp, we know that. No way to tell if it was race related either. But after Brittany Forrester's murder, there are people who will hear about a black man killing a white Somerset student and think it was some kind of payback."

"God," Jenna replied, baffled. "So, do you think the victim was the guy who killed Brittany?"

"Could be," Danny said, and shrugged. "It doesn't matter. There will be people who perceive the murder as an eye for an eye. You kill one of ours, we'll kill one of yours. The mayor and the city council were trying to figure out the best way to present Berman's murder to the public. They couldn't think of anything but the truth, but holding on to the information will only feed the suspicion that some people have been voicing."

"I wish I could be of more help," Slick said. "But Berman's autopsy reveals nothing beyond the method of his murder."

"It's on us, now," Audrey said grimly. She glanced at Dyson. "See, Dr. Dyson, you had a nice thought there. Not the same perp, so it wouldn't exacerbate the situation. I only wish you were right. In some ways, this is worse. Once the news really spreads, we're going to have a racial firestorm on our hands. Suspicion, anger, and grief can turn violent pretty fast."

Jenna felt sick as she stared at those gathered in the room. Her gaze stopped on Slick. "So we've got two killers to find, and no time to waste."

"You've done your job," Danny told the pathology team. "It's time for us to do ours."

Jenna made no response. Her mind was already working. It might not be her job to help solve these murders, but there was no way she could sit back and pretend they had not happened. No way she could ignore the chaos that she knew was about to envelop the campus.

She only prayed that nobody else had to die before it was over.

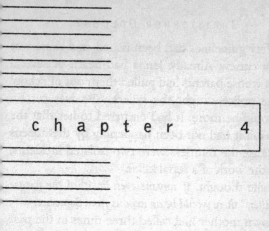

chapter   4

It snowed on Saturday night. Five inches of new white stuff was on the ground by Sunday morning when the sun finally broke through. So much for the hope that spring might arrive without winter ever returning full force. The wind was bitterly cold as Jenna cut across the quad heading toward the Campus Center for lunch. The sound of snow crunching underfoot set her teeth on edge, and she did not have to wonder too much why that might be. There were plenty of reasons to be tense. With two murders on campus in a matter of days, both of them apparently racially motivated, the atmosphere at Somerset had gotten more than tense.

The night before there had apparently been at least three arrests when a fight broke out at a party at Delta Upsilon fraternity. Night classes had been canceled. There was a much more visible police presence on campus, both the university police and Somerset P.D.

New safety guidelines had been issued, and there was talk of a curfew. Already, Jenna had heard of several students whose parents had pulled them out of school until the police caught the killers. She was certain there would be more. It had occurred to her that the only reason it had not been happening by the dozens was because the murders were two isolated incidents, and not the work of a serial killer.

God, she thought, *if anyone even breathed the phrase "serial killer," there would be an exodus from Somerset.*

Her own mother had called three times in the past twenty-four hours, trying to convince her to go home to Natick for a week or so. Then this morning her father had called from France, trying to get Jenna's take on matters. He had been on campus first semester, had lost one of his closest friends in a bizarre murder case. Jenna assured him that the administration seemed to be doing all they could, that the cases were not likely to be related, that it was probably all over but the grieving, and she did not want to fall weeks behind on her classwork when she was really in no danger. Her father vowed to call fellow faculty members to urge the administration to greater action. Jenna told him that she thought that would be helpful, though she doubted it.

The media, the administration, her parents, the tension and anger among the students—it was all practically unbearable. But Jenna had plans to meet up with Damon today, and she was determined not to let *anything* ruin their time together. Jenna was a little miffed at herself because she was running late, but for once there really was nothing she could have done about it. There had been an unexpected traffic jam waiting for a free shower in the girls' bathroom that morning, and no way had she been willing to go down to the guys' end the way Annette Charrier had.

Someone called out her name and her mood instantly brightened when she turned to see Damon jogging up the walkway toward her. He was wearing sunglasses and a dark brown leather coat with matching gloves. A plaid scarf was draped over his shoulder, giving him a rakish look. She smiled to herself. Her guy knew how to dress.

"Hey," Jenna called out, waving to him.

"What's up?" Damon asked. Before she could answer, he gave her a quick kiss on the lips. The tip of his nose was cold as it brushed against her cheek, but Jenna thought the kiss felt just fine.

"What's up is, I'm going to freeze my butt off if we don't get inside right now." Jenna laughed lightly between chattering teeth.

Clasping hands, they walked up the steps and entered the dining hall. Once inside, Jenna peeled off the woolen mittens her mother had given her for Christmas, and Damon took off his shades and leather gloves. They held hands as they waited in line side by side.

The dining hall seemed more crowded than usual. Jenna figured it was because so many people were lingering after a late breakfast, hoping to stay out of the cold as long as possible. Yoshiko was still feeling a bit under the weather, but Jenna and Hunter had talked about going traying later that afternoon on the hill beside the library. Now she was thinking that might be a bad idea, especially if it stayed this cold all day. Besides, it would be much more fun to hang out with Damon all afternoon. Maybe they'd even get a little studying done later.

Anything's possible, she thought, and shot him a conspiratorial glance that seemed to puzzle him. Which was all right. She would clear up any confusion later, when they were alone together.

As they moved through the Campus Center toward the back of the line Jenna took a moment to look around the room. There were only a few familiar faces, most of which did not have names attached to them in her mind. She recognized one guy from Professor Fournier's Shakespeare class who was sitting with several friends, laughing and talking as they ate. He looked up but barely registered the smile and friendly wave and soft "hey" Jenna gave him as she and Damon passed by.

What's up with him? she thought, feeling a sudden flush of confusion. He had spoken to her a couple of times after class, and she had thought he seemed like a nice guy.

The line was moving slowly, but Jenna was grateful just to be out of the cold. Whenever she looked over at Damon, she couldn't help but feel a warm glow blossom inside her.

The choices for lunch were typically uninspired, so Jenna settled for a bowl of chicken soup, a salad, and a root beer. Damon heaped his tray high with a meatball parmesan grinder, greasy French fries, a salad, some nachos, and two glasses of milk. Jenna wondered how he could eat like that and still look the way he did.

They looked around for a place to sit and saw an empty table in a far corner by the windows. As they walked over to it, the funny feeling Jenna had first gotten when she saw the guy from her Shakespeare class grew even stronger. She tried to convince herself that it was just her imagination, but she could not help but feel as though a number of people in the dining hall were watching her, staring at her . . .

Her and Damon.

You're being too sensitive, she told herself. But when she looked directly at a group of upperclassmen—guys and girls—clustered around a table, one of the guys leaned over to another and whispered something, all the while staring straight at Jenna. She bristled when the other student glanced up at her, then turned away and snickered behind his hand.

A terrible certainty filled her with dread.

They're laughing at us. Us being together.

Her face flushed as she followed Damon over to the table, shrugged off her coat, and sat down.

"You all right?" Damon asked, glancing at her as he emptied his tray onto the table.

Jenna almost said something about what was bothering her but then thought better of it and nodded.

You're imagining it, Blake, she told herself. *This is higher education in the twenty-first century, not a diner in 1960s Alabama or something.*

For a moment, she thought she might have at least

an inkling of what Olivia had been talking about on Friday, about how people look at you differently when you're black, but she quickly dismissed it.

Despite the weird vibe, Jenna forced herself to smile as she sat down with her tray in front of her. She closed her eyes and slowly inhaled the steam rising from her soup. The aroma reminded her of snowy-day bowls of chicken soup back when she was a kid in Natick. Despite the schedule her mother had to keep as a surgeon, she still managed to make soup from scratch sometimes instead of just opening a can of Campbell's. Jenna had not really understood as a kid how special that was, but now she did, and she missed it.

She opened a cellophane package of crackers and crushed them into her soup. "So how's Ant doing?"

"I stopped by the hospital to see him this morning," Damon said, a little tense. "He's doing okay physically, but he's still pretty upset."

"Can't say I blame him," Jenna replied, stirring the crackers into the broth.

She shifted uncomfortably in her seat and took a moment to look around. As she did, she saw that several other faces in the cafeteria were turned toward her, watching them. She squirmed uncomfortably, wondering why now, all of a sudden, a white woman having lunch with a black man was so damned interesting. Her hand was shaking a little as she scooped up some soup and sipped it tentatively.

Considering the atmosphere in the cafeteria—and she was convinced now that she was not just imagining it—she found it a bit difficult to make conversation.

Jenna braced herself, tried to shake it off, determined not to let anything or anyone ruin their time together.

"Hey, any idea if Olivia and Caitlin made up?" she asked.

At her question, Damon's face seemed to harden. He had a forkful of meatball sandwich halfway to his mouth, but now he paused and stared at her.

"They'll work it out," he said. His voice sounded flat and hollow.

"What did I say?" Jenna asked tersely. This was not what she needed. "I was just wondering. I thought it would be a shame if that argument Friday hurt their friendship."

"Olivia's a big girl. I'm sure she can handle it."

Jenna could not have missed the edge of sarcasm in his voice.

"Okay, you're not Olivia's biggest fan right now, but what about Caitlin?" Jenna asked, pressing. "All she's doing is trying to be a friend."

Damon swallowed, his expression grim. He looked away and pursed his lips as though he had some inexplicably sharp retort he was considering. Then he snorted softly and waved his hand in dismissal.

"She's a big girl, too. I don't think we need to play nursemaid to either one of them."

Confused by his behavior, Jenna sighed and turned to look out the window at the snow-covered campus. Everything seemed so peaceful, so picture-postcard beautiful. It saddened her to think how there could be so much hostility simmering just below the surface when even friends like Olivia and Caitlin could have a falling out. But of course she knew that her thoughts of the two girls were only her way of avoiding the tension she now sensed between herself and Damon.

They ate for a while in silence. Jenna hardly tasted any of her soup. The whole time, she could not erase the feeling that people in the room were watching her . . . staring at her and Damon.

"So, are we still on for the party tonight?" Jenna asked, shifting gears in hopes of lightening both of their moods.

Damon was in the midst of very carefully eating his meatball grinder, trying to avoid getting tomato sauce on his clothes. He glanced up at her, frowning. "Party?"

"Yeah. Off campus. I told you about it. At Tracy Hotchkiss's apartment on Summer Street?"

"Oh, right. That's tonight?" Damon cleared his throat. He picked up a napkin and dabbed at the corner of his mouth. "I can't tonight. Something's come up."

"What do you mean?" Jenna asked. She felt suddenly flushed, but it was not with anger; it was nervousness. There was no reason to think it, but she could not help but feel as though Damon was about to drop a bomb on her.

"There's a Somerset African-American League meeting at the Afro-Am House tonight. Brick and I were thinking we would go."

"SAAL?" Jenna said, genuinely surprised. "I didn't know you were involved with the SAAL."

"I haven't been . . . until now."

Damon looked at her with a confused, almost pleading expression in his eyes that communicated much more to her than he said. Jenna understood that the two murders on campus had raised some big issues, but it pained her to think that Damon was thinking about doing something that would exclude her not by his choice but because of her race. No one would speak the words, of course, but Jenna understood that she would not be welcome.

With a sigh, Jenna shook her head slowly.

"What?" Damon asked, his tone defensive.

She wanted to tell him the truth, that she had been hoping that they could put the turmoil and tension on campus behind them, at least for a little while; hoping to take back their relationship from those who would make it an issue. She wanted to remind him of the warning Ant had given him in the hospital, that he should keep back, keep out of it. But she did not feel that she could speak those words without making it even *more* of an issue. Jenna hated the way that felt.

"I promised Tracy that we'd come," Jenna said, by way of explanation. "She's in my gross anatomy class, and I just thought, you know, that it'd be nice to drop by. It's going to be mostly upperclassmen."

"You can still go without me, right?" Damon asked sincerely.

"Yeah, but it won't be the same."

Damon bit his lower lip as he considered for a moment; then he grimaced and shook his head.

"I'm sorry, Jenna, but this is important right now. You understand? Darnell Thomas called this meeting to address SAAL's position on all this stuff, and Brick and I just want to see what's going down."

Jenna could feel her stomach starting to tighten. Based on what little she had heard about him, she did not trust Darnell Thomas. But she knew if she addressed her concerns, Damon might take it the wrong way. The way things were on campus now, even the most innocent comments could be taken the wrong way. All she had to do for proof was remember what had happened in the dorm between Olivia and Caitlin. What had started out as a simple discussion had turned vicious fast, and hurtful words had been spoken. Words that Jenna feared might not be able to be taken back. There were enough wedges being driven between her and Damon as it was. She certainly did not want to start driving one of her own.

"Fine. Not a problem," Jenna said, although she thought her voice sounded as though it was very much a problem. "Hunter, Yoshiko, and I might go, anyway. We'll see."

"I hope you understand," Damon said.

"It's not that important," Jenna replied.

Damon reached out and placed both of his hands on top of hers. There was warmth and strength in his touch, and it made Jenna feel better . . . at least a little.

"Really, I'm fine with it."

She was burning inside, wanting to tell Damon that she was suddenly afraid . . . afraid that what was happening on campus *was* going to affect them, no matter how hard they tried not to let it. But Jenna could not accept that.

She *would not* accept that.

She was in love with Damon, and she believed that he was in love with her, and—damn it—love was supposed to be stronger than anything that might come up against it.

At least that was what she wanted to believe.

They made a little small talk while they finished their meals, but Jenna felt like there was a definite chill between them. When it was time to leave, he helped her on with her coat, and then they walked to the door side by side, holding hands. Jenna was painfully aware of the heads that turned to watch them. She had to fight back the sudden impulse to wheel around and yell at everyone there to mind their own damned business.

Outside, she and Damon kissed good-bye and went their separate ways. Walking into the wind that was blowing across campus, Jenna was glad she had the cold to blame when her eyes began to water.

Even though the SAAL meeting at the Afro-Am House had been put together on short notice, it ended up drawing a lot more people than anyone, even its organizers, had expected. The large meeting room on the first floor of the building was full to overflowing. Many people—including Damon and Brick, who arrived shortly after Darnell Thomas started speaking—had to stand out in the hallway to listen to him.

"We've come far, brothers and sisters," Darnell said in the same harsh, strident tone he had adopted when he had spoken on the quad the other day. Even without a microphone or bullhorn, his resonant voice filled the room and carried clearly into the hall. "But we still have a long way to go."

Darnell paused for emphasis and a low murmur passed through the room. Damon could feel emotions rising like an electrical current, steadily building up and looking to discharge. He glanced over at Brick, surprised to see how attentive his friend was. Brick was leaning against the wall with his arms folded across his chest, listening carefully. There was a firm set to his jaw and a light in his eyes that Damon had never seen before.

"We haven't got what we want," Darnell continued, "because we don't have true justice. And we haven't got justice because we haven't demanded it. And why is that? Why haven't we *demanded* the justice we want and *deserve?*"

Darnell paused, and in that slight pause, Damon looked from face to face among the people he was standing with in the hallway. They all seemed transfixed by what they were hearing, and for some reason, that bothered Damon. Darnell was earnest and charismatic and certainly he seemed to mean well, but he wanted to get things done by making people angry, and Damon had never agreed with that approach.

"It's simple math, D," his mother had always said. "Once you add anger, you're subtracting reason."

This isn't good, he thought to himself.

"It's not that we're afraid. Oh, no. We have the courage when we need it. But we haven't demanded it because we've become complacent for far too long in a white man's world. Our black pride has been put to sleep, lulled by the *illusion* that things have changed, that things have gotten better for our people."

Damon reached out and tapped Brick on the shoulder. Frowning, he shook his head, then nodded toward the front door.

"Come on, man," he whispered. "Let's bail."

Brick stared at him for a long, silent moment, then shook his head. "I'm staying."

Damon grumbled but for the moment he was reluctant to leave without Brick. He glanced at Olivia, who was pressed into a corner with several other girls on the other side of the room, and saw her nodding vigorously at everything Darnell said.

"We have computers and the Internet," Darnell went on. "We have cell phones and DVD players, and we think because we have all of these things that the world is no longer divided by race. We think that equality has arrived and that skin is finally only skin. But I'm telling you right now, we are *not* equal and we *never* will be equal until we have equal *justice!* And we don't have justice because we haven't *demanded* the *respect* we *deserve!*"

He punctuated his words with three loud raps on the podium at the far end of the conference room, and the people responded with enthusiastic applause and wild shouts of approval. Damon clapped along with everyone else but with little enthusiasm. He could not ignore the steadily tightening discomfort in the pit of his stomach.

This is getting dangerous, he thought. Most of what Darnell had said was true, but whipping up a furor was not the way to go about resolving anything. There were perfectly rational ways to address their concerns to the press and to the police, ways to find out if their fears that there might be some injustice taking place were founded in reality. But neither Darnell nor most of those listening to him seemed to have much interest in rationality. Damon understood that. After the cruelties, large and small, that he suffered every day for the color of his skin, it was simple for even the most intelligent person to fall back on anger.

It was so easy to be angry. It hurt less.

But anger denied reason. As Darnell went on, Damon listened with ever-growing unease.

"They try to pacify our concerns, our requests for information and cooperation with a few passing words. They smile patronizingly and move on, as if we don't have a right to participate in the process of justice. And what have we done? We haven't been out on the streets," Darnell shouted, his voice energized as he fed off the crowd's reactions. "We haven't taken their buildings by peaceful demonstration, and we haven't marched. If we have to get all sixties on the university's ass, then so be it. It's time we spoke up. It's time we took a stand. It's time we demanded full and equal justice on this campus, in this town, and in this country!"

The whole house erupted with wild cheering. Damon wasn't surprised to see that Brick was loudly shouting his approval as he applauded.

There was no doubt about it. This Darnell Thomas was quite a speaker.

But why does it always have to be adversarial? Damon wondered.

"Now there are some of you, I'm sure," Darnell continued, "who are thinking that this isn't the way to do it. That this won't work. You think that it might have worked in the sixties, but that it won't work now, that this is the twenty-first century, and things are different. But I'm telling you, brothers and sisters, things *aren't* different. They haven't changed. It's been four hundred years! *Four hundred years* of slavery and oppression, and the only thing that's kept our race from being destroyed is our *unity!* Our willingness to stand together and not lie down and roll over. It's time we all took action!"

The meeting room and hallway filled with applause and shouts of approval. Leaning close to Brick, Damon practically had to shout to be heard above the noise in the house.

"I'm out of here."

Damon wriggled his way through the crowd, anxious to get out in the open. Zipping his coat up in preparation for stepping out into the cold, he looked back in hopes that his friend had followed, but Brick had not moved. He was clapping with enthusiasm along with the rest of the crowd.

Darnell's voice faded to a dull buzz as Damon stepped out into the cold and swung the door shut behind him. After being in a room filled with the body heat of so many people, the chill wind hit him like a sledgehammer. Pulling the collar of his leather jacket up tight, he started across the street, heading back to

Sparrow Hall alone. If he was lucky, maybe Jenna had not left for the party yet, and he could still join her. If she had already left . . .

Don't go there, D, he told himself. *Stay far away from that thought.*

The sounds of applause and cheering gradually died away the farther he got away from the Afro-Am House, but that didn't disperse the uneasiness Damon felt. After listening to Darnell Thomas, he doubted that things were going to get better on campus any time soon. In fact, he was certain they were going to get a lot worse.

Even without Damon, Jenna was surprised to find that she was having a pretty good time at Tracy's party. Whoever was picking out the music had decent taste— Wallflowers, Beck, Smashing Pumpkins, and some Talking Heads for that retro feeling. Not necessarily what was in her CD player, but good stuff. Plus, there seemed to be no end to the munchies and drinks.

Especially after the pressure they had all been under lately, she thought the party was just what the doctor ordered. *Sometimes you've gotta just let things roll,* Jenna thought.

Other than Tracy, Jenna didn't know any of the people at the party except for Hunter and Yoshiko, who had come with her. Yoshiko was still not feeling well, so she and Hunter stuck pretty close together. Jenna was fine with them doing the couple thing, but it meant she was forced to mingle. She carried a glass of wine around with her, mainly to give her hands something to do. That was one thing private parties had over big fraternity bashes, she thought. No kegs and very few of the morons who usually surrounded them like flies.

She circulated through the crowd, smiling and nodding at everyone. Only a few times did she feel uncomfortable when one of the obviously unattached guys would try to hit on her. Not that it was bad for the ego to be flirted with, but she had a boyfriend.

I ought to wear a pin that says "taken," she thought, although she was far from convinced it would deter any of these guys. All in all it would have been much simpler and more enjoyable if Damon had come along.

She had to keep telling herself that she was not really upset with him for choosing to go to the meeting at the Afro-Am House over spending time with her. Things on campus seemed only to be getting worse, and he was doing what he felt he had to do to try to understand and work through the issues.

Besides, what was one night?

They had lots of time ahead of them to spend together.

Earlier in the evening, Jenna had noticed the small group of guys huddled together by the bay window that looked out over the city. A couple of them appeared to have had more than enough to drink already, but one of them—a stocky guy with short, blond hair and a ruddy complexion—kept glancing over at her in a way that she did not like at all. It reminded her of the looks she had gotten at the Campus Center during lunch.

Relax. Maybe he's just ogling you, she thought.

She smiled and gave him a slight nod as she made her way back for some more munchies. All the while, he tracked her with his eyes without moving his head. There was a dark, almost predatory look to his expression that was really starting to bother her.

Please don't try to make a move, Jenna thought.

She felt a sudden flush and told herself it was just that she'd had a little too much wine to drink, but she knew it was more than that.

I don't want to have to shoot you down.

But the guy never smiled at her. She couldn't be sure because the lights in the apartment were all turned down low, but it seemed like every time she caught him glancing over at her, he was scowling.

"What do you think *his* problem is?"

Jenna jumped, hearing Hunter speak so close behind her. She turned and smiled at her friend, not at all surprised to see Yoshiko standing beside him. She looked a bit pale and drawn, but she was smiling at least. Coming to this party had done her some good.

"Who?" Jenna asked, even though she knew perfectly well whom Hunter meant.

"That guy over by the window," Hunter said, indicating him with a slight hand gesture. "Frank something. He's in my political science class. Guy's been giving you the evil eye ever since we got here."

The seriousness in his tone of voice only served to make her more anxious.

"Maybe it's just a guy thing," Hunter went on, whispering close to her ear, "but I'll tell you right now, if you were a guy, that jerk would be over here in your face, picking a fight."

"Come on. I don't even know him," Jenna said, laughing and giving Hunter's sleeve a gentle tug. "He's just some cranky drunk. Speaking of which, how much have you had to drink?"

"He's been drinking Pepsi all night," Yoshiko told her.

Hunter turned and, leaning close to Jenna, lowered his voice. "I'm just saying—"

"Hey! You got a problem?"

All three of them turned and looked to see the blond guy making his way across the living room toward them. Jenna had no doubt now. There was a very dangerous look in the guy's eyes.

If looks could kill, she thought with a shudder.

"No problem, Frank," Hunter said. "No problem at all."

Jenna noticed that he purposely exaggerated his southern drawl, probably to let the guy know that he didn't want any trouble. He was just out having a good time.

"Wrong. There is a problem. I don't like the way you were looking at me," Frank said to Hunter. His scowl deepened, and the angry light in his eyes blazed.

"I don't believe we've met," Jenna said, getting between them and extending her hand for the boy to shake. "My name's Jenna—"

"I know who you **are**," the boy snapped.

When he spoke, his upper lip curled into an exaggerated sneer that under different circumstances Jenna might have found humorous. Now, all she could think was that this boy looked dangerous, like an injured dog that was going to bite the next thing that moved.

"Look," Hunter said, drawing himself up and squaring his shoulders. "I don't know what your problem is, okay? But nobody here was looking at y'all, nor do we have any real desire to do so. Why don't you just go back to your corner and pretend we're not here?"

The guy had been staring at Jenna, his eyes glowing with rage. He shifted his gaze slowly back to Hunter, then burst into a wide grin.

"I know what *her* problem is, man," he said. "But I can't get a fix on you. You being from the South and all, I'd expect you to know better, but—" When his eyes lighted on Yoshiko, his smirk widened all the more, and he nodded slowly. "No . . . no, I get it. You're just like *her*." He indicated Jenna with a quick flick of his head.

Their voices were getting steadily louder now—loud enough to be heard over the music and the other conversations. Partygoers in their immediate vicinity fell silent and just stood there, watching them. Jenna blushed from the sudden negative attention.

"I'm not sure I like what you're implying," Hunter said evenly.

Jenna had not often heard his voice this low and intense. Yoshiko stiffened by her side, staring at Hunter as if willing him to drop it, to just walk away.

"Hey, let's not spoil the party, all right?" Jenna said, forcing her voice to be light. "There's no reason for anyone to be—"

"*There's plenty reason!*" Frank shouted, cutting her off. His face, inches from hers, was bright red with anger. Spittle flew from his lips. "You're ruining this party for me and my friends! God! Are you too dumb to even realize that?"

"Hey Frankie, chill out," one of his cronies by the window called out.

"My advice to you, *Frankie,* is listen to your friends," Hunter warned.

Jenna could hear the slight tremor of fear in his voice, but she knew Hunter well enough to know that he wasn't about to back down.

"Relax," Hunter told the guy. "Go have another beer and contemplate your ignorance, and we'll stay right here and do the same. You don't want to ruin the girl's party, do you?"

"Too late," Frank snapped. He gave Hunter a hard shove that knocked him off balance. Hunter had to take a quick step back to keep from falling down.

"You make me sick," Frank said, glaring at Jenna. "Just walking in here you make me want to puke. I know you, girl. You think nobody's gonna notice you walking around pawing that black guy?" With a snarl, he turned to glower at Hunter and Yoshiko. "And you, southern boy. Go back and hide in your dorm or whatever and get cozy with your little yellow—"

Before he could finish, Hunter stepped in close and swung at Frank, connecting squarely with the bridge of his nose. The blow knocked Frank back a few paces. Groaning, the big guy leaned forward and covered his face with both hands. When he looked up at Jenna, she could see streams of blood seeping between his fingers.

"You son of a bitch!" Frank bellowed as he pulled his hands away and stared in horror at his own blood.

With a ferocious grunt, he cocked his arm back and came around with a wild swing that Hunter easily ducked. The momentum carried the drunken bigot around, and Hunter stepped in and gave him a shove that sent him flying back toward his group of friends.

"All right, you guys stop it! Right now! Or I'm gonna call the cops!" someone shouted.

Everyone turned to see Tracy, her face flushed with anger, her hands raised in exasperation.

"I thought we were all friends here."

Frank looked at her and sneered. Blood was still streaming from both nostrils, which gave his face a terrible masklike appearance. The angry fire still burned in his eyes, strengthened by the pain.

"I . . . I'm really sorry," Jenna said, turning to Tracy. She was stunned to find that her voice was trembling, and she was close to tears. "I . . . I don't know . . . I didn't mean to—"

"It's not your fault," Tracy said, lowering her voice but still keeping a steady eye on Frank and his bunch. "It's just that *some* people don't know when to stop. You know what they say. You can thaw a Neanderthal out in the twenty-first century, but he'll still want to live in a cave."

"I think we'll be heading on back to the dorm now," Hunter said. He stepped forward and put an arm around Yoshiko, then turned and grabbed Jenna's arm with his other hand.

"You don't have to leave," Tracy said. "I think we can all be mature about this and just chill out. Otherwise, I can always call the police."

Jenna forced a smile, even though she was trembling terribly inside.

"Thanks, Trace," she said, "but I think we'd better be going. Thanks for inviting us, though. I really had a good time until . . ."

She let her voice fade away, and Tracy smiled back at her. Grabbing Jenna's arm, she gave her a reassuring squeeze.

"I'll see you in lab tomorrow," Tracy said. "And I'm really sorry about this."

"Hey, don't sweat it," Jenna said with a little wave of her hand. "Like you said. Neanderthals. Can't live with 'em, can't feed them to ravenous wolves."

They laughed politely together, but Jenna could not help but feel uncomfortable as she, Hunter, and Yoshiko got their coats and walked to the door. She knew that every person in the apartment was staring at them as they left.

chapter 5

It was a little past midnight, and the wind from the north had real teeth to it. The campus was deserted and silent except for the faint hiss of traffic passing down on behind University Boulevard. The streetlamps cast little pools of blue light onto the sidewalk behind Keates Hall, but in between them, there was nothing but darkness.

I love undercover work, Audrey Gaines thought as she crossed the parking lot and started down the sloping walkway toward the tennis courts behind the graduate student dorms. *Especially in places so deserted your backup has to be goddamn invisible.*

Audrey was wearing several layers of clothes, but still, the wind somehow found a way to penetrate right to the bone. Her teeth were chattering terribly, and her eyes were tearing up from the cold. Right now, all she could think about was getting a cup of coffee and then maybe heading on home.

Tonight, anyway, had been a bust.

She hadn't really expected the killer to take the bait, but she thought it was worth a try. A black woman, alone on campus after midnight *should* be an easy target, if that was what he was looking for. But Audrey couldn't help wondering how much she really looked like a college professor. Even in the dark, maybe the person—or persons—she was trying to catch would recognize her as a cop who had been around campus. It was not very likely, but it *was* a possibility.

Audrey slowed her pace when she saw two couples approaching her. She smiled and nodded a greeting as they passed by, but they were all huddled so deeply into their coats and scarves as they raced back to their dorms or wherever that they hardly noticed her.

That was the problem.

How was she going to get the killer to notice her without being so conspicuous that she would tip him to the fact that she was bait. Somewhere else on campus she figured Claire Bellamy, a sergeant on the Somerset P.D., was having the same problem. Audrey was undercover trolling for whomever had been attacking blacks, and Claire was after the other guy.

What a weird night.

A line of trees interspersed by streetlights lined the walkway behind the graduate school dorms, but Audrey walked away from the light, cutting across the snow-covered grass and heading toward Sterling Lane. She was about halfway between the dorms and the street when she sensed a blur of motion in the darkness off to her left.

Hold on a second, now, she thought, feeling a sudden spike of tension. *Maybe we've got something here.*

She shifted her eyes to the left without moving her head. She did not want to alert the killer—if it was him—that she knew he was there.

Not yet, anyway.

Not until he made some kind of move, and she could bust him. Audrey was carrying a briefcase, so she stopped to shift it to her left hand, taking a moment to reassure herself that she could easily reach her service revolver, which she carried on her right hip. Taking a steadying breath, she resumed her walk. Her ears were pricked, just waiting to catch the sound of the man's approach.

If that's him, she thought, feeling the coil of tension winding up in her stomach.

"Your kind just doesn't get it, do they?"

The voice, speaking so suddenly from out of the darkness, was heavy with menace and hatred.

Audrey stopped short. She lowered her shoulders and cocked her head to one side, hoping to give him the impression that she was smaller and much more vulnerable than she really was.

Turning slowly, she saw a figure appear almost magically from the darkness of a small clump of shrubbery beside the tennis court. She couldn't see his face clearly, but she had the distinct impression that he was white. His skin seemed almost to glow translucent in the darkness.

"Are you talking to me?" Audrey asked, trying to give her voice a frail-sounding quality. She hoped that—if this was her man—she could lure him to do something. He had to act before she could put the collar on him.

"What are you, stupid, too?" the man said with a snarl. "Of *course* I'm talking to you!"

Even as he was speaking, he started moving toward her. He had his right arm raised above his head. In the darkness, against the night sky, Audrey could see that he had something in his hand, but she couldn't tell exactly what. A tire iron or something.

It doesn't matter, though, Audrey thought. *This is it. Show time.*

She acted scared, told him to get away, pretended that she was about to run. When the man was only a few feet from her, he swung whatever he was holding at her. Audrey easily ducked to one side and heard it whistle above her head. With a grunt she swung the briefcase at him and he staggered back momentarily. She reached under her coat and drew her service revolver with her right hand, and whipped her badge out with her left.

"Police officer! Freeze!" she yelled.

Her voice echoed back from the dorms, filling the night.

The man cursed and threw his weapon—a crowbar—at her as he turned and bolted up the hill, ducking low and zigzagging back and forth, keeping to the shadows.

"Stop right there! I'll shoot!" Audrey shouted, but she knew that he wasn't going to obey. It was difficult to track him against the dark building and trees, and

Audrey didn't want to risk squeezing off a few rounds in the direction of the dorm, so she started in pursuit.

"Backup!" she shouted. "Where the hell's my backup?" she yelled as she ran, but the fleeing man was already up the slope. Before she could shout again, he had disappeared around the corner of the dorm.

Damn he was fast.

Breathing heavily in the cold air, Audrey charged up the hill to the Keates Hall parking lot. Two unmarked police vehicles came roaring up, and she saw Danny running across the street behind her. Audrey paused to look around. The couples she had passed earlier had stopped in front of Keates Hall and were looking back to see what all the commotion was about.

"Are you all right?" one of the boys asked.

"Someone ran by here just a second ago. Did you see him?"

Audrey was still a little out of breath from the run. She leaned forward, bracing herself with one hand on her knee and held up her badge for them to see.

"I'm with the Somerset P.D.," she said. "I'm in pursuit of a suspect. Did you see anyone run by here? White guy, maybe six foot?"

"We've seen a few people, but nobody like that," one of the girls said.

Officers approached and Audrey sighed as she looked at them. "Get statements," she instructed, indicating the four students. Then she turned to face Danny, who stood looking guilty behind her.

"We had a false alarm with Bellamy," Danny admitted. He shrugged. "The other guys were here. I was gone like four minutes."

"Sergeant Bellamy had her own team. You were my backup on foot, Danny. These other guys were in cars, too far away to do me any damn good."

"I'm sorry, Audrey."

She scowled and shook her head. "I know. You figured if somebody jumped Bellamy, what were the chances? You could get the guy and be back in a couple of minutes. I probably would have done the same."

She glanced around again. The streetlights cast their cold blue splashes of light across the deserted walkway. The bare trees that lined the walkway trembled in the chilly wind.

"I don't see how these kids could have missed him. Never mind the unmarkeds. He ran right up here," Audrey said. She was trying to hold back her anger, but it was annoying to think that they could have missed him so easily.

"It's like he can turn invisible or something," she said, mostly to herself.

"The thing with Bellamy? Wasn't the only incident tonight," Danny told her. "A girl named Sally Cohen. Guy hit her from behind and knocked her down, but she started screaming, and a couple of students who were close by came running. They chased after him, but somehow the guy got away."

"Christ! Another invisible man. Did anybody get a good look at him?" Audrey asked.

She wished she had gotten a better look at her own assailant before he had taken off. Better yet, she wished she could have gotten off a clear shot at him. That sure would have slowed the guy down!

"All they could tell us was that he was black," Danny informed her. "It's weird. A couple of the students saw him pretty good, but even on the spot, they gave such different descriptions that I couldn't make much sense of them. Officer Pelky took them down to the station to try to get a composite sketch done, but I can tell you right now, based on what I already heard, we won't get anything we can use."

Audrey sniffed with disgust and shook her head.

"Man, I can't *believe* this," she said. "I mean, how can two or more people see the same guy and not even see the same thing?"

"What I don't get," Danny said, "is why he's doing this. I mean, it takes some balls to attack someone when there's other people around. If you ask me, it seems like he *wants* to get caught."

"Not he, *they*," Audrey said emphatically. "There's at least two of them out there, doing the same damned thing. All racial crimes. And it almost seems like they're doing it intentionally, just to keep things on campus tense."

"Yeah but . . . come on, Audrey. The things these guys have said and done?" Danny asked. "You can't think they could be working together on this."

"I didn't say that. It's just weird," Audrey told him. "But as far as that goes, Danny, you never know what people will do. I've worked with bigots every day of my life. Doesn't stop me from doing what I've gotta do on the job."

"Still."

"I know. Just making a point."

Audrey didn't smile when she glanced at him. She liked Danny, and she respected his work, but right now she did not want to get involved in a discussion about how much tougher it had been for her as a black woman to get where she was than it had been for him, a white male.

"I think a cup of coffee is in order," she said, "and then I'm heading home." She started to leave but then turned back to look at Danny.

"I hate this," she said softly. "The way it's got everyone thinking and second-guessing. Damn, I wish we'd been able to nab the guy tonight."

"Yeah," Danny said. "At least one of them. Until we do, it's only going to get worse."

Jenna's alarm clock went off much too early on Monday morning. She groaned and stuffed her pillow against her ears, but that did not block out the obnoxious beeping sound. Still, she did not move to switch it off until she heard Yoshiko roll over on the top bunk and mutter something about not having to get up this early.

With a mumbled apology, Jenna reached out and turned off the alarm. "How are you feeling this morning?"

"Better," Yoshiko replied. Her voice sounded dry and raspy. "Well, not better, better. But improved. Or I will be, as long as I can get a little more sleep."

"Sorry," Jenna said again more clearly. She couldn't

tell if her roommate was really irked or just being funny, but right now, she didn't want to talk about it.

She had other things to worry about.

What had happened at Tracy's party was still bugging her. On the walk back to the dorm, Hunter had told her more about the guy who had been harassing her. His name was Frank Abernathy. He was a sophomore in Hunter's poli sci class. In the short time they had been back from semester break, Frank had already established a reputation in class for being a bit of an agitator.

The previous Friday, Hunter had told her, the poli sci professor had taken some class time to discuss what was happening on campus. Abernathy had apparently argued—quite emphatically—that since blacks were only a little more than ten percent of the country's population, they had all the "special privileges" they needed and should shut up and be content. The majority of the class had argued against him. Some had even tried to shout him down. But Frank and two of his buddies—the same guys who were with him at the party—refused to back down until the professor cut off the discussion.

Okay, Jenna thought, *so there are a few racist jerks on campus. What's the big surprise there?*

But it was surprising, and it bothered her that a university like Somerset would attract anyone who had such racist views, much less an outright white supremacist. She reassured herself with the thought that there were probably only a small handful of them, and they were unlikely to make any more trouble. On the other hand, Hunter had given Abernathy a bloody nose, and loudmouthed jerks were rarely forgetful in such instances.

The last thing the campus needed was more cause for racial strife. The situation was already dangerously volatile and neo-Nazi idiots like Frank Abernathy could only make it worse.

The thought gave Jenna pause. One of the killers out there in the shadows attacking people for their skin color was a white male, about six feet tall, and strong. That described a lot of the men on the Somerset campus, but not all of them hated people whose skin was a different hue. Jenna wondered if there was real violence behind Frank Abernathy's hatred and intolerance. If not him, he had friends who felt the same way he did.

I'll call Danny later, she thought. *The cops should at least know about Abernathy's views.*

Even if the killings stopped right now, the damage had already been done.

And at that party, I just got a tiny taste of it, Jenna thought, groaning as she swung her bedcovers aside and stood up.

Yoshiko had her face turned to the wall. Jenna didn't know if she was sleeping or awake, but she decided not to find out. If she tiptoed out of the room, hopefully Yoshiko would be sleeping soundly enough not to hear her by the time she got back from the shower.

When she was halfway across the floor to her closet, the telephone rang. Jenna let out a surprised yelp and practically dove to answer it before it could ring a second time.

"Hello," she said, whispering close to the mouth-piece.

"Jenna? Is that you? Are you all right?"

"Oh, hi, Mom," Jenna said. She pulled the chair away from Yoshiko's desk and sat down. "Yeah, I'm good. What's up?"

"Why are you whispering like that?"

There was an edginess in her mother's voice that Jenna didn't like.

"I just don't want to bother Yoshiko. She's been fighting a cold."

"I see," her mother said after clearing her throat. "Well, I've been watching the morning news. Have you seen it yet?"

"No. I'm just getting up," Jenna said, covering a yawn with her hand.

The truth was, she hadn't slept at all well. She had been tossing and turning all night, stewing about what had happened at the party, and what she could have done or *should* have done to diffuse the situation before Hunter and Frank started throwing punches. That was so unlike Hunter, too.

"There's more coverage about what's happening on campus," her mother said. "I can't believe what I'm hearing. It sounds like the sixties all over again. I know what you're going to say. But honestly, Jenna, with everything else that's happened this year on campus, maybe you *should* come home for a little while. Take a few days away from the pressure cooker out there."

"Come on, Mom," Jenna said, though what she thought was, *not again.* "It's definitely not as bad as the media is making it out to be. Besides, things are out of control on campus, yeah, but I'm doing fine."

"You're sure?"

"Absolutely," Jenna said.

There was a long pause at the other end of the line. Then her mother sighed softly. "All right, Jenna. I just don't want to spend my days and nights worrying about you getting all caught up in this thing because . . . well, you know."

"You mean because I'm dating Damon?" Jenna said. " 'Cause I'm going out with a black guy, I'm supposed to run home and hide?"

She could not help but feel at least a little bit angry at her mother for even suggesting such a thing, though she knew it was all coming from genuine love and concern.

"Damon and I are doing just fine. There's no problem there. Honest."

"I'm sure the two of you are fine," her mother said. "But you know, we can't control what other people think and do, no matter what we may think about something. Do you understand what I'm getting at?"

"I do, Mom, and I appreciate your concern," Jenna said. "Believe me, Damon and I aren't oblivious to the problems. I've been trying really hard to imagine what it must be like, you know, to look at the world through a black person's eyes. I don't even know where to start. You taught me not to consider race in dealing with people, but black people don't have that option."

She glanced up and saw that her roommate was awake and watching her from the top bunk. "It's not just black people who have to see the world through different eyes," Yoshiko said in a whisper.

Jenna nodded. "It can't be easy, no matter what," she said, as much for Yoshiko as for her mother, "but I'm fine. You don't have to worry."

"Honey, listen," April Blake told her daughter in a no-nonsense tone. "I know that I've raised a bright, sensitive, and caring girl. I just hope you realize that sometimes the rest of the world isn't as bright, sensitive, and caring as we might like to think it is."

Remembering what Frank Abernathy had said to her, Jenna could not help but agree. She would have said as much to her mother, but a soft knock on the door drew her attention.

"Hey, Mom, there's someone at the door," she said, "and I'm going to be late for class if I don't get moving. I'll call you tonight, okay? Bye. Love you."

"I love you, too, Jenna," her mother said before hanging up.

Jenna opened the door to see Damon and Brick standing in the hallway. Damon leaned forward and gave her a quick kiss on the cheek. As she stepped back, Jenna saw that he was holding a piece of green paper. He held it out to her and she took it.

"These things are plastered all over campus," he said. "The Coalition for Racial Diversity is sponsoring a peace rally tonight at seven o'clock."

"We were thinking maybe we'd all go together," Brick said. "There's a memorial service for Brittany and that senior, Dave Berman, right before it. It was supposed to be at the chapel, but they're expecting so many people they're going to do it on the quad right before the rally."

Jenna glanced quickly at the announcement, which featured the international peace symbol with the letters CRD written above it, and the time and place below. Then she glanced up at Yoshiko, who was sitting up on the top bunk with the covers pulled up to her chest.

"You up for it?" she asked.

"Sounds good to me," Yoshiko said, smiling. "I'll drag Hunter, too."

"Cool," Jenna said, nodding to Brick. "But look, I'm going to be late for class if I don't hustle."

She folded the flyer in half and put it on the bureau behind her. When she turned, she was surprised to see that Brick had taken a step forward into the room. He looked uncomfortable, standing there scratching the back of his head, eyes kind of roving around the room.

"Look, Jenna," he said. "I want to apologize for what I said the other day."

Jenna opened her mouth and was about to say that he didn't have to apologize for anything, but he kept talking, cutting her off before she could speak.

"I've been thinking about it, a lot, and it's been bugging me that, you know, that you might think I was getting all bigoted myself because of what's happened. That's not the way it is. The whole world is Us and Them, but that's just saying good people and bad people, nothing to do with color. What I said was—"

"Apology accepted," Jenna said softly.

She wrapped her arms around him, and gave him a big hug.

"I know you're really upset because of what happened to Brittany and Ant," she said. "I don't blame you. And I have to thank you. All this has me so on edge that I'm seeing hate everywhere. I needed someone to remind me that the world isn't always like this."

Brick pulled back and smiled awkwardly, then looked away.

"You're a pretty cool girl, you know that?" he said. "I'm telling you, you hooked up with the wrong man here. When you see the error of your ways and you're looking for real romance, buzz me. You know where I'll be."

Damon punched him in the shoulder, and Brick gave a sinister little laugh. Yoshiko was chuckling as well and Brick shot a mock-angry glance up at the top bunk.

"Hey. Don't you doubt it a second, Yoshiko," Brick said.

"I don't know," Jenna said airily. "I don't think I could go out with a guy who had sex with Olivia Adams. You've got to be some kind of masochist to be with a woman that angry."

Brick protested, blasting Damon for telling Jenna about him and Olivia, and overall just acting very silly. Jenna and Yoshiko teased him mercilessly. It was a nice break in all the tension that had been running so high for all of them. But Damon shoved Brick out into the hallway, chuckling. Then he turned around and his gaze met Jenna's, and it hurt her to realize that not all of the tension was gone between them.

"I've got a full day," Jenna said apologetically, "but I'll hook up with you tonight for the service and the rally, okay?"

Damon nodded silently, then turned and followed his friend down the hall as Jenna watched them from the door. She wanted to call out to him, tell him to stop, to talk to her about whatever he was feeling. But then she realized that if he did stop, she would not know what to say.

At the top of Memorial Steps was a kind of forum made up of the sloping of the earth and the paths of the academic quad, surrounded by the nineteenth-century buildings in which most of the liberal arts classes were held. The far end of the quad was brightly lit by the fluttering orange glow of hundreds of candles, which the peace rally organizers had passed out for the memorial service that had preceded the rally. It had been a respectful, reserved service, and when it was over, the candles kept burning.

The rally was not quite as calm.

Jenna stood close beside Damon, their gloved hands entwined, while nearby, Yoshiko, Hunter, Brick, Olivia, and Caitlin huddled together as much from the cold as from the press of the huge crowd that had gathered.

Jenna had been surprised at first that Olivia was standing with them. Not only with Caitlin—the two seemed to have had no problem making up—but with the rest of them as well. The line had been so fervently drawn down racial lines in previous days that she had assumed Olivia would be with Darnell Thomas and the other more vocal SAAL members. It heartened her to see that was not so. This was an event sponsored by the CRD, after all. A celebration of unity and the shattering of color lines.

They were together. For the first time in days, Jenna felt that there was the possibility for the campus to draw together, for the students to rise above the tragedies they had recently experienced. It felt good.

Olivia and several other black students in the crowd were wearing black armbands, but even that militant symbol seemed lost in the overall good feeling of all the races represented on campus coming together.

At the top of the Memorial Steps, using a makeshift podium, stood Jules Barros, the president of the CRD. His amplified voice echoed and reechoed from the surrounding buildings, making it difficult at times to catch everything he was saying, especially with the crowd pressing all around them. So far, Jenna liked what she had heard about accepting racial diversity as a strength, not a weakness, but as Jules spoke there were pockets of restlessness among the crowd. As Jenna took a closer look at the crowd her good feeling began to dissipate, to be replaced by a gnawing sense of dread.

Most of the black students scattered throughout the crowd seemed calm and open to the spirit of the moment. Most, but not all. Many of them were waving signs over their heads. Some of the signs pictured Martin Luther King, while others had hastily scrawled images of clenched black fists with messages that read: FIGHT THE POWER and WHERE IS JUSTICE?

Grouped to one side, on the steps of Traynor Hall,

was a cluster of white males. When Jenna studied them a moment, she recognized Frank Abernathy, who was carrying a sign that read IT'S A WHITE WORLD AFTER ALL. There couldn't have been more than a dozen of them, but they were making plenty of noise as Jules tried to speak.

The majority of those gathered, all different races and creeds, seemed to embrace the words of the speaker. Jules Barros insisted that the Somerset campus had to set an example for the rest of the state and for the entire country by showing that all races could coexist peacefully, even in times of crisis. But still those small clutches of angry people looking for a conflict charged the atmosphere with volatile energy.

Jenna noticed that there were plenty of cops on hand in case things got out of control. Several of them were lined up in front of Traynor Hall, obviously trying to keep the white-power students separated from the nearby sign-waving SAAL members.

Several times, Jules had to stop speaking when one or another group began shouting or chanting, and then the others would try to shout them down.

"I don't like this at all," Jenna said. She leaned close to Damon and practically had to shout into his ear to be heard.

Damon looked at her and nodded his agreement.

"I like what the man has to say, though," he said, indicating Jules with a quick nod of the head. Next to Damon, Brick was standing stiffly at attention with his arms folded across his chest. His face was expressionless.

"Absolutely," Jenna said, "but I'm afraid that the ones who need to hear it the most won't get it."

She paused a moment and watched Jules. In the flickering candlelight, she could see that his skin was the color of coffee with too much cream. His handsome features suggested that he might be of Caribbean origin. He was wearing jeans and a bulky winter coat.

"What's his deal, anyway?" she asked, tapping Damon on the shoulder. "I don't think I've seen him around campus."

"He's not around much," Damon replied. "He's from Cape Verde, I think. He was my T.A. in American political thought last semester. I think he's planning to go to grad school for international diplomacy or something. Sounds like he's been practicing."

"Well, I'll tell you one thing," Jenna said. "I think what he's doing takes guts. You've got angry people on both sides looking for a fight, maybe willing to start one. If he keeps this up, they're all going to want a piece of him."

Damon frowned, then nodded his agreement.

At the front of the crowd, the group of white supremacists had started a chant that was gathering in volume as they waved their signs overhead.

"White power! White power!"

"Yes, oh yes, white power," Jules called out to them. "Absolutely. White power. Black power. Yellow, red, and green power. See, you've only got part of the puzzle figured out. Put it all together and it says 'Power,' true. Put it all together and it says 'Power to the People.' That's what happens when we're together.

Otherwise all we get is . . . well, look around you at the angry faces here today."

His amplified voice was almost drowned out by Abernathy and his fellow Neanderthals. Within seconds, the SAAL members started a counterchant: *"What do we want? Justice! When do we want it? Now!"* Olivia moved forward with the surge of the crowd. Her clenched fist was thrust high above her head.

"Man, it's gonna get ugly," Damon said as he pulled Jenna protectively closer to him.

"Listen to me, people!" Jules shouted, his voice straining to rise above the conflicting chants. "We have to *stop* this! Right *now!* This is *not* what we're about! Nobody wins like this!"

"White power!"

"Justice!"

"Hey!" Jules shouted. His face looked flushed in the candlelight. "I said 'Hey!' You want to kill each other? You want to make every ugly thing ever said about your people, white or black, come true? Go ahead. But I won't stand here and watch. That's not what we're here for today!"

Sneering with disgust, he threw the microphone down onto the granite steps. It hit with a loud *crack*, then filled the air with the shrill squeal of feedback until someone unplugged it. But even that didn't stop the chanters.

"What do we want? Justice!"

"White power!"

Jenna clutched Damon's hand tightly and started backing away, wanting to get away from the press of the crowd before a riot broke out. It looked like that was a real possibility. The cops had formed a protective ring around the small knot of white-power students, who were practically surrounded by black students and other white students who were shouting angrily at them.

Holding tightly to Damon's hand, Jenna pushed forward through the crowd. The fastest way out seemed to be past the podium and down Memorial Steps where they could make a wide berth and swing back around toward the dorms. They had just started down the steps when a shrill scream rose above the chanting crowd.

"What was that?" Jenna asked, looking around nervously.

A small group of people had gathered in the flickering candlelight twenty feet from the podium. They formed a ring and were looking down at the ground. Jenna caught a glimpse of Detectives Mariano and Gaines as they rushed over to the scene of the disturbance.

"I want to see what's up," Jenna said as she started back toward the commotion, dragging Damon along behind her. It took them a while to get through the sudden crush of onlookers, and when they finally did, what she saw made her heart flutter in her chest. A thick, sour sensation filled her stomach.

Sitting on the ground was a black girl. Her legs were splayed out awkwardly in front of her, and she was rocking back and forth, holding both hands to the side of her head where blood seeped out from between her fingers.

Jenna pushed up beside Danny Mariano. "What happened?"

Danny indicated another figure on the ground. It was

a white man wearing a dark sweatshirt and a woolen knit hat. His eyes were closed, and he wasn't moving.

"Looks like he jumped her," Danny said. "Even with a big crowd like this around." He shook his head. "I just don't get it."

The girl on the ground was crying as she rocked back and forth. Audrey and another uniformed police officer were kneeling down beside her, trying to comfort and tend to her.

"He tried to kill me! He tried to kill me," she kept saying through her tears.

"Is he dead?" Damon asked incredulously.

Danny glanced at him, then at Jenna, and she saw in his eyes that he made the connection instantly. Damon was her boyfriend. But this was hardly the time for introductions.

"One of the uniforms saw it happen," Danny explained. "He grabbed the guy, hit him once with the stick. The guy went down hard."

"So he is dead?" Jenna asked, unable to hide her nervousness. "Just like that? One whack with a nightstick and that's it?"

Danny shrugged. "As for what killed him, you and Slick can confirm that tomorrow. But yeah, he's dead."

"Yes! All right!"

Jenna jumped when she heard someone shouting so close beside her. She turned and saw Olivia, glaring at the man who was down on the ground.

"It's about time they dropped the bastard!" Olivia said, and then her voice rose into a victorious whoop.

"Ding dong, the son of a bitch is dead!"

chapter 6

Jenna stared at Olivia in horror. "God, what is wrong with you?" she asked. "This isn't a celebration. Something awful just happened here, and you're trying to be *funny*?"

Olivia's smile disappeared, replaced by a snarl. "We wanted justice, Jenna. Maybe the police weren't gonna work overtime to give it to us, but when it happens right in front of them, they sorta have to do something about it, don't they? This is about all the justice we can expect, so yeah, I'll celebrate."

"Maybe you could do it somewhere else?"

Both girls looked up to see Audrey Gaines glaring at them, positioning herself between Jenna and her friends and the chaos that constituted police business: the injured girl, the dead man, and the police who had gathered to keep the crowd back. Jenna glanced over and saw Danny watching her, and listening. She was embarrassed by the things Olivia had said about the police, but she shook it off. Danny knew how she felt. So did Audrey, for that matter.

Beside her, Damon cleared his throat, reached out for Olivia's hand, and started them all moving. Hunter and Yoshiko followed.

"Let's go Olivia. You want the police to do their job, that means we need to be out of the way," he said. "You might want to rein your mouth in a little, though. You don't even know if this is the guy who killed Brittany."

Olivia had been more or less going along with them, moving away from the chaos. Brick and Caitlin stood talking at the outer edge of the crowd—all but the most vocal students and the most curious onlookers had already left the quad. She was moving toward Brick and Caitlin, but when Damon spoke those words, Olivia spun around to face him, shaking his hand off her as though it were something filthy.

"You condescending SOB," she snapped. "Don't even touch me."

Brick and Caitlin looked up at her shout and started toward them. Yoshiko had the opposite reaction. She grabbed Hunter and pulled him away from the group. "We're out of here. See you later, Jenna."

"Later," Jenna agreed, barely looking up.

Olivia was fuming, and Damon just looked disgusted. Jenna took a step toward them, all her anxiety and sensitivity giving way to anger. "Olivia, what is it with you? Are you going out of your way to alienate your friends, or what? It's like being angry and staying that way is the most important thing in your life. Why can't we—"

"Why can't we what?" Olivia shouted, a cynical edge to her voice. "Why can't we all get along? Please, Jenna, don't tell me that's what you were going to say, 'cause I'll have to throw up."

Brick and Caitlin had come up beside her. When Caitlin touched her shoulder, Olivia turned to glare at her as well.

"Hey," Caitlin said quietly. "Can we crank it down a notch? You're drawing a lot of attention here."

"Oh, I'm so-o-o sorry!" Olivia said, even more loudly. "Am I embarrassing you?"

Jenna was surprised to see that Brick actually looked angry. She had known that he was inclined to side with Olivia when it came to racial issues, but this display on her part had apparently set him off as well.

"Olivia. You're close to crossing a line, here," he told her.

"She's already crossed it," Damon said bluntly. "I think she's getting off on all of this. I think she likes it."

"Go to hell!" Olivia roared at him.

Jenna glanced around nervously. Caitlin had been right. They were drawing attention, had become enough of a spectacle that some of the bystanders not close enough to the corpse and the police and the newly arrived ambulance whose lights strobed the trees and buildings around them had started to move over to watch the argument that was taking place.

"We should go," she whispered to Damon, moving up beside him and gripping him by the elbow.

"No!" he snapped, shaking her off.

Jenna stared in astonishment at the fury in her

boyfriend's eyes. She had never seen him this way before. He stalked up to Olivia and stuck a finger out, came just short of jabbing her in the chest with it to make his point.

"You're a screwed-up girl, Olivia," Damon told her through clenched teeth. "I may not agree with your political views, but I respect them. You have passion, and that's admirable. But when you start doing a little dance after a man dies practically in front of you, then I have to start wondering. You don't know what happened here. The cops don't even really know until they look into it some more. But it's like this is all a big game to you. Is this really about racial integrity, Olivia? Or is it just a cheap thrill for you?"

Even as the words left Damon's lips, Jenna felt the urge to catch them, to make him take them back. But it was too late. Olivia cocked her arm back and slapped him so hard across the face that Damon staggered backward slightly.

"How *dare* you?" she roared.

Jenna shrunk as the crowd around them, watching their ugly performance, grew even larger.

"You want to judge me? *You?*" Olivia screamed at Damon. Tears sprang to her cheeks. Brick backed off, shaking his head, but Caitlin went to try to calm her friend. Olivia only glared at her until she backed off, then turned her attention back to Damon and Jenna.

"Both of you!" she said, eyes narrowed. "You judge me? Take a look around you. Look at what's happened just on this campus. It's easy for you to pretend that racism doesn't exist. Just the way you two pretend. But guess what? Peaceful coexistence is about the best we can hope for, and maybe we really can accomplish that.

"But when a black man gets together with a white woman, when that line is crossed, it draws attention we don't need. It starts trouble. Being with a white girl isn't just turning your back on your people, Damon; it's irresponsible and it's dangerous. It inspires exactly the kind of thing we've all been protesting this past week."

They all stood around in a half circle, staring in disbelief at Olivia. Even Brick had an expression of horror and discomfort on his face.

"My God," Damon whispered, shaking his head. "You're—"

"Twisted," Jenna snapped. "You're out of your mind. Are you really suggesting that Brittany Forrester got killed because Damon and I are sleeping together? Other than in your fevered brain, how does that make sense?"

"It sets people off, Jenna. You're so goddamned naive. I heard what happened at Tracy Hotchkiss's the other night. Are you blind? Jesus! Frank Abernathy is scum. A lowlife, Nazi racist who deserves a beating and enforced chemical castration so he can't breed. But nothing would have happened there, not a damn thing, if not for you. There were plenty of people of color at that party, Jenna, but none of them set off a powder keg. *You* did—and the fact that your boyfriend is a black man."

"So we're supposed to let people like Frank Abernathy decide who can be together and who can't?"

Jenna replied, shouting, now, and not caring about the audience they had attracted. "Well, I don't want to live in that world."

"You already do!" Olivia snapped bitterly. "That's what I've been trying to tell you. Every time there's an incident, it's one more obstacle to overcome. All this chaos? It's your fault. You and people like you are responsible for all of this. You're always saying it doesn't have to be this way. You're right."

With that, she turned and stalked away, pushing at the people blocking her way. None of them cheered, which heartened Jenna, but none of them looked ready to dismiss her immediately either.

When Olivia was gone, Jenna turned to Damon and almost instantly glanced away. She could not stand the confusion and pain she saw in his eyes. Instead, she moved close and just held him. When he reached down and wiped at her eyes, she realized with some embarrassment and a great deal of anger that she had been crying.

At some point, while they were standing there locked in an embrace, their faces reflecting the turmoil in their hearts, somebody stepped in and snapped a few pictures in quick succession. Jenna turned, ready to scream at the photographer, but even though the audience around them had thinned considerably, she could not see who had taken the pictures.

"Guys, we should go," Caitlin said softly.

Angry and confused, Jenna was about to nod when she glanced back at the crime scene, now surrounded by yellow police line tape, and saw Dr. Slikowski sitting in his wheelchair, talking to Audrey and Danny, both of whom had crouched down to speak with him.

A change came over Jenna then. Where her mind had been chaos a moment before, the sight of Slick and the detectives talking seemed to clear her head. As a part of the mass of students upon whom the past days' horrors had been inflicted, she was helpless to do anything but react. Suddenly, however, she was reminded that she was not like the rest of the student body. She was involved in this professionally as well.

Damon touched her on the shoulder. "Jenna?"

With an almost imperceptible nod to herself, her features now more confident and composed than they had been all night, she faced her boyfriend. Jenna placed her right hand on his chest and stood on tiptoe to kiss him lightly.

"You guys go on back," she said firmly, finding the authority within her. "I'm going to stay and talk to Dr. Slikowski and the detectives. See what's up."

Damon frowned. "Jenna, come on," he protested. "There's nothing you can do right now."

The words were such a haunting yet negative echo of her own sentiments from a moment before that they made Jenna flinch. She shook her head in frustration.

"Yeah. I can. Look, I'll come by your room in a bit, okay? I want to talk to Slick and see what's up," she explained. Then she turned and walked away from them.

A moment later she glanced back to see him scowl, shake his head, and follow Brick and Caitlin back across the quad toward the dorms. Though she tried not to let it bother her, Jenna could not help but be disturbed by his reaction. Damon had never really been comfortable with the work she did for the M.E.'s office. And he had been vocally opposed to the lengths she had gone to, the danger she had put herself in for the job since she'd started working there in September.

For the most part, they'd gotten past that in their relationship. But as Jenna watched him walk away, she realized that it remained a much larger issue than she had believed.

With a sigh, she shook off the temptation to go after him, to talk it out now before it got worse. But the problem was not a superficial one. It was not something that could be mended in a single conversation. For the time being, it would have to wait.

Meanwhile, there were greater issues at hand. Jenna edged her way through the remaining students and the faculty and university administration people who had appeared on the scene now that the worst had actually happened. She spotted Professor Fournier, who taught her Shakespeare class, speaking in an angry whisper to the dean of students, but she had no desire to stop and talk to the man. Fournier had said a few things in class that implied that he wasn't exactly free from prejudice himself.

More police cars had arrived, driving down the wide paved paths that were usually reserved only for walking through the academic quad. An ambulance had taken the girl who had been attacked across the ridiculously short distance to Somerset Medical Center on the other side of campus. The lights of a second ambulance flickered ghostly red off the trees. Their passenger was in no rush, however.

As Jenna walked up she saw the attacker's corpse being zipped into a body bag. The EMTs had confirmed that he had no life signs, made a token effort to revive him, and now they were going to cart him over to the morgue. The last photographs had been taken, and now there was only an indentation in the trampled snow where the body had been.

Audrey was talking to a uniformed officer off to one side when Jenna walked up to Slick and Danny. The detective noticed her first.

"Hey," he said. "I thought you'd gone home." His tone made it clear that he was glad to see that she had not left. It only reinforced the clarity in Jenna's head, her feeling that this was where she belonged. As part of this.

Slick looked a bit tired, but otherwise well. She wondered if it was having to push his wheelchair around during the winter. It could not be easy. Even now he was on the paved path, unable to get any closer to the actual crime scene without help that he would never request.

He smiled when he saw her, though. Jenna and the M.E. had a kind of bond that was special to her. Their minds worked in similar fashion. Solving puzzles, helping people, pursuing a line of inquiry to its conclusion, no matter the consequences. In the past, during the most bizarre of circumstances, she had proven herself quite an asset to his team.

"Good evening, Jenna," the M.E. said warmly. "I'm

glad you're here." Then his smile faltered. He scratched at the back of his head, where the gray at his temples had yet to reach. The lights of the ambulance created an odd refraction in his steel-rimmed spectacles.

"Were you here when all this happened?" Slick asked.

Audrey got Danny's attention, and then Jenna and her mentor were alone together. She did not crouch to speak with him for she knew it made him self-conscious.

"A bunch of us were here," she told him. "We didn't see anything, though. It all happened pretty fast."

"It always does," Slick replied. "I'm glad you're all right."

Jenna was cheered by his concern for her. "I don't think I was ever in any danger," she said. "I was with a bunch of other people, including Damon. In a really morbid way, it's almost good that this happened. This was supposed to be a peace rally, but things got out of hand. A lot of really bad feelings, not to mention bad people on both sides, tried to get a riot going or something. They cleared out fast, that's for sure."

"I'm not surprised," Slick said. "It's also unfortunate. The police will never be able to determine precisely who was here when the crime occurred or exactly what happened."

Jenna frowned. She cocked her thumb over her shoulder to indicate the ambulance. Paramedics were loading a stretcher with a body bag on it into the back of the vehicle.

"Not like it's any great mystery," she said. "I mean,

the policeman who wailed on that guy saw him attack the girl. You can't get much more concrete than that."

"True," Slick said, looking thoughtful. "Still, the detectives like to have a clearer picture of the motivating factors in any homicide. More witnesses would help. We also don't know if the deceased was our killer or simply one of those 'bad people' you were talking about. I'm told there was a group of white supremacists in the crowd. He may well have been one of them."

"Maybe," Jenna replied, troubled. "Though I'd hate to think this wasn't our guy." She thought about it for a moment, her brow creased with dismay. Then she brightened suddenly. "Hey!"

Slick offered an odd smile, taken aback by her outburst. "Yes?"

"The perp who killed Brittany Forrester and put Anthony Williams in the hospital? Brittany scratched him. I scraped tissue samples from underneath her fingernails. We'll have no problem figuring out if this DOA is the same guy."

The M.E. smiled proudly. "My thoughts exactly. You aren't scheduled to work tomorrow, you know. I assume you'll want to come in for the autopsy?"

Jenna nodded grimly. The paramedics had loaded the dead man into the back of the ambulance, and the vehicle began to move away. The lights on top were turned off and the quad was suddenly darker. She glanced over at Danny and Audrey where they stood speaking to the other cops, and her thoughts began to drift again. Back to Damon and his frustration that she had chosen to stay behind. Jenna watched the way Danny and Audrey dealt with each another. They were partners, not lovers, but even so, it didn't seem as though it would ever occur to Danny to discourage Audrey from putting herself in danger on the job. That *was* the job.

Not that Jenna was a cop, certainly. But when she set out to help solve the mystery of a person's death, if for no other reason than to give comfort to those left behind, she sometimes got in too deep. Others in the kind of job she had would probably never leave the office or the autopsy room, but Jenna could not remain so clinical. For better or for worse, she had a mentor who felt the same way.

"Where've you gone?" Slick asked.

Jenna blinked, then smiled self-consciously. "Sorry. Just trying to work some things out."

"It's a difficult time," Slick said.

Jenna knew that he was referring to the racial strife and the attacks, not her personal life, but she did not correct him. When she glanced at him, though, she noticed his clothes for the first time. He was always well dressed, but tonight, beneath his winter coat, Slick wore a stylish red tie. She could tell by the crisp crease in his pants leg that he was wearing a suit, and it looked relatively new.

"Were you out with Natalie tonight?" she asked, smiling.

Slick straightened up a bit in his chair, then nodded slightly. "We were just finishing dinner when they beeped me."

"You left her to eat dessert by herself?" Jenna teased.

"Tiramisu," he confirmed. "She'll forgive me."

"Not if you do it often enough," Jenna warned. "On the other hand, it is sort of like Clark Kent running off to a phone booth, I guess. Sort of heroic."

Slick seemed to like that image. It amused Jenna, but only for a moment. Her mind went back to what she had been thinking about only moments before. Damon clearly did not want her running off to play Supergirl, or whatever.

Jenna uttered a tiny sigh.

Danny and Audrey had finished with the other officers, and Jenna looked up to find Danny standing beside her. "Long night?" he asked.

"For all of us, I think," she replied.

He nodded. "I guess we're all hoping this turns out to be one of our guys. Given the attack in the middle of a public event, he's reckless enough to be the same guy."

"One of them, yes," Slick added soberly.

"That's what's got me on edge." Audrey joined them. Her eyes darted around as though she were searching for something. "Even if this is our guy, there's still another one out there. It's making me damned irritable."

"So that's what it is?" Danny asked, razzing her. "What about every other day?"

Audrey glared at him, and they all chuckled.

From across the quad, where Fletcher Avenue ran past the language lab and Sparrow Hall, there came a screech of tires, the sudden blaring of a car horn, and then a shriek of tearing metal and shattering glass.

They all looked up instantly. Danny and Audrey started hustling toward Fletcher Avenue without a word. Another cop, closer to the action, looked back at the detectives.

"The ambulance!" he shouted.

Then they were all running.

All save Jenna and Slick. The medical examiner was incapable of running. Jenna moved behind Slick to help, but he was already in motion, pushing his wheels, propelling himself along the paved path as fast as he could manage. For a moment Jenna had forgotten how determinedly, almost angrily self-reliant he was. She took a deep breath, and then she followed at a run. The only reason the police beat them to the scene of the accident by as much as they did was that Slick had to stick to the paths, and the cops could just sprint across the snow.

Her course took her right past Sparrow Hall and the juxtaposition of her normal, college life with her job was oddly surreal. Then she was out onto Fletcher Avenue and turning right past her dorm. There was a small parking lot on that side of the hill, behind the dorms, and the ambulance had somehow veered off the road and plowed into a Pathfinder. Both vehicles had sustained heavy damage, but the ambulance had the worst of it. The back doors hung open. The hood was crumpled. The windshield was shattered, and the driver was standing in the street with a huge cloth over a bloody gash in his forehead. The other paramedic lay on the ground not far from the Pathfinder as though he had been thrown from the vehicle.

It was chaos. The cops all looked completely freaked.

Jenna's heart was pumping fast from trying to keep up with Slick as she ran up beside him. He sat in his chair a respectful distance from the accident, trying to stay out of the way of the police.

"What's going on?" Jenna asked, a little out of breath. "God, it's just one thing after another tonight. Could this night possibly get any worse?"

Danny spotted them and came over. He looked pale and drawn, almost nauseous, and his eyes were haunted.

"What happened?" Jenna asked incredulously.

"We're not sure," he admitted, eyes ticking from Slick to Jenna and then back again. "The paramedic up there on the hill? He's dead. Broken neck. Driver says someone hit him."

"Hit him?" Jenna repeated, incredulous.

"Yeah," Danny said, "and the DOA's gone."

"What do you mean 'gone'?" Slick asked gravely.

"He's gone," Danny replied. "He's not inside the body bag."

"You've gotta be kidding," Jenna said. She glanced at Slick and added, "Next time I'll know to keep my big mouth shut."

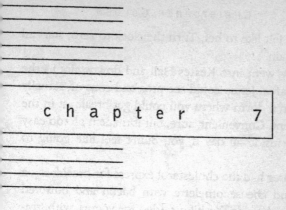

The weather in New England is always unpredictable, but never so much as in late winter as it begins to climb toward spring. On Tuesday morning the temperature rose significantly. The sun was out, and the snow had begun to melt again as Jenna, Hunter, and Yoshiko walked to Keates Hall for breakfast.

The snowbanks built up by plows after the recent storms were filthy with dirt and sand. Now that it was melting, the snow seemed even more of a mess. But that didn't bother Jenna in the least. Despite the events of the previous night, she looked up at the sky, clear and cloudless, and allowed herself to begin to hope that the pall that had hung over Somerset in previous days may have dissipated along with the cold, that it might be melting with the snow.

A music riff kept running through her head as she crossed the quad toward Keates, a new energy in her step. It was the Sting song, "Brand New Day." That was what it felt like to her. Turn the clock to zero; start all over again.

They went into Keates Hall and downstairs to the dining area. Jenna could see pros and cons of actually living in a dorm where you could get breakfast in the basement. Convenient, sure, but it made it all too easy to stay inside all day if you didn't feel like going to class.

Hunter had the cholesterol express for breakfast—a ham and cheese omelette with bacon and buttered toast on the side. Yoshiko settled for yogurt with granola and fresh fruit. Jenna wasn't in the mood to be healthy, but she also was not about to put the kind of junk into her system that Hunter seemed to thrive on. She got herself a big bowl of Cap'n Crunch instead. She figured you could never go wrong with the Captain.

They talked about little of significance over breakfast, mostly bemoaning how much studying they had to do, how far they had fallen behind, and which professors they regretted ever having met. It was small talk, and Jenna recognized it as such, but she also thought that maybe small talk was exactly what they needed right now. Despite how much they all felt they needed to catch up after recent distractions, they also needed to get away, to get off campus, even for a few hours.

"Hey, why don't we all get out of here tonight?" Jenna suggested. "We could hit a movie or just go into Harvard Square and hang."

"I wouldn't mind checking out a band or going to the movies," Hunter said. "If you two don't mind, that is. Why don't we see who's going to be playing at

House of Blues and Delgado's? If there's nothing that catches your eye we can have dinner at Miyamoto's or something and then go to the movies in Harvard Square. Best of both worlds."

"That sounds perfect. Just the three of us," Jenna said happily. "To be honest, I'd be happy with hot wings at the Cuckoo's Nest, but whatever you guys want."

"What about Damon?" Yoshiko asked, a tiny frown creasing her forehead.

Jenna shrugged and glanced away. "I think maybe it would be good for us to have some time to ourselves. Just to regroup, y'know? I'll talk to him about it."

Her friends nodded but made no further comment. The conversation turned back to the insubstantial, and life went on. Jenna was glad. She was already really looking forward to the night ahead. She allowed herself to drift off into the selfish world inside her head for a little while, but gradually Jenna became aware of an odd tension that seemed to exist between her two friends. Yoshiko and Hunter were fine while the three of them were talking, but during silences, and particularly now that Jenna herself had fallen silent, they seemed awkward with each other. For a guy and girl who were hopelessly in love, they also seemed to be sitting a little farther away from each other than she would have expected.

Jenna was done with her Cap'n Crunch, so while the others were still working on their breakfasts, she took the time to study them carefully. Yup. Something was definitely wrong.

"What's up with you guys?" she asked at last. "You okay?"

Yoshiko gave Hunter a sidelong glance and shifted uncomfortably. "Sure. We're fine. Why?"

Hunter looked at her oddly, then at Jenna. "Not really," he corrected. "I mean, we're doing all right, but this race stuff has been getting to both of us. It isn't easy, the way people look at you all the time. We'll be okay, I just can't wait for this to be over."

"No kidding." Jenna glanced around the dining hall. "Trust me when I say I know what it's like to be stared at. I hoped I was just being paranoid, but no such luck, I guess. It's all just been so bizarre. Then, last night, with that guy—"

"What about that?" Hunter asked, eyes narrowing. "I thought we went through the whole coming-back-from-the-dead thing *last* semester?"

Despite the tension, Jenna laughed at that. Months earlier she had worked on a case with the medical examiner that had involved a criminal using toxic powders to make individuals appear to be dead and then others to revive them and control their minds. There was no such thing as zombies. That was for sure. Still . . .

"I don't think this was the same thing. If he woke up that quickly and moved fast enough to overpower the paramedics and get out of the ambulance after it crashed, this guy had complete control of his faculties," she observed. "The snow prevented Dr. Slikowski from getting close enough to get a good look at him, and I didn't either. Lucky for him, I guess.

Slick would have known right away that he was faking it somehow."

"Faking it *how*, though?" Hunter asked, a confused expression on his face.

Yoshiko seemed contemplative. Jenna watched her. "What is it?" she asked her roommate.

"Just thinking," Yoshiko replied. "I guess we've all read about these swamis and stuff, people who can slow their respiration and heartbeat so they're in, like, suspended animation or something. I guess that's possible."

"It's crazy, but I guess that could be it," Jenna agreed. "However he did it, the guy is obviously not exactly what he seems to be."

Hunter chuckled. "Who is?"

Yoshiko shot him a hard look. "What's *that* supposed to mean?"

"Come on now, Yoshiko," Hunter said, reaching out to stroke her arm. "I wasn't talking about you or us. You know that."

Jenna took a deep breath and watched them with great concern. She found herself suddenly very passionate about the well-being of their relationship. Whatever happened with her and Damon, whatever happened on campus, it was important to her that Hunter and Yoshiko stay together. They were her two best friends, and she could not imagine what it would be like if they broke up, how difficult it would become for the three of them to hang around together. It was selfish of her, and she knew it. But it was also for them. They were perfect for each other. Hunter gave Yoshiko the measure of confidence she needed in herself; in return, he had the love and companionship that enabled him to go on day after day in the wake of his sister's murder the previous semester.

Jenna wanted to help, but she did not want to intrude. Instead, she turned the topic back to other territory.

"Whatever's going on with that guy last night is freaky," she said. "And you know once the freaky stuff starts happening, it piques Dr. Slikowski's interest."

"Not to mention yours," Yoshiko chided her.

Jenna shrugged. "Not to mention. Seriously, though, we're not going to let this one get by. We're going to find out what's going on here. I won't be happy until all of this stuff is put to rest." She narrowed her gaze and studied her two best friends. "Besides, are you really going to let morons like Frank Abernathy decide how you should behave? Who you can love? That's crazy. You think I'm going to let Olivia Adams tell me how to think and act? Forget it."

She waved her hand dismissively.

"This is the real world," she went on. "And in the real world, people need each other, and that's not defined by race or gender or anything else. Like Hunter says, there are only two kinds of people in the world. Assholes and others."

They all laughed at that, and then talk turned to other things. Lighter things. Jenna's birthday was coming up as well as Valentine's Day. There were things to celebrate, things to look forward to, and Jenna felt confident that somehow the chaos on campus would be over by then.

A few minutes later Jenna spotted the clock on the wall. Time was growing short, and she didn't want to be late for her eight-fifty Spanish class. She stood and took her tray up to the long horizontal hole in the wall where students left their plates and utensils and such. All she could see of the people back there who were washing the trays and plates was their hands. Jenna had always thought it a bit surreal.

Hunter and Yoshiko followed after Hunter gathered most of the trash off the table. As they walked up the stairs, they passed Aime Doyle and Keith Belinsky, who also lived in Sparrow.

"Hey, Jenna!" Aime said, a little too friendly.

"Hey," Jenna replied, taken slightly aback. They had never had more than a passing acquaintance, and it was odd for Aime to be so outgoing.

"So you're a celebrity now, huh?" Aime asked.

Jenna frowned. "What are you talking about?"

"You mean you haven't seen the *Daily* yet?" Aime looked uncomfortable, then she grabbed Keith by the arm and started dragging him down the stairs again. "Um, I'll see you later, okay?"

For a moment Jenna was confused, but only for a moment. Then she recalled with horrifying clarity the flash of the photographer's camera from the night before as she was holding Damon, kissing him and hanging on to him as if for dear life.

"Oh, my God," she croaked as a sick feeling blossomed in her stomach. "Come on, you guys." She grabbed Hunter and Yoshiko and dragged them upstairs and into the foyer of the building.

"What's going on?" Hunter asked, confused.

"Jenna," Yoshiko said, her voice filled with concern. "Jenna, slow down. What's wrong?"

There was a wooden stand just inside the front door of the dorm where free copies of the *Somerset Daily* were stacked. Even as Jenna approached, a few students grabbed copies from the stack. Most everybody on campus read the *Daily*. The queasiness in Jenna's stomach increased, and she winced. Even as her hand reached out for the top copy on the stack, Jenna knew what she would find.

She wanted to cry.

The paper was rough to the touch. Newsprint came off on her fingertips. She picked up the paper and looked at the front page, and there it was: a photo of her holding Damon, him kissing the side of her face. Behind them, to the left, the photograph also showed Olivia glaring at them. The headline read "Peace Rally Becomes Race Riot." What followed was the story of the previous evening's events, including the attack on a black female student and the apparent death of the suspect. There were interviews, articles, commentary, all discussing the racial strife of the previous days, culminating in the events last night.

None of that bothered Jenna. What disturbed her, hurt her, was the caption beneath the photograph. In boldface were the words "Racial Unity???" The triple question marks punctuated how much of a question they thought the phrase was. There was more: "Freshmen Jenna Blake and Damon Harris bear recent racial strife together even as others, like freshman

Olivia Adams (l.), wonder if such relationships are to blame for racial hostility." All the things Olivia had said to them, someone had heard.

Now it was news.

They were the poster children for all the issues that were fueling the tension on campus.

Jenna knew that there would be other opinions in the paper, that the writers would be thoughtful and fair, that most people would think Olivia's assertions were ridiculous. It was crazy, ridiculous to think that two people being in love would cause otherwise perfectly reasonable people to behave like animals. It was the nuts they had to worry about. The people who were already over the edge; the people who were already bigoted and violent. They had used the photo to represent something. It was sensational. The very idea of Olivia's theory would instigate more debate, more conversation, more anger.

It was the news.

Behind her, Jenna could feel Hunter and Yoshiko, looking over her shoulder at the paper. Hunter put a hand on her shoulder. Yoshiko sucked in a breath as though she herself had been insulted.

"God, Jenna," Yoshiko rasped. "You . . . that stuff Olivia said, you know that's not true. They just printed it 'cause it's . . . oh, my God, the *bastards!*"

"Jenna?" Hunter ventured, his voice almost breaking.

She turned and waved her hand in the air, eyes scrunched, trying to fight back the tears that were threatening to spill. She dropped the paper back on the stack and backed away from her friends as though she were retreating.

"Guys, I've gotta go. I just have to go back and lie down for a while."

"What about class?" Yoshiko asked. "You have Spanish right now, and you're behind. Can you really afford to miss it?"

Jenna just glared at her. "I really can't think about that right now," she said in a whisper.

They called out to her as she hurried away, but they had the respect and decency not to follow. Jenna walked quickly back to Sparrow, not willing to run, not daring to give in that much. In that way she was able to hold back her tears until she was climbing the stairs to the third floor. She rushed down the corridor toward her room, and only after she had shut the door behind her did the tears begin to come, burning twin paths down her cheeks.

The window was open. The girls had wanted to air out the room because it was such a nice day. But the fresh air and the warmth of the sun coming in did not make her feel any better. All the good feeling, the brand-new day she had hoped for, had been dispersed in one horrible moment.

Suddenly she and Damon had become the focal point of all the hurt and anger on campus. Their relationship was being used to address the issues, its validity called into question, and even blamed by some for racial intolerance. She felt like throwing up.

There was nothing she could do about the picture. Jenna knew that. They had reported the news as they saw it. Nothing they had said was untrue. Nobody could change what had been written; nobody could alter what had been done. But she cried. She lay on her bed and wept with a sadness she had not felt in a very long time. It was not horror, not grief, not mourning; not the kind of thing that adults cried over. It was just hurt. Bitter and painful, and to her mind, childish.

They were not tears she felt she could have cried in front of Damon, or even Yoshiko. They were little-girl tears. After she had lain on her bed and cried for what seemed like an hour, she sat up and wiped her face, then went to the phone and called her mother, the only person in the world she knew that she could talk to just then. There was nothing to be done, nothing to fix, no injury to kiss away. But she knew in some way that her mother could make it better. Just by listening, just by talking, just by being her mom, she could make it all right. Or at least as close to all right as it could ever be.

The doctors let Anthony out of the hospital on Tuesday at eleven o'clock. He still had a thick bandage over the stitches on his head as a nurse pushed him out to the lobby in a wheelchair. Brick and Damon teased him about it as they walked beside him. Brick flirted with the nurse, of course. It was not until Anthony stood up and walked out of Somerset Medical Center under his own power—though with the help of a cane he would have to use for a week or two—that he turned to ask his friends what was going on. He had heard some things about the near riot on campus the night before and rumors about the man who had allegedly killed his girlfriend Brittany dying, and then getting up and running away. How did that make any sense, he wanted to know?

Damon told Anthony all he knew. Brick filled in some gaps, things from SAAL, things people were saying. Nothing concrete. Anthony just listened and nodded.

"Don't worry, man," Brick told him. "SAAL is on the case. We're on the cops twenty-four seven, trying to make sure they don't let up for a second, make sure this guy gets what he deserves."

They walked a few more paces along the paved path that brought them to Carpenter Street, and then to the campus beyond. Anthony paused, a bit unsteady as he got used to the cane. His gaze ticked from Brick to Damon and back again.

"I don't think the cops need you on their ass, Brick. None of you. I'm sure they're trying to get this guy, trying to do their job. They've been in talking to me. I hear the questions they ask, see the looks on their faces. Nobody should ever have to go through what I've just been through, but they have. You see it in their faces. They go through it every damn day. I'm not saying they care about Brittany specifically or about me, but I can tell you this much: the fact that she was black, that I'm black, that's got nothing to do with it. They want to find this guy 'cause what he did is evil and inhuman. You oughta let them alone so they can do their thing."

Brick blinked, appearing uncertain for a moment, even confused. "Ant, I'm just trying to help, man."

"And I 'preciate that," Ant replied. "But making their job more difficult is not helping."

Brick nodded slowly in grim understanding. "All right, chief. I got you."

They walked on in silence after that, back toward Bentley Hall, where Brick and Anthony shared a room. Damon had never heard Anthony talk so much at one stretch or heard Brick be so silent. As they made their way downhill, Damon glanced at Ant.

"Sorry, man. I'm sorry she's gone. I know it's got to hurt."

Anthony scowled, added a little cynical chuckle. "It does," he said, "but I can't help feeling it should hurt more. Thing is, I didn't have time to get to know her all that well. Hell, boys, I didn't even know her birthday. Now I won't ever get to know her any better, find out what we could have been. People are saying, 'that poor guy, his girlfriend got murdered.' But she wasn't even really my girlfriend. We only went out a couple of times. I don't know. I almost feel guilty that it doesn't hurt more than it does."

He looked at his friends for understanding before continuing.

"But I can tell you this much. No matter what I felt for her, Brittany didn't deserve to go the way she did. She was a sweet girl. The worst part of it, worse than the fact that she's dead, is the fact that I was there and I couldn't do anything to save her."

"Ant," Damon said, shaking his head, "the guy got the jump on you with a shovel. You did everything possible."

"Yeah. I tell myself that," Ant responded, his voice getting deeper, sounding more forlorn. "Especially at night, when I think about her most. I've dreamed about her a few times. Not good dreams, either. I'm just sitting there doing nothing, and she's screaming. That's the worst of it. I'm a big guy. My whole life people have been getting out of my way. On the court or on the field or on the street, people get out of my way. It makes you feel invulnerable, indestructible. Maybe I am. 'Cause I'm alive and Brittany's dead."

He shook his head and chuckled.

"Maybe that's another reason I look at the cops different," he said. "I'm looking at the whole world different. I couldn't help this girl, but maybe there are people out there I can help. I don't know."

"What are you saying Ant?" Brick asked. "You gonna quit school, join the cops or the army or something?"

"I don't know." Anthony shrugged, then shot a glance at Damon. "I been thinking about Jenna a lot. We all go about our business in this tiny little college world, but she's got something real going on. Maybe she isn't saving lives, but what she does? It makes a difference. She's helping people to heal. That's doing something."

Damon shuddered and shook his head.

"What is it, D?" Ant asked.

"Nothing."

Brick tapped him on the shoulder. "No, really Damon, what's up with you?"

They had reached Bentley Hall, and they stopped on the front lawn. Damon glanced at Anthony, then quickly looked away. He shrugged again.

"I don't want to belittle what happened to you, Ant," Damon said. "I don't want to pretend Brittany dying wasn't horrible. But that was like getting hit by a truck or a tornado or something. There was no way you could have predicted that, or prevented it. With Jenna, though? I'm afraid she's gonna end up the same way, and if she does, it won't be anybody's fault but her own. It's like she's standing on the train tracks just waiting for the thing to come. Daring it to come."

After a pause, Damon lifted his eyes and studied his friends intently. "It scares me," he confessed. "I don't want to be in love with someone like that. I don't want to be in love with someone who's just asking to be taken off the board."

Brick scowled. "That's pretty selfish, don't you think, D? I mean, you can't ask somebody to change their life just 'cause you're afraid you'll lose them. We've all lost people before."

"Maybe you're right," Damon admitted, his face grim. "Maybe I'm just being a selfish jerk. Thing is, I don't know if I can love her the way she deserves to be loved if I'm afraid every second of every day that she's gonna do something stupid, and it's gonna cost Jenna her life . . . I don't know if I can give her that."

Just after two in the morning, the phone rang in Damon's room. He groaned and sat up at the second ring. On the third, he stumbled from bed and across the room to where the offending instrument sat on its cradle on the wall. His mind was fuzzy, thinking slow, but he glanced over at his roommate, Harry, who was still sound asleep, and growled. Damon only wished he had been sleeping soundly enough not to hear the phone ring.

He picked up, interrupting the fourth ring.

"Who is this?" he asked angrily.

Someone snickered on the other end of the line. "Saw your picture in the *Daily*," a voice said, muffled and low. Disguised. "You and your white girl. All over her with your filthy hands."

"Who the hell is this?" Damon demanded, furious.

He remembered what Jenna had told him about Frank Abernathy. One of those neo-Nazis, he figured. Typical of the kind of thing that had been going on around campus. After the paper that morning, it wasn't really a surprise. That realization did nothing to stem his rage.

"Come on, you coward. You gotta call me on the phone, disguise your voice. Why don't you show your face? Come on up here and say what you've got to say," Damon dared the caller.

That snicker again. "Oh, I'll show my face all right, Harris. You're a celebrity now. Front-page news. And it won't be the last time. You'll make the news again real soon. I've got my eye on you."

Damon paused, dumbstruck. He had thought this was nothing but a crank call, some bigoted jerk having a bit of cruel fun with his buddies. Suddenly he was fully awake as he considered the possibility that this guy was the real thing. The killer.

"See you soon, Harris," the voice said. "Oh, and one last thing. Tell your friend, Anthony, that Brittany had tears on her face when she died. Tell him that."

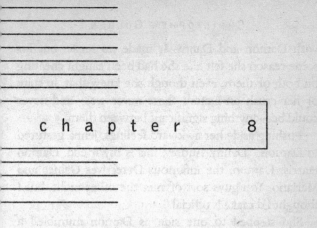

chapter 8

Early Wednesday morning, before classes, Jenna and Damon met with Dr. Slikowski in his office. They had been there only a few minutes when there came a light rapping on the door.

"It's open," Slick called out. The latch clicked, and the door swung open. Detectives Gaines and Mariano entered, acknowledging the gathering with grim smiles and slight nods. Jenna thought they both seemed exhausted, especially Danny, who looked like he could use a good night's sleep. Then again, she supposed they all could.

"Sorry we're late," Audrey said. "We had some paperwork to finish up at the station." She was carrying a Styrofoam cup of coffee and took a quick, slurping sip of the steaming liquid as she looked around the room.

Jenna's stomach churned with tension. She was not at all comfortable being together in the same room with Damon and Danny. It made no sense, but for some reason she felt like she had been caught cheating on both of them, even though she knew that, in spite of her crush on Danny, there never was—and never could be—anything significant between them.

Pushing aside her awkward feelings, Jenna gestured to Damon. "Danny, Audrey, this is my friend, Damon Harris. Damon, the infamous Detectives Gaines and Mariano. You guys sort of met the other night, but I thought I'd make it official."

She stepped to one side as Damon mumbled a greeting and shook hands first with Audrey, then with Danny. When the two guys were shaking hands, Jenna thought she detected a hint of mutual mistrust flash between them, as if they each knew more about the other than they were letting on. It was behavior she had seen before in other people, a weird competition she figured was probably based on each feeling that he knew her better and was more concerned with her welfare than the other.

Not a good way to start the day, she thought.

Though Slick had been working in his inner office when Jenna and Damon had arrived, he had come out into the main area of the medical examiner's office space so that they wouldn't have to crowd into the smaller room. Soft jazz piano played by Dr. Slikowski's desk, and Jenna thought it was Marcus Roberts, but could not be sure. Some of his favorites she had gotten to know pretty well, but there were plenty of others she had not heard enough of to know just by hearing a few minutes of music.

Slick was seated at the center of the room in his wheelchair. Everyone else sat down except Danny, who remained standing by the door. He leaned back against the wall and folded his arms across his chest. The stress he was under was starting to show. He looked like he would be perfectly capable of falling asleep standing up.

Jenna's stomach was feeling coiled and tense as she sat down next to Damon, but she resisted the impulse to take his hand. It had been nice of Slick to allow them to use his office for this meeting. She felt good here, safe, as if the room were a haven from everything that was happening on campus. It also made her feel like they could keep things on a more professional level, but also a more private one.

Audrey cleared her throat as she flipped open a small notebook and clicked the pen she had taken from her pocket. "So," she said, getting right down to business, "you got this call around two in the morning, right?"

Damon nodded but said nothing. His face was set with a stern expression as his eyes darted back and forth between the two detectives. Jenna was surprised at how nervous he appeared. Usually Damon presented himself with such strength and confidence but she could tell by his demeanor now that he was still very unsettled by what had happened last night.

"And you're positive you didn't recognize the voice, right?" Audrey asked.

Once again, Damon nodded. "He was doing something to disguise his voice. It was really distorted."

"Too bad you don't have caller I.D. on your phone," Audrey said almost casually as she scribbled a note.

Slick, who had been sitting quietly with his hands on the armrests of his chair, glanced over at Damon. "I seriously doubt that anyone would be foolish enough to make such a threatening call from a phone that could be easily traced," he said.

"That's assuming all sorts of things," Danny replied. "We don't know if the caller was a crank or the real thing. If he's one of the guys we're after, we don't know which one. Either one of the perps in this case might focus on Damon."

"No, this guy was white for sure," Damon said, his voice gathering strength. "I see what you're saying, that because I'm with Jenna that could piss off either one of them, but I could tell by his voice, and what he said, that he was not a brother."

Jenna saw Audrey smile slightly. The expression was more gentle than she had come to expect from the detective, and she wondered if it was because she liked Damon or because she also found it a bit odd hearing such a self-possessed, clean-cut guy refer to another black man as a "brother."

"Damon, normally we go about this all a bit differently," Audrey said. "And we're going to want you to submit a formal report on this, so it's in the files. But since this is sort of in the family here, let's get down to it. Jenna partially related it to Detective Mariano earlier, but tell us again what exactly the caller said to you."

Damon laced his hands behind his head and leaned back in his chair, narrowing his eyes in concentration. "I'd been asleep, so when the phone rang and woke me up, I was pretty groggy. I said something kind of snappish—"

"What exactly did you say?" Audrey asked, interrupting him.

"I'm not sure. I don't like being woken up in the middle of the night. The first thing he says is that he's seen my picture in the *Daily*. 'You and your white girl.'"

"'You and your white girl.' Those were his exact words?" Audrey asked.

Damon's mouth was a thin, hard line as he nodded.

"But he said the *'Daily'* . . . not the 'newspaper,'" Jenna interrupted. "That's what all the students call it. I'd guess that means he's a student here at Somerset, not someone from off campus."

"Could be," Audrey said, nodding as she jotted something else down onto her notepad. "Not necessarily a student, though. It could just as well have been someone who works at the university—a professor, say, or one of the cafeteria workers or someone from buildings and grounds."

While Audrey and Damon were talking, Jenna took the opportunity to glance over at Danny. He appeared not even to be listening, but she knew better. He was taking in every word; she could see the wheels turning behind his eyes. She was certain he was thinking about the case and yet a small part of her almost hoped he was also thinking about her. Jenna was pretty much over the crush she had had on Danny, but it would make her feel good to think he might have the tiniest bit of jealousy when it came to Damon.

With an imperceptible shake of her head, Jenna

chided herself for thinking about such things in the midst of a crisis. *Get your mind on business, Blake,* she thought.

"We'll take all of this into consideration while we're working on the case," Audrey said. "Right now, though, our priority has to be figuring out if this phone call was a serious threat to you or just some jerk's idea of fun."

"Oh, it was serious, all right," Damon said. Jenna noticed that he stiffened slightly as he spoke. "This guy wasn't messing around. He was definitely trying to scare me."

"And did he?" Audrey asked.

"Did he what?"

"Did he scare you?"

Damon scowled and waved her off with a casual flick of his hand. "All he did was piss me off."

"So what now?" Jenna asked. "I don't see why you can't just give him police protection." There was a sharpness to her voice that made her wince. She did not want them to realize just how on the edge she was at the moment, but she genuinely feared for Damon's safety. These were her friends. They would have to know that, and to understand.

"With all you've been involved in, Jenna, I sometimes forget you don't know all the rules. I'm sorry, but there just isn't enough evidence for us to justify police protection." Audrey's tone was cool and restrained but her expression, at least, was apologetic. "I can hear the lieutenant now. No way is he going to assign men to Damon on the basis of one phone call. If we tried to

protect everyone on campus who might be a target . . .
well, you see where I'm headed with this."

"You don't think having our picture on the front
page of the *Daily* and then this phone call shows we're
a more likely target than the average Somerset student?" Damon shook his head slowly. "Look, I'm not
worried so much about myself as I am about Jenna.
Maybe she didn't get a phone call, but if I'm in danger,
then so is she. More, maybe, because this guy seems to
be targeting women."

"True," Danny replied. He glanced at Audrey. "Most
of the attacks have been either against couples or single women, white and black."

Jenna looked at Damon in surprise, then glanced at
Slick for some sort of moral support. His expression
was troubled, but he said nothing. It seemed silly to
her now that they had asked to have this meeting in his
office. He was her friend and employer, and her relationship with the police was mainly based on his
authority and her experience with him. But what could
he really do in a case like this? His job had little to do
with the living.

Jenna sighed and looked at Danny and Audrey. "I
understand what Damon is saying," she said. "I just . . .
nobody's called me. If someone wanted to terrorize
me, my number's listed, y'know? But the guy didn't
want that. He wanted to scare Damon. If he's the real
deal, Damon could be next on his hit list. And you're
telling me there's nothing you can do?"

Audrey looked at her and shrugged helplessly.
"We'll do what we can," she said mildly, "but the lieu-

tenant won't authorize it unless we come up with something more substantial. If this guy keeps calling, we can set up a trace. In the meantime, since we don't know if the guy is legit or not, my advice to both of you is to be careful. Don't make yourself a target. Don't walk around alone, particularly after dark."

"Even that may not help," Dr. Slikowski added.

The medical examiner gave Audrey a hard look, and Jenna knew it came from his concern for her. Strangely, she found the protective instincts of this reserved man in his wheelchair more comforting than those of her boyfriend or the two police detectives. Slick cared about her, but he was more objective than Damon, and not as bound up in the rules of the game as Danny and Audrey were because of their job.

"If what you say is true, these killers—both of them—are brazen enough to attack people in the middle of a crowd," Slick said bluntly. "Audrey, we've known one another for some time. You've used your imagination to get around the rules more than once. Couldn't you simply suggest to your lieutenant that since young Mr. Harris here is a probable target that putting *him* under surveillance could lead you to the killer? That would give de facto police protection to Jenna and Damon, without it appearing to be extraordinary measures."

Audrey seemed to consider that, but all the while her expression was doubtful. Jenna was going to snap at her; she felt her anger growing, and then all at once it was expelled in a burst of realization.

"They can't do that," Jenna said. "At least not around the clock."

Damon shot her an angry look. "This guy could be after us. I'm not all that worried for myself but I don't want you ending up like Brittany."

The others were staring at her as well. Jenna shrugged. "Audrey and Danny are the best chance the Somerset P.D. has of finding these two. The other detectives I've met are either too inexperienced or too jaded to see through a mess like this." She looked at Danny and Audrey. "It would be one thing for you guys to pull double shifts, but it would be hard to explain to guys like Ross and Cardiff why they had to follow us around."

Jenna sighed and shook her head. "I'm afraid for Damon, mostly. And I hate all of this. I know how insignificant it sounds, but it just makes me feel so . . . foul. I think the fastest way for this to be over is for you guys to do your job without having to worry about us. Let's get it over with. I mean, right now we have no clue who to even be suspicious of. It could be anyone here on campus. If one of the killers isn't this neo-Nazi Frank Abernathy, then it could be anyone. I mean, it could even be my Shakespeare teacher, Professor Fournier. The other day in class we were discussing *Othello*, and he said a few things that could be interpreted as racist. Not to mention he seems like a pretty angry guy on a good day."

Jenna ran out of steam then. She offered a small shrug and sat back in her chair. After a moment Damon reached over to her and twined his fingers with hers. Much to Jenna's dismay, it did very little to reassure her.

Danny had been mostly silent during the meeting. Now he stepped away from the door and moved a few steps farther into the room, eyes on Jenna and Damon.

"We'll do everything we can to try to keep you two safe. I'll check in with both of you by phone. We'll drive by. We can call in some favors from a few uniforms as well to check up on you now and then. But unless something more happens, we can't protect you."

He focused on Jenna. "Thanks for understanding that."

"We're going to have a chat with Mr. Abernathy right after we leave here," Audrey revealed. "And maybe we'll drop by and have a talk with Professor Fournier."

"Couldn't hurt," Danny added. When he looked directly at Jenna, she saw the concern in his eyes. "In the meantime, you can help all of us by not making yourselves seem like available targets."

"We didn't do that," Jenna said angrily. "The *Daily* did when they plastered our picture on the front page."

"Ahh . . . the joys of the free press," Slick said bitterly. There was a sarcastic edge in his voice that Jenna had never heard before.

He was angry for her. She knew that and, again, she was heartened. Slick was more than her boss. Over the months as they had worked together, she felt a growing bond with him. It was more than how they approached their work, more than professional respect or even affection. Jenna recognized that she and Slick were kindred spirits. During the previous week's chaos she felt as though she had distanced herself from him and her job. Now, though, she realized that she should have looked to him first. She determined to talk to him later, to see if he had any ideas about ways in which the two of them could help pursue answers in this case. It was not their job, really, but that had never stopped them before.

Her job empowered her. Jenna had done well as Slick's assistant, even saved lives. But she had been so distracted by her relationship with Damon, her emotional response to what was happening on campus, and by her growing realization that she was extremely naive when it came to issues of race that she had allowed herself to feel powerless.

No more, she thought. *Maybe I won't find anything the police haven't found, but that doesn't mean I shouldn't try.*

As for Damon, Jenna knew that he was more scared for her than he was for himself. It was weird, though. To most girls, she knew that concern would seem romantic and passionate. Jenna felt some of that. But somehow Damon's attitude was putting even more distance between them, and she couldn't explain it. All this time she had been worrying that with all the racial issues on campus, their skin color might somehow come between them. It had never occurred to her that there could be other issues. The truth of it was that they had not really known each other that long, did not know each other nearly so well as Jenna had imagined.

What would put an end to all the tension and anxiety was solving the murders, finding the killers, and bringing them to justice. Nothing else would do. After that, they could all get on with living their lives.

"We should get going," Audrey said. She flipped her notebook shut and rose from her chair. "You both have our phone and beeper numbers. If you get any more calls, or anything else happens, call us immediately. I know this isn't an easy time for either of you, but you just have to hang in there. These guys are both slippery, but they're enjoying themselves too much. It's only a matter of time before they screw up. We'll get them."

"Thanks," Damon muttered as he stood up.

"I appreciate you guys going out of your way," Jenna said, mainly to Danny.

After the detectives had made their departure, Dr. Slikowski put on his own jacket.

"Jenna, I'm late for an appointment in Dorchester. Do you mind locking up?"

"Of course not," Jenna replied.

Once Slick had left, closing the door quietly behind him, Jenna turned to Damon. "So, I guess it's up to me to protect you," she said with a smile, making an effort to dispel the tension between them.

From the look she received in return, her words had done the opposite. "Yeah. Great," Damon said. "Thing is, I'm supposed to be protecting you. So if you're watching out for me, who's covering *your* back?"

Jenna flinched. "Wow. I didn't think you had that whole manly man Neanderthal gene."

Apparently, Damon did not appreciate her attempt at humor. He frowned, then sighed and sort of shrugged. She wondered if his comments about covering her back were at all motivated by jealousy. After all, if anybody was going to watch her back, it would likely be Danny.

"I'm just scared for you," he said at length.

Jenna knew it would be useless to remind him that he was the one who had received the phone call. After a moment Damon shook his head and uttered a soft chuckle.

"We need a vacation," he said. "What do you say we head over to Keates and grab a late breakfast?" Damon stepped close to her and placed his hands on her shoulders.

She almost said yes. But then she reminded herself of her earlier thoughts about prioritizing. Jenna narrowed her eyes and looked down, shaking her head.

"Thanks, but no," she said softly. "I think I'm going to spend a little time going over these autopsy reports. Maybe there's something in them that I've missed. Something that will give us the clue we need."

Damon sucked in a breath and was silent for a moment. He almost said something, but then, with a sigh of frustration, he turned and opened the office door.

"I'll catch up with you for lunch," Jenna called out brightly, but he shut the door behind him without looking back and was gone.

Moving slowly, Jenna walked back to Slick's desk and took out two files from the top drawer. There was still a tight fist of tension in her stomach, but she told herself not to worry as she sat down in Slick's chair, took a deep breath, opened the top file and began to read.

I'll find out who you are.

Why couldn't this have happened in April or May when it was warmer? Audrey thought.

It was a little past eleven o'clock at night, and she was shivering terribly as she moved along the dimly lit walkway beside Brunswick Chapel, heading toward Memorial Steps.

Wonderful. I get to freeze my butt off out here while my partner spends the night cruising the campus in a nice, heated unmarked?

But she knew why.

She was the bait.

Audrey had changed her look some since the last time she'd gone out on campus undercover trying to lure the killers. Tonight, she wore a long, frumpy woolen coat with a stocking hat pulled down low over her eyebrows. She carried a paper shopping bag filled with books instead of a briefcase, hoping to look more like a harried graduate student than a visiting professor, but she had her doubts. How much different could she look? Maybe the perp would recognize her from the CRD rally on Monday night, and maybe not. Time would tell.

Just stick close by me, Danny-boy, she thought. But even with Danny not far away, Audrey didn't have a good feeling about doing this. There had to be a better way to nail these guys.

The lighting was much better along the walkway that led up to Mayer Library. Stepping out of the shadows, Audrey paused beneath one of the streetlights, letting her shoulders slump as she placed her bag of books down by her feet. Turning so the light was shining from behind, she knelt and started pawing through her bag, pretending to be looking for something. Then she straightened up and uttered a loud, "Damn!" as if suddenly realizing that she had forgotten something.

She looked around quickly and tensed when she heard a light cough behind her, but then she relaxed when she saw a black man walking toward her also heading toward Mayer Library. One of the killers they were looking for was black, but the crimes were all across racial lines. They had Claire Bellamy undercover elsewhere on campus, trying to bait the black perp. Audrey had nothing to worry about from unfamiliar black faces passing by. It was white faces that she needed to be on alert for.

She nodded a silent greeting to the guy as he passed but did not pay much attention to him. He wasn't her concern.

Grabbing her shopping bag by the handles, she started walking back the way she had come, back toward the shadows where, hopefully, the man she was after—the guy who had escaped from the crashed ambulance after the CRD rally the other night—was lurking. She had walked no more than twenty feet when she heard a whispered curse close behind her. Before she could even begin to react, she felt a violent push from behind that sent her staggering to keep her balance.

"We'd all be better off without *your* kind around here," the man said as he closed in on her.

A streetlamp was shining behind him, so Audrey did not get a good look at him. All she saw as he rushed at her was the white blur of his face beneath the dark hat he was wearing.

Where the hell did he come from? Audrey wondered,

but she did not have long to contemplate it. She saw the wicked gleam of a knife blade reflecting in the light just before he jabbed it into her ribs. There was an instant of cold, stinging pain on her right side. Audrey thought crazily that this must be what it was like to be bitten by a snake. Then her legs felt like they'd come unstrung, and she was falling.

Her face struck the cold concrete of the path and her eyes fluttered. Nearly unconscious, she stared at the steps leading back up toward the academic quad. They were empty. Someone had passed her only seconds earlier, but now there was no one there.

She was on her own.

Danny had swung around campus and parked on Sterling Lane just a short way down from the library. He had Audrey in sight. He was no more than a hundred yards away from her when she was attacked, and still that wasn't close enough. He had noticed the black man who had walked by, and then, no more than a second or two after that man had disappeared up the stairs, a second man appeared, coming down them.

A white guy wearing a dark hat. From the way he moved, Danny had known it was their man.

Jesus, that's him!

The man came down the walkway, moving fast and closing in on Audrey from behind. Danny reacted instantly. He picked up the radio mike and snapped it on.

"Backup, we've got him. Close in now. He's right in front of the library."

He didn't wait to hear any acknowledgment. Danny

jumped out of the car and ran up the slight rise toward the walkway. There was no sound other than the crunching of his feet on the snow until he heard Audrey scream. The guy was on her. Danny saw him shove Audrey, almost knocking her down, and then lunge at her.

As he ran, Danny drew his service weapon.

"Officer down!" he shouted, looking around desperately for some sign of the other officers who were supposed to be in the area.

The guy rabbited, heading across the lawn and then into the shadows behind Brunswick Chapel. There was a line of trees there. Danny wanted to run him down, but Audrey was his first priority. She was not moving.

"Officer down!" he screamed again.

A couple of uniforms came running down the library steps from the academic quad, and Dwight Ross, an aging detective Danny hated, puffed along on the near side of the chapel. Danny shouted and pointed the way the perp had run, and they all took off after the guy. Ross was closest, but he was also slowest and least motivated. Danny saw the perp disappear between the chapel and the trees just as Dwight turned the corner. He must have had the guy in his sights.

As he watched, Dwight leveled his gun, aiming at a spot Danny could not see. Then the old detective cursed, lowered his weapon and started running again. The killer was quick. He must have gotten around the other side of the chapel. Dwight gave chase, and so did the uniforms. In all likelihood Dwight's partner, Mike Cardiff, was on the other side of the chapel.

But Danny knew the guy had given them the slip again.

"Audrey," he rasped as he knelt by her, almost too afraid to touch her in case she was injured as badly as he feared.

Her eyes flickered open and she winced with pain. "He got me, partner. Too damn slow. Let my guard down," Audrey said with a broken gasp, wincing again as she clutched her side.

Danny's heart gave a cold squeeze when he saw the dark red flow of blood that was soaking through her heavy coat. He grabbed his portable radio from his belt and flicked it on.

"We have an officer down and need immediate medical assistance at Mayer Library on Sterling Lane," he barked.

"Go get him," Audrey said. She struggled for breath as she looked at Danny with pain-glazed eyes. "He just nicked me. I'll be all right until the ambulance gets here. Don't let him get away."

Danny glanced over his shoulder in the direction the man had gone, but there was no one in sight. From Sterling Lane, two more uniforms were rushing toward them. He could not bring himself to tell Audrey he was sure they had lost the guy who had stabbed her. With a curse, he turned and practically shouted at them, "Stay with her until the ambulance gets here." Then he was off, running up past Brunswick Chapel and into the quad.

As he ran into the quad, he saw Dwight Ross and the uniforms. They were standing with several students they had obviously detained. This late at night, there weren't many people around, but he saw another couple walking toward them from the direction of Sparrow Hall. That was no help, so he jogged over to the other cops and studied the students they were speaking to. A guy and a girl, both white, were holding hands and looking perplexed.

The third was a Latino guy, though he could not have been any more specific than that just by looking at him.

"The guy ran by here thirty seconds ago," Dwight was growling. "And none of you saw him?"

All three shook their heads.

"You're sure? You didn't see or hear anything?" Danny pressed.

Dwight shot him an angry glare that Danny thought had more to do with the fact that Cardiff was not there than anything else.

"We're just getting back from Espresso's," the girl said. "We didn't see anyone. Right, hon?"

Her boyfriend shrugged and shook his head. "No one."

"How about you?" Danny said, turning to the Latino boy. "What are you doing out here this late?"

"I was visiting a friend in one of the dorms and was just heading back to the T," the boy said without a trace of nervousness in his voice. "I live in Cambridge."

It was obvious to Danny that none of them was going to be able to help him, but it baffled him that Audrey's attacker could have gotten away without being seen. Dwight and the others were right behind him. It was as if he had never been there or could melt away into the shadows without anyone seeing him. Considering that he had been pronounced dead at the scene of the attack on Monday, and then clawed his way out of the body bag, attacked the ambulance driver, and escaped, it wouldn't surprise Danny to learn that he could fly as well.

"All right," he said, giving up. He was still concerned about Audrey and anxious to get back to her, so he decided not to waste any more time here. "Give the officers your contact information. We may need to contact you later."

Danny touched Dwight on the arm and indicated that the other detective should walk with him. A few yards away from the others, he stopped.

"Where's Mike?"

Dwight glared at him sourly, then shrugged. "He went for coffee. But it wouldn't have mattered, Mariano. I was right behind this guy. He's like freakin' Houdini or something."

"It would have mattered if your partner had been waiting on the other side when you chased him around the chapel," Danny said through clenched teeth. "So he went for coffee. And my partner is on her way to the hospital with a hole in her gut."

The other detective seemed suddenly less adversarial. He swallowed and looked down. "Oh, come on, Danny, I didn't know. How . . . I mean, what'll it look like when you write it up?"

Danny shot him a cold, withering glance. "It'll look like what it is."

By the time Danny got back to Audrey, he could see the flickering red lights of the approaching ambulance as it sped down Sterling Lane toward the crime scene.

Huddled in the shadows, away from the light, the young man waited. He took small sips of air and exhaled them slowly so the mist of his breath in the cold night would not give him away. Every nerve in his body was tuned and humming with expectation. In his gloved left hand, he gripped the tire iron he had used a few nights before.

I'm not done yet, he thought, fuming with frustration and rage. *Not by half.*

He was wearing a dark woolen hat, pulled low over his eyebrows. Glancing down, he smiled as he flexed his right hand inside the glove he was wearing. He enjoyed the creaking sound the leather made even as it set his teeth on edge. In his other hand, he hefted the tire iron.

He was ready.

It was late, well past midnight, and the temperature was dropping.

Must be near zero, he thought.

The night air cut through his coat and reached its icy fingers down his back. He tried to stop his teeth from chattering but couldn't.

Come on. . . . Someone's gotta come along. . . . I can't wait here all damned night!

He heard the faint snap of boots on cold asphalt before he saw her. Easing forward just enough to see onto the lighted walkway between the buildings, he made out a dark shape headed in his direction, moving away from the Campus Center. She was huddled against the cold, a thick scarf masking her face; but when she passed under one of the streetlights, he caught a quick glimpse of her features.

Yes! She's white!

That was all he needed to know. His blood sang with anticipation. Coiled and tense, he waited for just the right moment to step out of the shadows.

The woman was moving at a brisk pace. He wondered if it was just because it was so late and she wanted to get in out of the cold or if she knew that it was foolish and dangerous to be out alone like this so late at night.

Bottom line, it didn't matter.

All it meant was she was walking that much the faster toward him.

As she got closer, passing under another one of the lights that lined the walkway, the light illuminated her face, and he clearly saw her features. Her eyes gleamed in the darkness as she focused straight ahead. The young man held his breath as he prepared himself and waited until she was several paces past his hiding place.

Then he stepped out of the darkness.

Approaching her from behind, he tried to walk silently, hoping that she would not hear him coming until it was too late. He was getting good at that. His grip on the tire iron tightened, sending a painful, electric throb racing up his wrist. His anticipation had built up so much inside him now that he finally could not hold it back anymore. He was close enough now; close enough so she would not be able to escape him.

"*Hey!*" he called out. His voice sounded heavy with menace in the darkness as it echoed from the surrounding buildings. He liked that.

The woman stopped short and started to turn around. He could tell by the way she hunched her shoulders that she sensed danger and was preparing either to run or fight.

As long as she doesn't scream, the young man thought as a wicked grin spread across his face.

The woman turned, looking back at him. The spark of fear he saw kindle in her eyes filled him with joy.

"What do you—" she started to say, but that was all.

He rushed her, tire iron raised. He swung it down toward her in a wide, whistling arc.

"Don't you know?" he shouted as the tire iron made contact, striking a glancing blow off the side of her face.

The skin tore, and blood flowed. The stunned woman dropped down on one knee, bracing herself with both hands like a track runner in starting position.

"This is to even the score," the man said in a low growl.

The woman looked up at him, her eyes glazed with pain, unfocused, as she tried to shake it off. A trickle of blood ran down her face and soaked into the fabric of her scarf. The only sound she made was a tiny whimper in the back of her throat as she cringed protectively, tilting her head to one side.

It didn't do her any good.

The man cocked his arm back over his head, and then swung again, viciously, bringing the tire iron straight down on the top of her head. The night filled with a loud crunching sound as her skull caved in, and the woman collapsed face-first onto the cold asphalt. Her arms were spread out in front of her like she was clinging to a life raft. Blood oozed down the sides of her head and ran like spilled ink across the frozen ground.

"Maybe *now* you get the point," the man hissed, bending down and leaning close to her senseless ear.

Before he straightened up, his wool hat fell off and landed on the woman's back. After taking a nervous glance around to make sure no one was watching, he picked up his hat and inspected it for blood. The material was dark, and he didn't see anything. Just to be on the safe side, he stuffed the hat into his coat pocket. He'd get rid of it as soon as he could. He sure didn't want to be found wearing a hat with bloodstains that matched the victim's blood.

Satisfied and filled with a feeling of exhilaration, the man stood up and took a deep breath of the cold night air. After thoroughly wiping the tire iron on the woman's coat, he hid it under his jacket, braced under his arm, and started walking away. He had to restrain himself from running. That would only draw attention to him if any of the cops on the prowl for him happened by.

He felt good. *Really* good.

chapter 9

I just can't believe I was so *stupid*," Danny said.

"I can," Audrey said with a sly smile.

It was Thursday morning, and sunlight was streaming in through the window of her hospital room. She was sitting up in bed, a tray with the remains of her breakfast on the bed stand beside her.

"You were there, Danny," she said softly. "I appreciate it." She paused and winced as she took a breath. "I just can't believe I let the guy get behind me like that. I never even heard him coming until he was right on top of me."

"He's quick," Danny said. "I'll grant him that. Dwight called him Houdini, and that's about right. Guy appears out of nowhere and disappears the same way."

Audrey looked at him with a tight smile. "And I'm the one with the punctured lung to prove it." She shook her head with disgust. "I just can't believe I was that slow. So who was this solo student you questioned last night?"

"Student I.D. says his name's Paul Vasquez, but there's no one by that name living at the address he gave me. Also, there's no one with that name registered as a student at Somerset."

Audrey frowned in contemplation and shook her head, letting her gaze drift over to the window. Her eyes clouded with pain as she shifted her position in the bed.

"Of course," Danny went on, talking to himself as much as to his partner, "I might have questioned him a little further if I hadn't waited until this morning to read the statements the couple gave the uniforms last night. The only person they saw around the chapel before our guys came running around there was Vasquez."

Audrey turned and glanced at him with one eyebrow raised.

"See," Danny said, mentally reenacting the scene, "they were walking right toward the chapel. Now they were together, so they might not have been paying attention to much other than each other. But they didn't see anyone except Vasquez and Somerset P.D."

"So you're saying he just appeared on the quad out of nowhere?" Audrey winced as she took another breath and pressed her hand against her wounded side.

"Pretty much. Damn! I should have questioned all of them more closely. But Dwight and the uniforms were there to take statements, and I wanted to get back to you."

"So Vasquez isn't who he claims to be. Then who *is* he? The guy who jumped me was Caucasian."

"You sure?"

"No doubt of that," Audrey said. Her eyes clouded again with a wave of pain. "We're out there looking for two killers. One of them's white. The other one's black. We have plenty of witnesses who have seen both of them, and still no one can identify them. Now we've got this Latino guy on the scene and his I.D. doesn't even check out."

"Yeah, and I let him walk away," Danny said.

He grunted with frustration and smacked his fist into his open palm as he started pacing back and forth at the foot of the bed. The worried look in his partner's eyes was almost too much for him to bear. All he could think was, *Why wasn't I just a little bit faster? I could have saved my partner a knife in the ribs.*

Audrey sighed and let her gaze shift back to the view outside her window. "Just don't tell me," she said in a low, trembling voice, "that we've got *three* killers on campus."

On Friday afternoon Jenna hurried across Carpenter Street to Somerset Medical Center, almost breaking into a jog. She went upstairs as quickly as the elevator would allow, and down the hall to the medical examiner's office. The campus was in an uproar unlike anything she had ever seen. There were reporters everywhere, cameras and news vans everywhere she looked. Cars and trucks were pulled up in parking lots and along the streets. Students carried boxes and suitcases and TVs and

VCRs. People were moving out or being withdrawn from the school by their parents.

A third murder meant that it was more than two isolated incidents. There was a predator on campus. Even if one killer had taken two lives, that did not necessarily fit the definition of serial killer. But to parents and many students definitions no longer mattered. The university president, deans, and trustees were on every network, talking about the measures that were being taken by police and on campus in regard to safety. But it was too little too late.

That morning April Blake had practically begged her daughter to come home. But leaving now was the last thing Jenna would do. She could not walk away from all this any more than she could walk away from Damon. She had met him for lunch the previous day, they had sat around the dorm watching a movie the night before, and everything seemed okay. But it wasn't. Jenna could not have pointed to any one specific word or action, or even explained it, but things were simply out of sorts between them. She truly believed that all the tribulations they were facing should have been making the bond between them even stronger, but as much as they denied it, more and more she felt like they were being driven apart. And there was nothing she could do about it.

Morbid as it was, she was almost relieved to have something even worse to contend with.

At Slick's office door, she pulled out her key card and slipped it into the lock. After the beep Jenna withdrew the card from the mechanism and turned the handle.

"Hey," Dyson said. He was seated at his desk and barely glanced up as she entered. A cup of steaming coffee at his elbow, he pored over the contents of a file that were spread before him.

"Where's Slick?" Jenna asked when she noticed that Doctor Slikowski's office door was open, but the room was empty.

"He had a lecture at the med school this morning, but he should be along in a minute," Dyson said, looking back down at his work.

Jenna slung her book bag onto the chair in front of her desk, then removed her hat and gloves. "Good. So you haven't done the autopsy yet?"

Dyson held up a finger, read another line or two, then closed the file and slid it to one side on his desk. He spun around in his chair and faced her directly, picking up his coffee. Now that he was not concentrating on his work, his expression had softened. His gaze was gentle.

"We could have done it early this morning, but he wanted to wait for you," Dyson told her. "Did you know her?"

"No," she said. "God, when is this going to be over? I mean . . . How can people be so intolerant? What motivates someone to do something like this?"

They were silent for a moment, each looking at the other. In that brief interval, Jenna noticed for the first time how exhausted Dyson looked. His eyes seemed darker than usual, and his expression looked a little lost, almost forlorn, as if he had a lot more to say to her but was at a loss how to say it.

"Ignorance, I'd say," Dyson replied dryly. "Ignorance and fear. Fear of people who are different."

Jenna nodded her agreement.

"You have to deal with that all the time, don't you?" she asked, her voice low and soft. "You and Doug, I mean."

"Some," Dyson said with a casual shrug.

"So how do you handle it?" Jenna asked.

She suddenly felt guilty. Here she had been all self-involved, trying to figure out how she would handle people's reactions to her dating a black man, and every day of his life, Dyson had to deal with the discrimination that came from being gay.

"How do we handle it?" Dyson echoed. A faint smile twitched the corner of his mouth. "We don't have a choice. Bottom line is, you have to be stronger than the bigots."

Jenna could see in his eyes that there was more—a lot more—to this issue than what he was saying. He was always so protective of her, and she felt selfish for never having spent much time reciprocating. She might have said more to him about it, but the office door lock beeped, and the door swung open. The moment was instantly broken.

"Ah, Jenna. You're here. Excellent," Dr. Slikowski said with a warm smile as he propelled his wheelchair into the office.

Jenna looked at her boss and smiled thinly. "Reporting for duty," she said, her voice low and constricted.

Slick's face softened with sympathy. "I thought to

wait for you on this. I know how stressful this has been for you, and I sensed yesterday that you wanted to become more involved with this case than you have been. You'll have to tell me if that instinct was off base."

Dyson ran a hand through his curly black hair. "It's not pretty."

"I can handle it," Jenna said, bracing herself. "I've seen the worst there is."

A slow smile spread across Slick's face. "I didn't expect you'd say anything else."

Ten minutes later, with Miles Davis playing softly over the sound system in the autopsy room, the three of them were scrubbed up and wearing surgical gowns and gloves as they began the autopsy.

"Subject's name is Patrice Connors," Slick said, speaking into the tape recorder so Jenna could key in the full report later, once they were done. "Caucasian female. Age twenty-two. Severe cranial trauma with a blunt object, apparently the cause of death. Decorative tattoos on left hand and left ankle—"

"They're temporary," Jenna said.

Slick glanced at her, eyebrows raised.

"Henna tattoos. Just dye. The pattern is mendhi. It's kind of trendy, worn almost like jewelry," she explained. Jenna had noticed the tattoos immediately.

"Thank you for the clarification," Slick replied.

They moved on.

By now, Jenna was used to the grisly aspects of her job, and she worked silently alongside Slick and Dyson. Though the brain was traditionally the last part of the autopsy, the M.E. reversed that order in this case. When they removed the brain for weighing and dissection it was so severely damaged that it fell apart like jelly in Slick's hands as he tried to extricate it from the shattered skull. Jagged pieces of bone had to be picked from the dead girl's gray matter. More than once, Jenna shuddered.

This could have been me, she thought. Yet instead of frightening her, it only made her angrier and more determined.

Jenna weighed the brain, and Dyson took tissue samples. Slick used the controls that moved the stainless steel table and bent over the cadaver with a scalpel. He was about to cut the Y-incision into the woman's chest cavity when Jenna stopped him.

"Wait a second," she said. "What's this?"

Leaning close to the body on the autopsy table, her eyes narrowed as she closely inspected the bloodstained strands of the victim's blond hair. They were clumped together, held by dried blood, but she picked up a pair of forceps and started gently pulling the hairs apart.

"What is it?" Slick asked, moving his wheelchair closer to her.

Up until now, the autopsy had been nothing out of the ordinary, and she had been simply going through the motions. They certainly did not expect to find any cause of death other than the severe blow to the head, but Jenna recognized a note of restrained excitement in Slick's voice.

"Look. Right here," she said, pointing with the tip

of her forceps to the thick clumps of coagulated blood and matted hair. At first Slick looked like he didn't register what she was trying to show him, but after a moment, he smiled and nodded.

"Black hairs," she whispered, her breath warm against her face inside her surgical mask.

Slick's eyes shone brightly over the top of his mask as he nodded.

"Excellent. Excellent," he said, adopting a professorial tone. "I was so intent on examining the brain and the pattern of the blows that I missed that completely. Well done, Jenna."

On closer inspection, she discovered three strands of short, dark, curly hair that were stuck to the blood that had clotted in the woman's long, blond hair.

"They could be woolen fibers from her hat or scarf," Slick suggested.

"True," Jenna said. "And they might be lint from the chair or couch she was sitting in before she started her walk home." She paused, taking a breath, then added, "Or they might be strands of hair from her killer."

They glanced at each other, and Jenna couldn't miss the look of almost fatherly pride in Slick's eyes.

"I'll get you an evidence bag," he said as Jenna leaned forward and very carefully plucked the strands of hair from the dried blood. Her hands were trembling with excitement as she dropped the specimens into the poly-bag that Slick held open for her. He zipped it shut and carefully placed it on the table beside the operating table.

"You really have a knack for this job," he said, and

Jenna could just imagine the wide smile behind his surgical mask. "Of course, it goes without saying that it's all the result of having such a knowledgeable and skillful teacher to show you the ropes."

Dyson chuckled. "Well, I do what I can."

Jenna groaned and swatted at him playfully, but drew up short when Slick cleared his throat.

"Please," he said, indicating the woman lying on the table. "Let's remember why we're here."

Chastened, Jenna nodded and got back to work as Dr. Slikowski prepared to make the first incision into the woman's chest.

At a quarter to five Friday evening, Jenna was seated in one of the booths by the front window of Paula's Bakery Café watching the sky darken to a deep purple above the city. Danny had called and asked if he could see her, and she had chosen to meet him here because the atmosphere was relaxed and subdued. After the day she'd had, it was about as much stimulation as she could handle.

Danny sat across from her, his hands wrapped around a cup of coffee that he had barely touched, as if he only held on to it for the warmth it provided. He wore a navy blue V-neck sweater over a T-shirt and jeans. In the harsh fluorescent light, his face looked sallow and thinner than usual. Jenna did not like that she was finding it difficult to look him directly in the eyes. She felt a strange kind of tension between them, as if there was something unspoken but of utmost importance suspended over their heads.

And there is. She could not stop thinking about how on the night of the CRD rally, and then again yesterday in Slick's office, Danny had looked at Damon . . . how?

Like he's checking Damon out, trying to decide if he's good enough for me or something.

Over the last month or two, as her relationship with Damon had blossomed, she had tried to tell herself to forget all about Danny. Okay, so she had a little crush on him, and maybe he even felt a little more than friendly toward her. He had his life, and she had hers. Just because things were tense with Damon did not change anything.

"Audrey's going to be all right, isn't she?" Jenna asked.

She had been stunned to learn that last night, not more than an hour or two before Patrice Connors had been attacked and killed, Audrey, who had been working undercover, had been stabbed by a white assailant.

"Oh, she'll be fine," Danny said, casually waving a hand at her. "The knife punctured her right lung, but it missed any major blood vessels. The doctor says she'll be out of the hospital within a week, and back to work, at least on light duty, a week or two after that."

"If I know Audrey," Jenna said with a chuckle, "she'll be back on the job in a couple of days."

Danny smiled at her, but his smile looked thin and forced. Jenna felt compelled to get up and give him a reassuring hug, but she decided to stay where she was. It was just not like that between them, and she did not want to make things any more complicated than they already were.

But beneath his brave front, Jenna could see the

hurt and worry in Danny's eyes. She knew without him having to come right out and say it that he was tormented by the thought that he had let his partner down. Of course, both he and Audrey knew from day one that they were putting their lives on the line with their jobs, but that didn't make it any easier when it came so close.

"It's not just that Audrey got hurt, either," Danny said, staring down at his folded hands. "It's . . . I think I caught the guy and didn't even know it."

"What are you talking about?" Jenna asked, stunned.

He seemed so deeply troubled that she wanted to reach out across the table and take his hands, but once again, she held herself back. She was here because Danny had asked her to meet him. He said he needed to talk to someone, and she was pleased that he had thought of her first. The last thing she wanted to do was confuse the issue by sending the wrong message.

The leatherette creaked as Danny leaned back in his seat. He took a deep breath and let it out slowly. When he looked at her, his eyes seemed dull, haunted.

"Once I got up to the quad, I stopped and questioned three people," he said softly. "One of them was a young guy, a Latino. Paul Vasquez. Come to find out, the name and I.D. he gave me were fake. He isn't registered on campus, either. I just can't help thinking that he might have been the guy I was looking for."

"But Audrey's attacker was white," Jenna said. "You said you were sure of that. And there have been plenty of witnesses from the other assaults. You've got one white suspect and one black."

"I know, I know," Danny said, shaking his head with frustration. "But none of their descriptions seem to match. I mean, how can we have several people all see the same person at the same time, and still get different descriptions of the guy?" He clenched his hand into a fist and punched the cushioned seat beside him once, hard. "It doesn't make any sense. It's like he's a chameleon or something. But with this Vasquez guy being such a ghost, I feel like I may have let the guy we're looking for get away. I don't like that feeling."

"So what are you saying?" Jenna asked, leaning forward intently. "Are you telling me that maybe in the dark and the confusion of seeing your partner attacked, you might have *thought* this guy was white? Thing is, Danny, Audrey saw him too."

Danny sighed and shook his head but said nothing. He just sat there slumped in his seat, staring blankly ahead. After a moment, he picked up his cup of coffee and took a gulp. "Oh, man," he said, wincing and shaking his head with disgust. "I can't believe I let a four-dollar coffee get cold."

Jenna knew that he was trying to lighten things up, but she was still bothered, both by what he had said and at seeing him so upset.

"Look," she said, and this time she didn't stop herself from leaning forward and clasping his hands in hers. "You're not going to find these guys if you spend all your time regretting what you did and didn't do. Regret is for suckers. Didn't you tell me that?"

Danny frowned. "I never told you that."

"Well, someone did," Jenna replied. "Maybe it was in an old Humphrey Bogart movie or something. The point is, it doesn't matter. There are two murderers out there that we know of, and with or without your partner, you're going to find them. I know you will."

Danny's eyes seemed to snap back into focus as he looked at her and then smiled a warm, genuine smile.

"Thanks," he said softly. He shifted his hands around so he was cupping her hands, and gave her a reassuring squeeze. "How about I give you a ride back to the dorm? I don't want you out walking alone after dark."

"Good idea," Jenna said with a smile.

Yoshiko and Hunter had meant to stay in the library longer. Both of them had papers to research, and it was much nicer when they were able to do such things together. With all the security measures and so forth, she had almost been afraid that the library might be closed after dark. Hunter had assured her they could not do such a thing, considering the impact it would have on the students, but Yoshiko was not convinced until she pulled on the front door and it opened.

An hour later she wished it had been closed after all. Nothing truly outrageous happened. No one attacked them or even ridiculed and insulted them the way Frank Abernathy had. But that did not mean people kept to themselves. In spite of the usual rules about silence in libraries, there was a group of students hovering around a study carrel nearby who argued loudly about race relations and the administration's tactics. Mainly they talked about prejudice.

To them, it was all black and white. Quite literally. It was an issue for black students and white students, because those were the races of the kids doing the arguing.

Twenty minutes of that was enough. Yoshiko glanced up at Hunter, who was trying to focus and failing. "Can we move?"

"Thought you'd never ask," he muttered.

When they rose with their books, quite obviously relocating, there were plenty of stares in their direction. Yoshiko told herself she was letting it get to her, but she felt something more in those stares than mere curiosity. Now that they had come to the attention of the debaters, she and Hunter were a subject of great interest.

Male and female. Asian and Caucasian. *They even rhyme,* she thought bitterly.

As she sat down and spread her books out again, Yoshiko glanced up and saw that the students who were involved in "The Great Race Debate" were not the only ones who found her and Hunter so fascinating. A number of other people were also looking at them.

Yoshiko scowled and looked down. For as long as she had been able she had kept her own feelings out of it. In some ways, it *was* an issue of black and white. And Hunter did not need to deal with anything else while he was being constantly surrounded by reminders of Melody's murder. But eventually it had become too much for her. Theirs was an interracial relationship, with all the difficulties that implied.

Hunter had tried to pretend that was not true and, in some ways, so had Yoshiko. But lately it had been inescapable. Several times she had wanted to talk to Jenna about it, but her roommate was having such a difficult time of her own that Yoshiko did not want to add to that. She had a feeling that things between Jenna and Damon were entering the danger zone.

"Hey," he said softly, reaching out to lay his hand gently over hers on the study table. "You okay?"

His voice melted her. Yoshiko grimaced slightly, then rolled her eyes and smiled. She had never known a boy so sweet while she was growing up. She certainly was not going to let something like this take that away from her. There had been some stress for both of them, but they had worked through it. They were going to be all right.

"I'm fine," she said. "Just distracted. Why don't we check some books out and study back at my room?"

Hunter grinned and waggled one eyebrow. "Think we'll get any studying done?"

Yoshiko tried to frown but only half managed it as she fought not to smile. "No dice, Mr. LaChance. Jenna's home and we didn't schedule any private time tonight, so I'm not just going to ask her to step out for a while."

"Well, then studying it is," Hunter replied with a mock-heavy sigh.

They packed up their books, checked out the most important ones, and slipped on their jackets as they stood by the front door. Yoshiko paused with her hand on the glass, looking out at the night.

"What is it?" Hunter asked. "You see something?"

She shook her head. "It's just . . . it would be kind of crazy to wait for a shuttle going the wrong direction just to go a couple hundred yards, right?"

Hunter laid a comforting hand on her shoulder and squeezed. His grip was firm, a reminder to her that her boyfriend was stronger than he looked. It did not escape Yoshiko that that was a trait that extended beyond physical strength. Hunter's father had died young, his mother had fought alcoholism most of her life, and his sister . . . Yoshiko felt lucky to have someone of such heart and character.

"It isn't crazy if it makes you feel safe," Hunter told her. "Let's wait."

With a glance at the clock, Yoshiko shook her head. "We just missed one, I think. We can be back to the dorm in five minutes or wait twenty-five. Let's just go. There are plenty of lights. And I have you."

"You're sure?" Hunter asked grimly.

"Very."

But when they left the library, and while they walked up the stairs toward the chapel and then across the academic quad toward Sparrow Hall, she regretted her certainty. Though it was relatively early, there were very few students out and about. Right then Yoshiko would have put up with any number of degrading stares from people who looked down on interracial couples if it meant she would not have had to feel the frisson of fear that ran through her.

She was spooked.

Hunter held her hand tightly, and they walked at a brisk pace, and they made it to Sparrow in *four* minutes.

But Yoshiko silently vowed that, with or without Hunter, she would be taking the shuttle at night from then on, until the police said it was safe again. And maybe even for a while after that.

Damon was attending a meeting at the SAAL house, so Jenna spent the evening studying alone in her dorm room. Around ten o'clock, Yoshiko came back from the library where she had been studying with Hunter. They had asked her to come along, but she had declined. Yoshiko was pretty much over her cold, but she went to bed early, anyway. Jenna had fallen behind quite a bit with her class work and had a lot more studying to do, but she was feeling so burned out that she crashed a little before eleven o'clock.

Still, as exhausted as she was, sleep wouldn't come. She couldn't stop thinking about everything that was going on—the tension between her and Damon; the autopsy of Patrice Connors; her talk with Danny; and just the thought that there were two killers loose on campus. Everything blended in her mind, and kept her tossing and turning in bed until the alarm clock beside her bed showed that it was well past one in the morning.

Come on, just go to sleep. You're not going to solve any-thing tonight!

But she could not turn off her mind. What both-ered her most was something Danny had said at Paula's Bakery Café, about his instinct that this Vasquez was his guy, even though he was Latino and the perp was white. It was impossible, but it was obvi-ously eating away at Danny. It was not just him, either. Everybody saw the killer differently. Both killers, in fact. And the way they eluded police, like magicians. Not to mention masters of disguise. The similarities were so bizarre, it was almost like the two of them were working together to drive the entire campus into a firestorm of racial hatred.

It was not until Jenna had finally started to drift off to sleep that what had been stewing in her head finally hit her. An idea struck her so suddenly she let out a gasp and sat up in bed.

"No way. That's crazy," she whispered in a dry voice.

She cast a nervous glance at the upper bunk to see if she had disturbed Yoshiko. Thankfully, her roommate slept on.

That's too weird, Jenna thought. *It's out there, even for me.*

But as crazy as her idea was, when she plugged it into the situation at hand, it made an eerie kind of sense. She rubbed her eyes vigorously, feeling now just how tired she was in spite of her insomnia. But now that the idea was lodged in her brain, she could not get rid of it. Moving slowly, she got out of bed, walked over to her computer, sat down, and switched it on. As she waited for the machine to boot up, she kept trying to convince herself that she was so stressed out about everything that her brain had slipped a few cogs. She wasn't thinking straight. Just to satisfy her curiosity, though, she got on-line and started doing a little research.

Just in case I haven't totally lost my marbles.

c h a p t e r   1 0

On Saturday morning, the impossible happened.

Jenna had stayed up far too late surfing the net, and when Yoshiko shook her awake just after nine A.M., she had done little more than murmur and swat at her roommate as though she were a pesky housefly. Shortly thereafter, when Damon came knocking, she had managed to shuffle to the door and let him know that she really needed to sleep. It was after eleven o'clock when she finally dragged herself out of bed, by then fairly buzzing with her discoveries of the night before and instinctively certain that, outrageous as her theory was, she was right.

None of that was the impossible part, however.

The impossible was what Jenna was confronted with when she stepped out the front of Sparrow Hall and started toward the medical center. The day was sunny, in the mid-fifties, and the sky was a clear, crisp blue. A perfect late winter day. Across the residential quad, someone had parked one of the school's now severely overworked safety shuttles.

Standing on top of that shuttle bus, in front of a veritable ocean of human beings—students and faculty from Somerset University and wave after wave of local and national media—was Jules Barros, president of the Coalition for Racial Diversity. On either side of him were SAAL frontman Darnell Thomas and white supremacist Frank Abernathy, both of whom were suspects in the various crimes on campus.

The CRD had planned and was now executing a second peace rally. That was courageous enough, considering how ugly the previous one, five days earlier, had ended. But they stuck with it, spent the time to organize it correctly, guilt-tripped the right people into behaving responsibly, and the result was a bona fide miracle, as far as Jenna was concerned. The sight of those three students together, on top of the shuttle that must have been lent to them by the administration, lifted a shroud that had been weighing heavily upon her.

Jenna had known about the rally for days, but she hadn't given it much thought, considering what had been going on. She had planned to go with Damon, but also did not feel very guilty about sending him away when she decided to stay in bed that morning. Now she was sorry to have missed the beginning and to have missed him. As she moved down from Sparrow and into the crowd, all of whom seemed much less grim by the light of day, she watched for him.

But there was no sign of Damon. Jenna knew that

she needed to see Dr. Slikowski as soon as possible, and she had no intention of staying for the entire rally, but she could not resist spending just a few minutes listening to the students with megaphones on top of the shuttle and mingling with the mass of people on the quad. The fury of earlier in the week had given way to a kind of proud determination. As Jules Barros said, whatever the differences, whatever the anger in the individual members of the student body, this was an attack against the campus as a whole. It was a series of savage incidents that reflected poorly on all of them.

Darnell and Frank agreed that in order to protect students of all colors on campus it would be necessary to table their differences until the killers were caught and dealt with. To that end, the CRD brought on Ron Baylor, a Somerset trustee who headed the safety committee, to talk about all the recent security measures and to announce that the administration had leased seven *additional* shuttles, bringing the total up to fourteen. For days, the administration had been recommending that students obey a voluntary midnight curfew. Now Baylor announced that the curfew had been made mandatory until such time as the rule was rescinded.

An astonishing number of students cheered. Jenna was amazed and pleased.

After that, Lieutenant Gonci of the Somerset P.D. got up with the chief of the campus police, Art Kelley, to discuss an even greater increase in patrols. A student patrol called Campus Watch was also being formed, with signups being temporarily handled by the CRD as the rally's organizers.

While Jenna was taking all of that in, Yoshiko spotted her and came over, pulling Hunter along behind her.

"Hey!" she said. "You're awake!"

Jenna nodded. "I have to go in to work this morning. This is amazing!"

"No kidding," Hunter said. "I can't even believe it's the same campus. I guess people just got tired of being angry, huh?"

"Or tired of being afraid," Jenna replied, studying those around her.

The three friends stood and watched together for a few minutes longer. After Jenna had glanced at her watch half a dozen times, Yoshiko tapped her on the shoulder.

"Go. If Dr. Slikowski's expecting you, I'm sure he doesn't like to be kept waiting."

Jenna smiled. As she left the crowd and headed past Keates Hall and across Carpenter Street, her only regret was that she had not seen Damon at the rally. Otherwise, she felt happier and lighter than she had in quite some time. Not only had the campus apparently begun to throw off the anger and fear and hate that had haunted it for the previous week and a half, but she felt that she might have found the key to the murders that had plagued Somerset. It might all be over soon, if she was right. And if the police could put the knowledge to use. Getting someone to believe her was the first step, and that's why she wanted to talk to Slick, first.

Slick stared at her as though she might be feverish. "Not to put too fine a point on it, Jenna, but have you been getting enough sleep? I know you well enough to be certain you realize the incredible nature of what you're proposing. Even if such things are possible, what are the odds?"

Jenna frowned and glanced away awkwardly. "I know," she said. "Believe me, I know. But it makes so much sense. Okay, not as much as it made at three in the morning, but . . . look, just do the tests, okay? Please? Humor me, at least."

Dr. Slikowski took a deep breath and let it out slowly. He scratched the back of his head, then removed his glasses and began thoughtfully to clean them on an edge of his white smock that was still spotless.

On the table in front of him was a dead man. The corpse reeked of a week's worth of body odor, the stench tinged with whiskey. Jenna guessed from the smell alone that the man had been homeless, but that hardly explained the quartet of messy stab wounds in his chest. It reminded her that there were other things going on in the Somerset area, other murders, other cases for Slick to be concerned about. Apparently the corpse had turned up in a Cambridge subway station, and the Cambridge P.D. had asked Slick to do the autopsy and consult on the case, because it was the third homeless man stabbed to death in their fair city in five months.

"Tell you what," Slick said, replacing his glasses. "Be so kind as to help me with this autopsy—which was, after all, the reason I asked you to come in this morning—and then we'll run those tests together. Wild or not, I've come to trust your instincts enough not to simply ignore them, even when they sound so outrageous."

Jenna smiled and said, "Thanks . . . I guess."

The autopsy went smoothly except for a couple of small problems. The camera setup above the steel table was out of film, and it took her several minutes to search the cabinets for more. Worse, the massive overhead vent with its charcoal filter began to make strange sounds right about the time Slick was opening up the subject's chest cavity, and the air became stagnant with the stench of the corpse and formaldehyde that always permeated the room. Jenna had gotten almost as used to the nostril-burning chemical odor as the doctors, but today it seemed even Slick was bothered by it.

"We'll have to have that looked at right away," the M.E. said more than once during the autopsy.

They were able to ascertain little from the autopsy, save to compare with the records of the previous murders and confirm that the blade used to kill their subject was similar or identical to that used in the earlier killings. The gray matter of the John Doe's brain had an oddly shaped tumor in it, but Slick was certain that had as little to do with the man's death as his alcohol-devastated liver.

They did what they could. That was the job.

After the skullcap had been replaced upon the body—its head resting on black rubber—and all the notes had been dictated, photographs taken, tissue and organ samples cut and bagged, Dr. Slikowski had Jenna do something she had never done before. Dyson had the day off, but it was not the first time she had assisted without the other doctor there. It was simply that, this time, Slick wanted her to take another step.

With him guiding her, she used a thick needle and surgical string to sew up the Y-incision in the subject's chest. Though she wore gloves, the skin felt stiff, lacking the pliability it would have had in life. It was thicker than she had imagined as she plunged the needle through and tugged the string to suture the incision. Though the flesh around the needle moved as she worked, the rest of the corpse was so still that it began to seem surreal to her. This was death. This empty husk of a human being. She thought she understood it a little more, now, but tried not to pursue her thoughts on the subject, for they were disturbing. If the John Doe's mind and spirit had gone from the body, where were they now?

No wonder so many people believe in some kind of afterlife, she thought. *The alternative is too horrible to even consider.*

Even through her mask, the smells in the room, the plastic thickness of the skin, and the fact that she had eaten nothing more than a bowl of Cap'n Crunch in her dorm room when she first woke up nearly caused her to faint. But she managed to finish the job.

"All right," he said when she was done. "I promised Natalie I would call her when I was finished, but let's get those tests done first."

Jenna felt her heart skip a beat. "How long before we get them back from the lab?"

Slick grinned mischievously. "What do you say I buy you lunch in the cafeteria? If I rattle a few cages upstairs, we can have answers in an hour or so."

"Yumm, hospital cafeteria food," Jenna said, teasing. "I hope you aren't that cheap when you take Natalie out."

Both of them laughed, and as Jenna studied Slick, she realized something. He did not think her crazy idea was out of the realm of possibility. Not that he believed it or would even be willing to call it anything but crazy, but he was going to suspend his disbelief until the tests came back, based mainly on a hunch of Jenna's and a few hours' Web research.

He had not heard the anguish in Danny's voice, the certainty about what he had seen. He was not willing to jump to conclusions based upon something as simple, yet baffling, as the conflicting reports of crime witnesses.

But he was also not going to dismiss Jenna's theory out of hand, no matter how bizarre it was.

She found that she loved him for that. Jenna had grown up with a father who saw her once or twice a year, at best. Frank Logan was a professor at Somerset, but he was on sabbatical in France for the semester, and planned to be remarried in the fall. But even when Jenna had first arrived at Somerset, and he had made an effort to get closer, she had never felt that he knew who she was and what she was made of.

Slick did.

Her sarcasm had elicited a laugh from the man, and then a grimace. "All right. Pizza then. We'll order in."

And so they had. The M.E. rattled some cages, ordered the tests Jenna had asked for, and the two of them sat in Slick's second-floor office listening to

Diana Krall and eating pepperoni and mushroom pizza.

Slick must have rattled the cages hard, because the test results were back in under an hour. As Slick spoke to the lab on the phone, his always pale skin became even more so. He frowned so deeply the lines on his face looked like they were drawn there.

"My God," he whispered as he hung up the phone. He stared at Jenna at a momentary loss for words, then said, "You were right."

Jenna's heart gave a slight kick in her chest, and she swallowed.

"Now what do we do?" she asked, surprised that she could even speak.

"We call Danny Mariano, and we try to convince him that *both* of us aren't out of our gourds."

"I think you're both nuts," Danny said, staring wide-eyed at Jenna and Dr. Slikowski.

Jenna and Slick shared a glance; both of them wore faint smiles. When they had first called the Somerset police station, Danny was in the midst of another case. Slick had left him a message that they were on their way down to the station and needed to speak with him as soon as possible. In Dr. Slikowski's specially equipped van—there was a hydraulic ramp that lifted him into the back of the vehicle, and the brake and accelerator were on the steering wheel—they drove straight to the station, stopping only long enough for coffee and doughnuts.

They went bearing gifts, and although Danny was

not averse to a chocolate doughnut or two, he still thought they were completely insane. Jenna supposed the smirks on both of their faces and their almost giddy manner didn't help matters. She had never seen Slick so . . . *tickled* was the word her mother would have used. But she felt they both had reason. They hadn't solved the case, but they had cracked it, Danny's doubt notwithstanding.

"You know, I warned Jenna that you'd say that," Slick told the detective.

"Actually, you said he would think we were both out of our gourds," she corrected, then turned to frown at Danny. "*Nuts* is such a crude word, don't you think?"

With a sigh, Danny shook his head. "Look, Jenna . . ." He paused, then turned to Dr. Slikowski instead. "Walter. I don't know what to think anymore. With Audrey in the hospital, maybe you two are just trying to get me going, make me laugh. Other than that, insanity is the first thing that comes to mind."

It was the M.E.'s turn to frown. Slick raised one eyebrow and fixed Danny with a cold stare. "You will really have to pardon my demeanor, Detective Mariano. But we have known one another for several years. Would I have made the trip down here on a mere social call, even on a benevolent mission to improve your own mood? Though I may seem unusually lighthearted at the moment, I assure you that springs from my own initial staunch disbelief. Which, I should note, was not unlike your own. It seems incredible, Detective Mariano, but it is nevertheless true."

Mouth slightly open, Danny glanced from Slick to Jenna and back again. Speechless.

"Danny, don't tell me this doesn't make sense to you," Jenna said. "Vasquez, remember? All the witnesses saw something different, but you were sure Vasquez was the guy. The killer keeps giving you the slip. Look me straight in the eye and tell me that when you questioned Vasquez and then let him go, you didn't wonder if, no matter what anybody had seen, this was the guy all along. That all those times you thought he'd given you the slip, he was right there in front of you, with a different face."

"Jesus," Danny almost moaned. "He really is Houdini."

"Nothing so mundane as magic, I'm afraid," Slick told him. "In fact, there are scientific explanations for everything you've encountered. They make an incredible tale, but not an impossible one."

Danny's gaze drifted for a moment; then his eyes locked on Jenna's.

"It's true? You're sure?" he asked, obviously still having trouble digesting it.

She nodded. "It's true," she said. "You're not looking for two killers. They're the same guy."

With a grunt Danny, stood up and started pacing the police station's break room. He went from the vending machines against one wall to the long table with the coffeemaker against the other, then back again. Several times he hesitated and seemed about to say something; then he would catch himself and run his hands through his hair. He was thinking so hard

Jenna thought he looked like he was about to run out of the room.

With a sudden jerk, he came to a halt and returned to the small table and sat down across from them.

"Okay, then explain it to me," he said. His blue eyes flashed darkly. "Explain it to me in a way that I can tell Audrey . . . hell, that I can tell Lieutenant Gonci about it and not have them think I've completely snapped."

Slick nodded grimly. "The first dead girl, Brittany Forrester, scratched her assailant. Jenna was able to scrape a sample of his skin tissue from under her fingernails. On the latest victim, Patrice Connors, we found—again thanks to Jenna—several hairs that we believe belong to her killer."

"So far you haven't told me anything I don't know," Danny said, listening intently.

"The guy who murdered Brittany was white, and the guy who killed Patrice was black," Jenna said. "But after all the things you were saying, about the witnesses and all, I couldn't sleep thinking about it. Your instincts are usually dead on. I was trying to figure out how you could feel so strongly about Vasquez and be so totally wrong. Then I turned the problem around the other way, trying to figure out how it might be possible that you were right. There was really only one way."

"They're the same guy," Danny said, nodding grimly. This time, however, he did not sound quite as doubtful. "But it isn't makeup," he countered. "The guy would never have had time to do that, not in any of these circumstances."

"No," Slick agreed. "It isn't makeup."

"Then?" Danny asked slowly, spreading his hands with a shrug.

He was looking at Dr. Slikowski, but the M.E. turned his own gaze upon Jenna.

"They're your theories," he said.

Jenna nodded, ignoring the pleasure it gave her that he would yield to her and let her explain. She considered how best to explain as Danny regarded her closely.

"Do you know why an albino looks the way he does?" she asked.

Danny nodded. "Pigment."

"Well, lack of pigment, yes. They have no pigment in their skin. No color at all, really. Skin color is completely determined by pigment. There are a number of conditions that affect skin pigment. But there are also one or two in which the amount of pigment changes gradually in response to external stimuli, like extreme temperature changes or even altitude."

Jenna swallowed. She glanced at Slick, who nodded for her to continue. Danny was giving her his full attention, so she plunged on.

"In 1978, in Istanbul, there was a case reported of a man who had a condition just like that. He used the same kinds of meditation techniques that fakirs use to control pain receptors and other supposedly unconscious functions of the brain, and he reached the point where he could control the amount of pigment in his skin so that it would no longer react to external stimuli the way it once had."

Danny's eyes were wide. "You're serious about this, aren't you?" he said, astonished.

"Completely," Slick said. "The case Jenna's referring to was the most extreme that she found in her research, but it was not the only one. The basic condition is called *varius derma pigmentosum*. The ability to control that condition is rare enough that science has not yet given it a name. But if a person so afflicted could use such purposeful control to prevent changes in skin pigment—"

"Then they could probably also change it on purpose if they wanted to," Danny finished for him.

Jenna nodded vigorously. "Blushing, or the way your pupils change, those are involuntary functions. But I think this guy was like the one in Istanbul, that he took an involuntary function and somehow made it voluntary, the same way some people can cry on command."

"From black to white, or vice versa, and my buddy Vasquez in between," Danny said. "That's . . . incredible. Can you test for the condition you're talking about?"

"Every time we test, we destroy part of our sample. If we test for it now, you won't have any evidence left to make your case when you catch him," Slick replied. "But it truly does seem the only logical explanation. You might ask your primary suspects if they're willing to be tested, however."

Danny grumbled. "I'm not sure we even have primary suspects anymore. Darnell Thomas and Frank Abernathy butt heads on a regular basis, but we have no real reason to suspect either one of them." He seemed to be struck by a thought and looked up at

Jenna oddly. "So you think our guy used these meditation techniques, like the . . . what do you call them, fakirs? That also might explain how he was able to stop his pulse during the rally to make everybody think he was dead."

"He didn't stop it," Slick said. "He merely slowed it down."

"Okay, but that still doesn't explain why his face looked so different every time he committed a crime. Skin pigment is one thing, but you can't change facial structure."

"Actually, you can," Jenna told him. She smiled uncertainly. "He wore a hat or a hood all the time so nobody could see his hair, which he couldn't change. But I thought about that, and I looked it up. There's a condition called *facies mollis* that makes some of the bone of the skull malleable, strong but soft, almost like cartilage. It always reverts to its natural shape, but when manipulated it can be briefly shaped. Within limits."

"Come on!" Danny shouted, throwing his hands in the air and jerking back in his chair, the legs squeaking loudly on the linoleum floor of the break room. "What are the odds of someone having both of these things? For God's sake, Jenna—"

"Incalculable," Dr. Slikowski told him. "Nevertheless, that is what we believe. You are free to disregard our theories, however. After all, we are not police officers."

Danny frowned. "Hey, Walter, don't do that. I just . . . you've got to understand how hard all this is to believe."

Before Slick could reply, Jenna stood up. "We do. But now that you know, Danny, maybe you should give us the benefit of the doubt and stop wasting time. Have we ever steered you wrong before?"

He stared at her for a moment, obviously taken aback by her manner. Then he smiled. "Kid, you are something else," he told her.

Jenna bristled. Danny chuckled. When she said, "Don't call me kid," he said it right along with her. Jenna glared at him a moment, then let out a long breath.

"I'll get you for that one, Mariano," she said.

"Oh, I'm sure you will," Danny replied.

There was a moment between them that was almost electric, a moment where each recognized something in the other that was powerfully compelling. Danny shook his head and looked away, and Jenna thought she might have blushed a bit.

Bad pigment, she thought, hoping Slick had not noticed her blushing. *Bad timing.*

"All right," Danny said as he resumed his pacing. "Assuming I go along with this, I'll have anybody we consider a suspect tested. We can start doing a little research, see if anybody with either condition has been talked about in local medical journals, that sort of thing. Meanwhile, we don't talk to the press, don't let the guy know that we're on to him. I guess we keep up our undercovers, but if he goes after one of them again, we grab up everyone nearby. With the number of Somerset and campus cops roaming the grounds, it'll be like a damn dragnet."

"I wonder if the number of police officers will deter him," Slick said.

Danny shook his head. "Not this guy. He likes it too much. He's not afraid of us because he thinks we don't know his secrets."

Jenna smiled. "Talking like a true believer, Detective."

He scowled at her. Jenna laughed, but only for a moment. Her expression grew quite serious, and Danny noticed. He stopped pacing and moved toward her.

"What is it?"

After only a moment's hesitation, she told him. "I should be the bait."

Slick reacted even more quickly than Danny. "Now just a second, Jenna!" he snapped. "We have done our part of this job. More than our part. Thanks to your hunch and your research, the police will have a much better chance of capturing the killer. You've put yourself in danger far too often on my watch, and I can't let you do that again."

Danny nodded and gestured toward Slick. "What he said. Jenna, no way. Do you understand? No. Way. There are a million cops out there, let them do the job, and you stay out of the way."

Though Jenna had expected their reaction, she found herself growing furious in spite of that. She walked across the room away from them, then turned and stalked back. When she stopped, she pointed at Slick angrily.

"I work for you," she said, voice tight and controlled. "You are not my keeper and you are not my mother."

Then she turned on Danny. "And as for you, Detective, I want you to think about something. I was ecstatic to see that rally this morning, to see how everyone's pulling together, to see the support of the administration, and to hear about all the security measures that are being instituted. But you can bet your ass that your killer was there too. Probably front row, center."

"He fell for the undercover thing twice already," Danny reluctantly added. "I think he's smart enough that maybe the second time wasn't a mistake."

"Exactly!" Jenna said. "Maybe he knew that Audrey was a cop and was just toying with you. Without knowing what he can do, you didn't have a chance. *He* knew that, too. Now you've got a campus full of cops, a midnight curfew, and a fleet of safety shuttles moving across campus. For the next week or so, there are going to be damned few students walking around after dark unless they're in big groups. He'll know most everyone who's solo that late at night is a cop, and now that there are so many of you, he'll know it's a bigger risk. And if he goes long enough without being able to hurt anyone, he'll probably go underground or even move on to another town or another college."

With a hard look at Slick to let him know that he should stay out of it, she sat down at the table again and glared at Danny. "You roll that around in your head, Danny, and then you tell me that you don't need me."

Fuming, she studied Danny's face. He was angry, that was for certain. His jaw was tight, and his nostrils flared. His eyes ticked from left to right as if he were searching for an answer to be simply given to him. After what seemed a very long time, he shook his head slowly and breathed an angry sigh.

"How did you get so far ahead of me on this?" he asked her.

Jenna blinked. Then she offered a tiny shrug. "You just found out what the key to this thing is. I've had twelve hours to think about it."

Slick stared at Danny, then glanced anxiously at Jenna. "Now just a minute," he said quickly.

She did not let him continue. Softening, Jenna leaned forward and placed her hand over Slick's where it rested on the arm of his wheelchair. "I know you're worried about me. I appreciate it. Way more than you know. Truly. But the only way to be sure they catch this guy is to use a student as bait."

"Yes, but why you?" Slick snapped, his lips a thin white line where they were pressed together.

"It has to be her," Danny said, his tone filled with reluctance and what sounded like actual anguish.

"What?" Slick demanded, turning on him.

Danny glanced at Jenna sadly and then regarded Slick with a steady gaze. "I can't believe I'm saying this after what happened to Audrey, but it has to be her. If she's volunteering, anyway." He looked at Jenna again. "You know why, too, don't you? You've got it all worked out."

She nodded. "Because of the newspaper."

"See?" Danny said with a helpless shrug. "She's got it all worked out. We can't be sure if we picked another student that our perp would recognize the bait as a student and not think she was a cop. But we know that he knows who Jenna is because of that picture of her and . . . and Damon, in the *Daily*."

"If this guy is really the one who called Damon, and I think he is," Jenna said, "then I'd be an irresistible target."

After a very long silence in the room, Dr. Slikowski looked over at Jenna. His fear for her was plain on his face. "You should tell your mother and father. And if you do, make sure you tell them that I was opposed to it one hundred percent."

Jenna agreed.

They headed out of the break room. At the door, Danny paused and turned to Jenna. "If I was your boyfriend, I'd be terrified for you," he told her, and there was weight to his words. "What are you going to tell Damon?"

Quickly Jenna glanced away.

"I wish I knew."

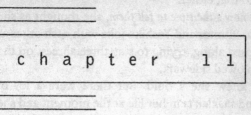

chapter 11

Though it was supposed to be warm and sunny the following day, on Sunday morning the sky was still overcast. Jenna could easily believe it when the weatherman said it might snow by evening. The low-hanging clouds looked like a mat of dense, gray cotton. But even the dismal weather didn't dampen her spirits. She was determined not to let it as she, Hunter, and Yoshiko walked down Fletcher Avenue, heading to breakfast at Nadel Dining Hall.

She was also determined not to allow herself to be distracted by the thing foremost in her mind, though she was not succeeding very well in that respect. Quite purposely, she had been avoiding Damon since her meeting with Slick and Danny the day before. The thought of telling him what she had agreed to do filled her with dread. Although she had not yet found the opportune time to talk to Yoshiko and Hunter about what she had proposed to do, Jenna already knew what their reaction was going to be, and she was not looking forward to that either.

Maybe now's the time to tell them, she thought as she listened to Hunter and Yoshiko joke with each other as they traipsed along, trying to stay three abreast on the narrow, plowed sidewalk.

Jenna knew she should. But there were a lot of *shoulds* and *shouldn'ts* in her life at the moment and she was having a hard time paying attention to any of them. So she had not told her best friends that she was planning to play the worm on the Somerset P.D.'s fishhook. She should have. The fact that she had not told Damon was even worse. Damon was going to freak out.

And who could blame him? she thought, wondering for the thousandth time why she had offered herself up as bait. *Because you're the perfect target,* the answer came back. Which, she was quite well aware, was not an argument that would score points with her friends, her boyfriend, or her mother.

She took some satisfaction in the knowledge that at least there was just one murderer, rather than two, as they had initially thought. But he was still out there, no doubt waiting for another chance to strike. The mood on campus had been so much better since the second CRD rally on Saturday morning, and Jenna was positive that the perp would not allow that feeling to last for very long. With his ability to alter his skin color and facial structure, he seemed to be purposely manipulating emotions on both sides of the racial lines.

But for what? Jenna wondered. *What does he get out of this?*

Did he enjoy the racial strife, or was he simply using it as a smokescreen to hide his brutal acts? It had to be the killing that he enjoyed the most.

Bottom line, though, it didn't matter. Jenna's insight had given the Somerset police the piece of the puzzle they needed to solve the crime. Now she was going to be the bait to finish it.

Resolute, she took a deep breath. "Guys, listen—"

Yoshiko waved her arm over her head. "There's Caitlin and Olivia."

"And Brick," Hunter added.

Jenna saw that he was right. The two girls and Brick—more Damon's crowd than her own but still her friends—were walking up toward them from the dining hall. The moment was broken, and Jenna resigned herself to telling Yoshiko and Hunter later—if at all. She forced herself to smile as the six friends came together on the corner by the President's House. There were friendly greetings all around, but Jenna felt distracted by Damon's absence. There had been no answer when she knocked on his door this morning to see if he wanted to join them for breakfast, and he certainly was not at the library first thing on a Sunday. She had sort of assumed he was off somewhere with Brick, maybe down at the gym or hanging with Ant, who was still healing.

Now here was Brick, and still no Damon.

With only the slightest pause, Jenna shook off the lingering question and nodded a friendly greeting to Olivia, Caitlin, and Brick. "How's it going?" she asked. There was still a slight chill coming from Olivia, but Jenna ignored it, telling herself that maybe, in order to be happy, some people just had to be a little bit angry all the time.

"No need to hurry," Brick said with a thin smile on his lips. "The eggs will still be cold and rubbery when you get there."

"Where's your better third?" Jenna asked. "I missed him this morning."

"D?" Brick said. He shifted from one foot to the other, and cast a funny look at Olivia and Caitlin. He offered a halfhearted shrug. "Haven't seen him. Could be hanging with Ant, I guess." He hesitated and, once again, looked back and forth between Caitlin and Olivia. "I figured he'd be having breakfast with you."

"Yeah," Caitlin said, Jenna thought a bit too quickly. "We thought for sure he'd be with you."

Jenna frowned as she shook her head. "He didn't answer when I knocked on his door."

"He's probably gone off with Ant," Olivia offered. "He's been visiting him a lot."

Now that was even more bizarre, because suddenly Olivia was being a little too helpful in light of the chill that had been between them before. Jenna was tempted to ask her what was going on but decided to let it drop.

You're just nerved up because of what you're going to do, she told herself, but she couldn't deny that all three of them—Brick, Olivia, and Caitlin—were acting sort of strange, like they were uncomfortable being around her or something. She wondered if Damon had talked to them about the tension in her relationship with him at the moment.

206

"Well," she said finally, "we probably better get over there before they stop serving."

Hunter and Yoshiko nodded their agreement, and after a round of "later," they separated. As she walked away, though, Jenna could not help but cast a nervous glance at her retreating friends. Caitlin was also looking back and their eyes met for just a moment before the other girl quickly turned around. Jenna frowned. Everyone was acting way too fidgety for her. It made her feel a little skittish herself.

Fifteen minutes later, when she, Yoshiko, and Hunter sat down at a long table after suffering through the breakfast line for yellow bits of rubber that were scrambled eggs in name only, Jenna was still feeling a bit off center. Brick had certainly been right about the eggs. Jenna ended up with nothing more than a bowl of cold cereal, a glass of OJ, and a cup of coffee.

After they had settled in, and Hunter was plowing through breakfast, Jenna sat back in her chair and cleared her throat to get their attention.

"What's up?" Yoshiko asked, regarding her with one raised eyebrow.

"Look, guys," Jenna began. "I don't know how to say this—"

"Is it about Damon?" Hunter asked as he wiped his lower lip with a paper napkin.

"Damon? Why would you say that?" Jenna asked. She did not miss that Yoshiko jabbed him in the ribs, making him jump.

Hunter eyed Jenna for a moment, then tried to dismiss what he had said with a casual shrug of the shoulders.

"No reason," he said. "I just thought . . . You know . . . you asked Brick about him and . . ." He let his words trail off, then busied himself with jabbing another forkful of eggs.

"So what did you want to say?" Yoshiko asked.

Her roommate's attention was still focused on her, and that made Jenna squirm uneasily. She did not enjoy feeling like she was under such intense scrutiny.

"I . . . umm, I need your advice on something," she said, shifting uneasily in her chair. "Well, not your advice, really, because I've already decided to do it, but—"

"You're going to dump Damon, right?" Hunter asked, glancing up at her.

"*No*. I'm not going to dump Damon." Jenna felt a surge of anger but pushed it aside, knowing that it probably came from her nervousness about telling them what she planned to do. In as few words as possible, she explained everything.

"I think you're out of your mind," Hunter said, scowling deeply as he shook his head.

Jenna could not help but chuckle. "You're not the first one to say that to me," she said.

"You mean to tell me that even after what happened to Audrey you're going through with this?" Yoshiko asked incredulously. She had a blank stare, and her mouth hung open as she looked at Jenna and shook her head. "She's a trained police officer, and that didn't stop her from getting hurt. And you're going to go out there looking for this guy?"

"This is all strictly confidential," Jenna said, leaning

forward and lowering her voice. "I'll have ten times as many cops in the area, so I should be safe."

"But why not send someone else out?" Hunter offered as he gnashed away at a mouthful of chewy eggs.

"I told you. With all the extra police coverage, he's not going to risk just attacking anyone. Oh, he'll be out there looking. But with all the cops around, he's not going to be dumb about it. The guy's crazy, but I don't think he's stupid. After all that stuff in the paper, I'll be the perfect target to draw him out." She shivered and cast a nervous glance around the still crowded cafeteria.

"I still say you're nuts," Hunter said.

Yoshiko swatted him on the shoulder. "Stop saying that!" she said, keeping her voice low only with effort. "That's all you've got to say, knowing that Jenna's putting her life on the line like this?"

"I should be okay," Jenna said, even though she wasn't entirely convinced herself. "Like I said, there'll be plenty of cops around. I should be fine."

Hunter snorted, but when he caught the withering glare from Yoshiko, he said nothing. Instead, he only looked at Jenna with grave concern and doubt in his eyes.

"Look, Jenna," Yoshiko said. She leaned across the table and, taking her friend's hand, gave it a tight squeeze. "I'm sure you've thought this all through, and even if you haven't, you're going to go through with it, but I just want you to know that—"

Her voice caught in her throat, and for a moment

she was unable to continue. Before she could finish what she'd been about to say, Jenna smiled back at her.

"Don't you worry," Jenna said shakily. "Danny will be there. He'll make sure nothing bad happens to me."

"Hello. You awake?" Jenna whispered as she eased the hospital door open and entered the dimly lit, silent room.

Audrey's head was turned to the left, facing away from the door. Either she was asleep or else staring out the window at the darkening clouds. She made a low grunting noise as she turned to see Jenna standing in the doorway.

"Hey," she said. A wide smile spread across her face, and she boosted herself up in the bed. The fresh sheets made a loud crinkling sound. "Come on in. I was just lying here, bored out of my mind."

"I can come back later if you're not feeling up to having a visitor," Jenna said as she inched into the room.

"No. Don't be silly," Audrey said as she ran her fingers through her hair. "I haven't had enough visitors, and to tell you the truth, a little bit of daytime TV goes a long way."

"I know what you mean," Jenna said, finally feeling as though the welcome was genuine, not just Audrey being polite. One thing she knew and respected about Audrey was that she would always speak her mind, no matter what. It was a trait Jenna admired and often wished she had a little more of. On the other hand, she figured that Slick and Danny and lots of other people thought she already had plenty of that particular trait.

"So," Audrey said, watching as Jenna walked over to sit down in the comfortable chair by the side of the bed. "Danny tells me you helped crack the case."

Jenna felt a flush of embarrassment and glanced down at the floor. "I didn't really solve it," she said, noticing that her voice sounded lower and huskier than usual. "But—yeah, at least we figured out that it's really just one guy, not two."

"A guy who can change his skin color from black to white," Audrey said, lips pursed as though she were tasting the absurdity of the words.

When she said it, she looked at Jenna with an expression that made her feel even more embarrassed. But then Audrey laughed and shook her head.

"Let me tell you, I wish I'd known how to do *that* trick when I was going through police training." She cocked her head to one side and sniffed with laughter, her dark eyes sparkling. "Sure would've made that part of my life a lot easier, anyway."

Jenna looked at her and smiled, but she still felt wary. She could not ignore the fact that there had been some tension between her and Audrey ever since she started working for Dr. Slikowski. That had had something to do with the feelings that had started to develop between herself and Danny, but Jenna and the detective had put a stop to that. Since then, Audrey had slowly seemed to warm up a bit. And Jenna had never doubted that Audrey at least respected her as someone dedicated to her job.

"And while we're at it," Audrey went on, still chuckling to herself, "maybe it's too bad that we couldn't have done something about me being a woman, at least during that time. That would have made things a *whole* lot easier."

Jenna was not sure what to say to that. It was obvious that race had been and still was an issue for Audrey, especially since she had chosen to work in a profession traditionally run by an old-boy network of white men. She could have argued that things seemed to have been changing in that respect for some years, but the last thing Jenna wanted to do was get into a debate about police department politics with a homicide detective. Particularly one who had never really been that fond of her.

"So you think my idea is nuts, too?" Jenna said.

Audrey did not answer right away, and Jenna started squirming under the detective's steady gaze. Finally, Audrey cleared her throat.

"Just because I've never heard of something like this before, that doesn't mean it can't be real. Besides, if Walter Slikowski backs you up on this, who am I to argue?"

"We've been able to test to confirm that he does have this mutable pigment syndrome. Something *derma pigmentosum*. As for the malleable facial bones, that part we can't prove, but we researched it really carefully," Jenna said. "Everyone is pretty much in agreement on how crazy it sounds, but there are actually more known cases of that than the pigment thing. Plus, it's the only possibility anyone's come up with that fits the facts we've got from people who have witnessed the attacks."

"I know, I know," Audrey said, her voice taking on a little wistful tone. "And I got the scars to prove it. Unless our perp is some kind of quick-change makeup master—which now that those words are out of my mouth sounds even more absurd than what you're suggesting—we don't have a choice but to go with what you've got."

The injured detective smiled thinly. "Of course, that's got nothing to do with the fact that without the carefully researched scientific opinions of the medical examiner and his staff, the Somerset P.D. look like absolute morons for letting this guy slip us so many times."

She paused and sat up straighter in the bed. Leaning foward, she held her hand out to Jenna, who got up out of the chair, came over to the bedside, and clasped Audrey's hand firmly.

"You're not a cop, Jenna. You don't have to go the distance on this thing."

Jenna swallowed. "Yeah," she said firmly. "I do. Anyway, it was my theory."

Audrey nodded and squeezed her hand. "Whether you're right or wrong, you've got more guts than most people I know twice your age, and most of them are in uniform. Just be careful. I've been at this a long time and the guy suckered me."

"Thanks," Jenna said, giving Audrey's hand a reassuring squeeze. "But we didn't know then what we know now. If this guy had been an ordinary suspect, you'd have had him easy."

Audrey nodded slowly. "Everyone's telling you you're stupid or crazy or both, right?"

Jenna bristled. "If we don't get this guy now, he'll figure out that we're on to him and set up in another town, and we'll never even know who he was."

"Hey," Audrey said. "I wasn't arguing. You're going to be okay, you know. Danny's going to be practically in your coat pocket, and you'll have ten times as much backup as I had, probably more. They'll have you covered. No way is Danny going to let anything happen to his favorite girl."

Jenna ignored that last comment. Too many complicated feelings surrounded it. She set her jaw and looked Audrey straight in the eyes. "That's what I'm counting on."

"So."

Jenna resisted the urge to say *so what?* She simply leaned forward and looked deeply into Damon's eyes. Her own eyes were burning as tears gathered, but she held them back, telling herself not to cry. It certainly wouldn't help matters right now to get all emotional.

"So you're telling me that race isn't a factor in what's happening between us," she said.

It was a little after ten o'clock at night, and they were sitting alone in the common area on the third floor. When they had first entered and sat down in the stuffed chairs in the corner by the window, there had been a few students sitting on the floor playing cards. As soon as it was obvious that there was a very intense discussion going on, however, they ended the game and walked away, one of them muttering something about having a lot of homework to do.

"Absolutely not," Damon said, looking at her with a firm set to his jaw.

Through the window behind him, Jenna could see thick snowflakes falling, illuminated against the night sky by the pale blue glow of the streetlights.

"So why am I sensing this . . . this distance between us?" she asked. Shifting closer to him, she placed her arms around his neck and drew his face close to hers. Damon looked back at her, his eyes moist and dark.

"I don't know. All I know is it isn't you and me. It . . . it's just . . . everything. All the crap that's been going on, you and I have just been handling it differently. That's all. And maybe not well."

"Differently?" Jenna echoed, looking past him at the falling snow for a moment as she let his words sink in.

"Look, Jenna," Damon said as he reached out and, touching her chin, gently turned her face back to his. "It's just been a real tough time for both of us, right? But I promise you, I'm willing to work to fix it. I . . . I don't want to lose you."

"Do you really mean that?" Jenna asked even as she let herself slip into his embrace. Her shoulders shook as they hugged. She could feel the warmth of his breath on the back of her neck. They both remained silent for a long time, with Jenna burying her face into his shoulder to hold back her tears while Damon ran his hand up and down her back, pulling her close against him.

"There's something I have to tell you, though," Jenna finally said, her voice muffled from her face being pressed so hard against his shoulder.

Damon suddenly released her, and they both sat back, facing each other.

"What have you got to tell me?" he asked icily. His whole posture had stiffened, and Jenna could not have missed the tightness in his voice. In a flash, she thought she caught a flicker of something new in his eyes.

Guilt? Worry? Anger?

Jenna had to look away from Damon, because she found it so hard to say what she was going to say if she was looking straight at him.

She said it.

Damon jerked away from her, his expression a mixture of anger and surprise. He tried to say something more, but words failed him, and he ended up just stammering.

Jenna braced herself, squeezing her hands into tight fists. "I know it sounds dangerous," she went on, "but there are going to be undercover cops everywhere, and it's the only—"

"No, no," Damon said as he shook his pointed finger at her. "It doesn't *sound* dangerous. It *is* dangerous. It's absolutely insane."

Jenna gritted her teeth and shook her head.

"No, it's not," she said, struggling hard to keep her voice even. "Look, we think we've figured out—well, not who the guy is, but something about him that will guarantee he won't get away again. But with all the cops around, we need bait he won't be able to resist. After he threatened you on the phone . . . it's me. Call me irresistible."

"No. You don't get to do that. You don't get to tell

me you're putting your life on the line, and it isn't even your job or anything, and then make jokes about it and pretend it isn't stupid. Damn it, Jenna!" Damon clapped his hands together. No longer able to contain himself, he got up from the chair and began pacing back and forth across the floor. "That's it exactly! *That's* what's driving me nuts about you."

"What?" Jenna asked, bristling inside but genuinely confused. "You're upset that I want to help solve these murders and stop them?"

"No, no . . . I get that you want to help," Damon said, shaking his head with frustration. "But there are limits, for God's sake. I . . . you know, just the other day, I was saying to Ant how we . . . how I'm not sure I can take this." He lowered his voice and stopped pacing as he turned and looked at her squarely. "You throw yourself into this like . . . like you can't get hurt or something. But you know what? You *can* get hurt. You could get yourself killed, and I don't know if I can take being in a relationship with someone who's constantly doing things like that.

"I'm eighteen, Jenna," Damon said softly. "Stuff like that is not what being eighteen is about."

Although it was a struggle not to lash out at Damon, Jenna said nothing. What could she say? She knew that she loved him, and she wanted him to know that she would never do anything to hurt him. But he also had to understand who she was and how she functioned. How could he *not* appreciate that she had to do everything she could—even if it meant putting herself in danger—if it would help stop this *chameleon* from killing again?

"I'm doing it for us, too, you know," she said, her voice controlled but barely above a whisper.

"No, you're not!" Damon said, almost shouting. "You're doing it for yourself and you know what? I think you like it. I think you get a thrill out of it."

Jenna grimaced and shook her head sadly. "What this guy has been doing has driven a wedge between us," she said, "just like it's driven wedges between everyone on campus. No one trusts anyone anymore, no matter what we say and no matter how many rallies the CRD has."

"That's not it, Jenna, and you know it," Damon said, simmering with anger. "You do this all the time. You get yourself into these dangerous situations, and—I swear to God—sometimes it seems to me like you enjoy them so much you seek them out."

"No, I don't seek them out," Jenna said, barely containing her fury at the suggestion. "But when they happen, I don't run from them, either. I do what I can to help solve them. Are you telling me you don't want them to nail the guy who killed Brittany? Who put Ant in the hospital?"

"Of course I do," Damon said bitterly, "but that's the cops' job, not yours."

"I'm just doing what I can, to help."

"There, you see?" Damon straightened up and crossed his arms over his chest, closing himself off from her. "That's *exactly* what I'm talking about. You jump right in. You're eighteen, Jenna! Eighteen. A kid. This job you've got, maybe it puts you in contact with this stuff, but that's where it should end. You don't have to get any deeper than that."

Jenna opened her hands, helpless, and glanced down at them. "I do, Damon. I can't explain it to you, but you're wrong. I have to. If I can make a difference, then for the families of the victims, and for the people who might eventually be victims, I have to help if I can. And you know what? I have made a difference. In this case—and in others."

Damon stood fuming a moment, his chest rising and falling. He seemed to have completely run out of words. Then he threw up his hands again.

"Know what, Jenna? Maybe you want all this fear and pain and stress in your life. Maybe you want to just skip eighteen right on up to thirty. But I don't."

Jenna stood up from the chair and held both of her hands out to him. Tears spilled from her eyes and ran down her face. After a moment's hesitation, Damon moved close to her and took her hands in his, holding them tightly.

"I love you, Damon," Jenna said, her voice cracking with emotion. "And I don't want to lose you. More than anything in the world, I want to work this out. But before I can do that, I have to go through with this."

Damon let out a long sigh and stared at her for several seconds. Then, without another word, he released her hands, turned, and walked out of the lounge.

chapter 12

"Do you really think our suspect isn't going to notice all of this activity on campus?" Jenna asked Danny incredulously as she looked around the room. "He'd have to be blind not to see what's going on."

They were standing in Sparrow Hall's basement rec room, but it didn't take much imagination to mistake it for an active police station. The Somerset cops, working with campus security as well as cops and detectives from several surrounding towns, had turned the large room into their command headquarters. The Ping-Pong table in the center of the room was now strewn with a detailed map of the campus as well as assorted laptops, cell phones, and two-way radios. The window shades were drawn, and there were guards posted at each door leading down into the basement. A group of ten police officers and detectives were gathered in the room, talking and drinking coffee as they prepared for the stakeout, and there were many more on standby, already positioning themselves along the agreed upon route.

"Don't worry," Danny replied. "We know what we're doing."

"I know that," Jenna said snappily, "but he knows what he's doing, too."

She couldn't help but notice the sharp edge in her voice and told herself to calm down. *Don't say anything stupid just because you're nervous,* she cautioned herself, but even Danny's comforting presence didn't seem to be enough to take the edge off. A slippery coil of tension twisted in her gut whenever she let it sink in that all of these preparations and all of these cops were here for her.

No, not me, she thought. *They're here for him . . . for the killer . . . so they can catch him.*

"This is all part of his game," Danny said, his voice low and reassuring. "He knows the place is crawling with cops, but he's going to try to kill again anyway. He *has* to if only to show that he's smarter than we are. Our ace in the hole is that he doesn't know that *we* know his secret."

Jenna was about to reply, but she jumped when a voice spoke suddenly behind her.

"I've got to hand it to you, kid. You've got sand."

She turned around quickly, surprised to see Detective Sergeant Joe Flannery from the Cambridge Police Department walking toward her. His thin gray hair looked almost silver in the glare of the overhead fluorescent lights, and there was a sparkle in his eye. Remembering how she and Flannery had clashed on a previous case that had involved the Cambridge police, Jenna was surprised that he had answered Danny's request for help on this detail.

"I'm not exactly sure what 'having sand' means," she said, trying to hide the tremor of anxiety in her voice, "but I'll take it as a compliment."

"Oh, it is. Honest," Flannery replied with a reassuring smile. "There are several other expressions I could use, but that one's most acceptable for mixed company."

"Thanks," Jenna said.

As far as she could tell, Flannery was being one hundred percent genuine with her, and she could not help but be touched by his obvious respect and concern. Somerset was out of his jurisdiction. Like many other cops, he was here to help. It was impossible to know if Flannery had opted in on the evening's festivities to help watch out for Jenna. It didn't seem likely, and yet at that moment, it felt true. Jenna did not know what to say. But that was all right. Flannery would only have grumbled something nasty if she had tried.

"Break a leg," the aging cop said.

Jenna smiled. "Thanks."

Danny had made his way over to the Ping-Pong table and was leaning over a large map of the campus. As Jenna approached, she saw that the map was covered with arrows marked in blue felt-tip pen. In numerous places all across campus, there were red Xs on several buildings and along the sides of the street.

"Okay," Danny said, taking a deep breath and not bothering to look up at her. "This is the path we want you to take tonight." He tapped the map with the tip of a marker and started tracing out the route. It went from Sparrow Hall down Fletcher, then turned left by the President's House and headed toward Brunswick Chapel and the library. The return route swung around onto Sterling Lane, then cut across the tennis courts behind the graduate student dorms, and went past Keates Hall and finally back to Sparrow.

"The killer's struck in several locations around campus, but so far it's always been on campus, and he's always stayed close to buildings or other structures like the bleachers on the football field," Danny said.

"That's so he can hide in the shadows while he changes his appearance," Jenna offered.

"No doubt," Danny said, glancing at her quickly and nodding. "We've got undercover cops stationed all along the route as well as every place that's marked with a red X. We have one corridor all along the route you'll be taking, and another, wider perimeter around that so we can catch him if he makes it through the first line. Remember, though, we're just going to scare him off at first. Make him run. We'll give him some rope so we can be sure he's far enough away from you. Let him think he's safe while we make sure that you're safe. But we will not let him out of our sight."

Jenna suddenly felt uncomfortable and realized that someone was standing too close behind her. She turned and saw Flannery, his arms folded across his expansive gut as he craned his head forward and listened to Danny. When he noticed that Jenna was looking at him, he gave her a grim half-smile.

"No way this guy's gonna get away from us tonight," Flannery said sternly.

There was an intensity in his gruff voice that Jenna found reassuring. She thought of the things Damon had said and though she knew that they were fundamentally untrue, she could not help but feel a little guilty at the exhilaration she felt just being in on this. While the rest of her classmates were studying or sleeping or playing cards or watching TV in the lounges upstairs, she was directly involved in a police operation. She was part of the team, a professional working with other professionals to nab a vicious killer. As scary as that thought might be, and as impossible as it may have seemed to her just six months ago, Jenna found that beneath her fear and anxiety she was actually enjoying what was about to transpire.

"I hope you're right, Detective," she said softly as she looked Flannery straight in the eye.

"It's almost ten o'clock," Danny said, straightening up and rubbing his hands together. He picked up his cup of coffee from the edge of the table and, leaning back, gulped it down. "What do you say we move out?"

A hard lump formed in Jenna's throat, and her body felt suddenly much colder than normal as she pulled on her black leather jacket. Even twenty-four hours before she would have needed her heavy winter coat, but as predicted, that Monday had been startlingly warm, a promise of spring right around the corner. All the snow that had been on the ground and the few inches that had fallen the night before had melted away by midafternoon and the sun had seemed to linger a bit at the end of the day.

Danny handed her a small spray can that she slid into the right front pocket of her coat. Then she pulled on her gloves, hat, and scarf. Despite the warmth of the day, by now it would be near freezing outside.

"Okay," she said, bracing herself. "I'm ready . . . I guess."

The tremor in her voice was unmistakable, and she was thankful that neither Danny nor Flannery commented on it or reacted to it. They knew the stakes better than she did, and she had no illusions about what she had gotten herself into. She told herself that she had to have faith that Danny and the other undercover cops would be close by. All she could hope was they would react fast enough when—and if—the killer made a move.

Jenna was tingling with nervous anticipation as she slung her backpack over her shoulder and settled it into place. She kept telling herself not to think it, but her mind wouldn't let it go.

I'm the bait, and if these people let me down, I'm going to end up right next to Audrey in the hospital. Or worse, laid out on top of Slick's stainless steel autopsy table.

As she started toward the door, the cops all watching her, the image that came to mind filled her with icy dread. Gritting her teeth, she closed her eyes for a moment and shook her head, trying to force it away, but she couldn't stop imagining herself, stiff and pale, laid out on the cold metal table as Slick and Dyson performed an autopsy on *her*.

* * *

He waited in the shadows, his pulse racing, his breath coming fast and shallow from anticipation. It was a little after ten o'clock on Monday night, but the campus was so deserted it looked more like it could be three o'clock in the morning. There wasn't a soul around. Even the traffic passing by on University Boulevard seemed sparse and distant.

It's all because of those damned cops! he thought angrily as he flexed his hands inside his gloves, listening with pleasure to the creaking sound the leather made.

They've got so much security around here, everyone's afraid to be out after dark unless they're in large groups or riding around in those damned shuttles!

But he was determined to get someone tonight. It didn't matter if it was a man or woman or if the person was black or white. What mattered was, he had to show them. Show them all. He had to prove to the cops that he could outwit them every damned time.

He had it all planned out, just like he had all those other times. He was wearing a black, hooded sweat-shirt, the hood drawn down tightly around his face. Beneath the sweatshirt, he was also wearing another, lighter-colored jacket so after he made his kill, he could shed the sweatshirt. He was also wearing two woolen hats—one dark blue, and the one beneath that, bright scarlet—so he could discard one if any witnesses saw him.

The important thing, he knew, was to keep the hood and hats on tightly so his hair was covered. No matter what shade his skin was, he knew that he couldn't change his hair color or texture, so he had to make sure that no one saw his hair. That was the only way someone might be able to identify him.

But waiting was the worst part. He hated it. It filled him with a nervous anticipation. And there was only one way to get rid of that feeling. That was to find someone—fast—and do what he had to do before he froze his ass off.

Impatient, he peeled off one of his gloves and looked at his hand in the darkness. Narrowing his eyes, he concentrated and, before long, the pale white flesh on the back of his hand began to darken as though an ink stain were spreading beneath his skin. Then he reached up to mold the bones of his face with his fingers and felt his features shift beneath his touch. Even after all these years of practicing and refining his talent, the sensation was strange and vaguely disgusting. Sometimes he imagined that there were living things crawling beneath his skin, shifting and writhing as his facial bones and muscles assumed different shapes.

Come on . . . Come on! I don't have all night!

He shifted nervously from one foot to the other as he scanned up and down the dark, deserted walkway that led down from Cantor Street between Coleman Auditorium and Langer Science Center to the parking lot behind the auditorium.

No one was in sight.

Maybe I should give it up for tonight, he thought. Maybe the campus security was too good, and everyone was too alert to the danger. It might even be time to move on to another campus. After lying low for a few months, he could see if he could get things started again. He knew leaving Somerset was a good idea, but he wasn't quite ready to do that yet. He had plans, long-term goals that made staying necessary, at least for a while. If he was to benefit in the end from all of this, he had to stay.

But if he wanted to stay he would have to stop the killing. At least on campus. No question, he had to do it or put all his goals in jeopardy. First, though, he had to show those goddamned cops and everyone else that he was smarter than they were. As long as the police were confused as to who the targets would be and what color the suspect was, he could stalk and kill with impunity.

And here comes one now, he thought when, off in the distance, he saw a solitary figure moving in his direction.

It was a woman.

Alone.

A tingling thrill ran through him as he craned his head forward, trying to see if she was black or white. He scanned the area but didn't see any cops lurking nearby, but that didn't really matter. As soon as he knew her race, he would adapt himself and do what he had to do, quickly. Then, once he had killed her and shucked his outer layer of clothing as he ran, he could change his skin color and bone structure and become another innocent bystander who just happened to be in the area.

It worked every time, and he didn't see any reason why it wouldn't work again tonight.

The woman was drawing nearer, and when she

passed under the streetlight, the man got a good look at her face. A cold rush of excitement filled him.

I can't believe it! he thought, trying hard to keep from laughing out loud. *This is perfect.*

He moved slowly, savoring the moment, and reached into the pouch of his sweatshirt to withdraw the knife he carried there.

It took Jenna a great deal of effort to walk with a casual stride, as though she were unaware of—or didn't care about—the dangers of being out alone this late at night on campus when there was a killer on the loose. She knew that there were plenty of undercover cops and detectives nearby. She had seen their positions marked with red *X*s on the map. As she walked along her preplanned route, she glanced around to see if she could spot any of them, but Danny had warned her not to do too much of that. A little looking around was okay; it would seem like normal caution. But too much would be suspicious and might give them away.

Well, if they're anywhere around, Jenna thought nervously, *they sure are good at keeping out of sight because I feel absolutely alone out here.*

It had snowed the night before, but just enough to make the roads a mess that day before melting completely. It had been warm all afternoon, but now it was growing cold again and she shivered. New England winter was so unpredictable, but she could not remember another like this. She tried not to think about how many times she and Damon had walked this way, going to or from class, holding hands and talking, so happy to be in love.

Now, she was not sure what was happening with Damon. Something was wrong, but she could not figure out exactly what. There were so many forces at work here, pulling at them both.

She could not understand why he was so angry at her for doing *this*. True, she was deliberately putting herself in danger. She was well aware of the risks, and if she wasn't, Danny and Slick had made sure she knew how dangerous what she was doing was.

But why couldn't Damon see how important it was to her? She had a duty, an obligation to do everything she could to help the police catch the killer. Although it wasn't technically part of her job description working for Slick, she felt committed to doing anything and everything she could to catch the killer before he could strike again. That was the only thing that was going to end the racial tension on campus, and—maybe—help heal her relationship with Damon.

Don't get distracted, she cautioned herself as she looked left and right, poised for danger. *Just focus on the staying alive. You can deal with all that other stuff later, once this is over.*

Jenna considered staying on Cantor Street, but she knew that she had to stick to the planned route. Even the slightest deviation could spoil the police protection. Danny had made it perfectly clear that even a few seconds variation could mean the difference between help arriving in time . . . or not, and she knew what *that* meant.

Telling herself to relax her shoulders and walk casually so as not to alert the killer in case he was lurking nearby watching her, Jenna made her way down the pathway beside Coleman Auditorium. It did not escape her that Melody LaChance, her best friend, had been murdered in the auditorium. The lighting was poor on the path, particularly in a small, pine tree-covered slope off to her right, by the science building. The wind sighed softly through the branches, making the black shadows shift menacingly across the snow. She made it into the parking lot behind Coleman, though on this end it was not very well lit. A sigh of relief was about to escape her lips when she sensed movement behind her.

"You're not too bright, are you?" someone said.

Jenna turned. There, in the shadows, emerging from the path she had just walked down, was an angry-looking black man.

At least right now he's black, she thought, and in that brief instant, she wondered how she could have believed such a crazy idea enough to actually put her life on the line for it.

"What's your problem?" she asked, raising her voice loud enough so whatever cops were nearby would hear her. She hoped the man didn't detect the fear in her voice.

"My problem?" the black man said, his voice high and mocking. "My problem is stupid little white girls. *That's* my *problem!*"

Without waiting for her to respond, the man made his move, coming at her fast with something—a slender knife—clasped in his right hand.

You picked the wrong little white girl to mess with, Jenna thought.

She shifted one foot in front of her and took one of the fighting stances her marine corps brother, Pierce, had shown her. Preparing for the attack, she raised her fists and clenched them, keeping one tucked close against her body, and the other in front, ready to block.

Seeing her stance, the black man laughed out loud. Moving swiftly, he came at her, grunting as he punched the air with the blade. Jenna reacted quickly, ducking low as she dodged to her left. While she was down, she reached into her right coat pocket and grabbed the spray can that was there. She could hear the sound of running feet now. Glancing behind her, she saw two cops moving toward her, fast, running from the other side of the rear of the auditorium. One of them looked like Danny.

Her attacker saw what she was looking at and instantly understood what was going on.

"You bitch!" he shouted, almost spitting the words. "You set me up!"

Without a word Jenna stood up quickly, raised the can, stepped close to him, and pressed the button, squirting him in the face.

He let out an enraged shout as he backed away from her, his face covered with both hands. Wiping his eyes frantically, he glared at her. Then a wide smile spread slowly across his face. "I think you'd better check the expiration date on that can of Mace, honey," he said softly, "because I don't think it's working any-more."

He pointed a finger at her, angry but grinning just the same. "I'll see you again."

After taking a quick look around at the cops hustling across the lot toward them he started running, heading across the lot and out of range of the light. Jenna was panting heavily and felt a strange tingling throughout her body as the cops joined her. It was Danny and a patrolman she didn't recognize.

"You okay?" Danny asked, his brow creased with concern.

For a moment, Jenna wasn't able to speak, but she gave him a thumbs-up as he stepped close to her and gripped her by the shoulders.

"Yeah," she said, gasping for breath.

Before she could say anything more, an intense wave of relief washed over her, making her feel suddenly cold and weak.

It's over, she thought. *I've done what I can do.*

She staggered backward a few steps and almost fell down, but Danny darted forward and caught her by the arm, giving her support.

"For a second, there," she said, hearing the tremor in her voice, "I was afraid that you weren't going to make it." Her body felt curiously light and was tingling all over. Little zigzagging dots of white light danced in front of her eyes.

"You sure you're okay?" Danny asked, his expression softening as he held her tightly in his arms. "He didn't hurt you, did he?"

"No, no. I'm fine. Just give me a minute," Jenna said, shaking her head and taking a few slow, deep breaths. "I tagged him good," she said, unable to suppress a sly grin. She couldn't believe that she had pulled it off and was still alive and breathing.

"All right," Danny said, smiling and nodding. He still had an arm around her and, even though she didn't really need the support anymore, it felt good. "Let's go see if they nailed the bastard."

chapter 13

The bitch!

His throat was dry as he ran up the walk between Coleman Auditorium and Langer Science Center, sticking to the shadows and hustling to reach the corner of the old science building. If he cut across the darkness right in front of the older building, that would take him to Somerset Circle, a theater-in-the-round utilized by the university's drama clubs.

All of which would be easier if he could see. The Blake girl had sprayed something in his eyes—it wasn't mace or pepper, far as he could tell, but it still stung!

He should have known better. That was what pissed him off more than anything. That article in the *Daily* had had enough information about Blake and the job she did that he should have expected her to be prepared for an attack. She had been attacked on campus before. Damn it! He should have known. He had known. But she had been too perfect a target to pass up, particularly after how tight things had been on campus.

In the darkness of the walkway he wiped at his eyes and then swabbed the sticky liquid off his hand and onto his pants. A moment later and he was finally able to blink the stuff out of his eyes, though it was stringing between his lashes. The path was hard and rutted beneath his feet, but he ran swift and sure.

Swift and sure, because he promised himself he was not done with Jenna Blake. He would have another chance at her. Soon as he was able, he would finish what he started tonight, and it wouldn't be the wham-bam-thank-you-ma'am of his previous kills either. He'd enjoy doing Jenna. She would bleed a lot before she died.

All of that went through his mind in the seconds it took to move up the walk and then across the lawn in front of the science building. His heart had been clenched and pounding at first, but now as he reassured himself he began to slow. Once again he had gotten away with it. And, after all, a kill was better but the attack alone was enough to serve his purposes for the moment.

Yeah. It was going to be all right.

Car doors slammed somewhere nearby but he heard no shouting, no sirens. With a final thrust of energy he ran into the tiny paved lot in front of the Somerset Circle Theater. It was an ugly old building, brown and, of course, round. There was a light on right in front and the door was unlocked.

Just as he entered he heard the shouting start close

by. The police, shouting. A siren, though still at least a block away.

He smiled. Wiped at his face again.

With a quick glance into the dimly lit foyer of the theater to be sure no one was watching, he pulled off his sweatshirt and quickly stashed it in a trash can. The jacket he had worn underneath it was a light blue, and by the time he had settled his dark red knit hat on his head, tossing the other into the trash with the sweatshirt, he had concentrated long enough that the hue of his skin was pale white, though flushed a bit pink from exertion.

Smug and quite satisfied with himself, he turned to appreciate his appearance in the reflective glass of the box-office window. Even in the dim light, his visage shocked him.

A streak of white paint was smeared across his face. It was on his hands, so now it was on his cap, his jacket, and wiped on his pants.

Suddenly he could not catch his breath.

"Oh, shit," he whispered to himself.

At the back of the theater he heard someone shouting. There was a back door. He had seen it before, cutting behind the building on his way to class.

"You're interrupting a rehearsal!" someone cried in a whiny voice.

"Police. No one move!" came a shout in return.

So there would be no refuge inside the theater. A cold sweat had broken out on his forehead, yet he managed to maintain his composure . . . his concentration. That was important. Frantically he whipped off the watch cap and tried to wipe the paint off but he knew it was fruitless. He would not get it all, and it was on his clothes regardless. Worse, he could not spare the seconds. He stared at the double doors through which he had entered the theater. Each had a square window high up, but he could see only the night beyond. No flashing police lights. That was good.

"Just go," he snarled at himself.

He swore again as he bolted at the doors and pushed through, out into the night.

In an instant the world lit up with a blaze of illumination. Spotlights, headlights, and the blue swirl from atop police cars. There were cops all over the place, weapons leveled at him.

"You've been marked, mister. It's over!" shouted a policeman over a bullhorn. "Put your hands above your head and—"

There would be more to the commands, he knew. But he did not wait for them. He had seen and heard enough. In the sheath he wore inside his belt at the small of his back, his knife felt very warm.

Inside the theater, in the dark, he had a better chance. With a cry of fury and frustration he turned and dove back through the doors. There was a shout behind him and he knew the police would follow immediately. Follow cautiously, in case he waited for them in the dark, but follow him just the same.

His mind whirled, planning. With a flash he drew his knife. There were two sets of doors entering the theater straight ahead, but also a set of stairs off to the right that would lead up into the higher rows of seats. By now the police would have evacuated the students rehearsing through the back door. Or would think they had, at least. But there might be one more.

With a moment's pause he focused his mind. It would be something he had rarely attempted, but also something they would not expect. Even then, in order to keep his concentration . . . but he had no choice. Centering himself mentally, using meditation techniques he had spent fifteen years perfecting, he altered his skin pigment to a hue that would appear roughly Asian. Then, without benefit of a mirror or much practice, he used his fingers to manipulate the soft, cartilage-like bone tissue of his face, raising his cheekbones, thinning his entire jawline.

Then, with a shout of fear and alarm, he took the knife and stabbed himself in the right side, at an angle where he could be reasonably sure not to kill himself.

The killer screamed as his own weapon pierced his flesh.

"This way!" he heard a police officer shout from up the stairs.

He focused again, forcing his skin tone to remain a bronze hue, and stumbled up the stairs and into the walkway at the top of the rows of seats, looking down on the circular stage in the middle of the theater. A police officer ran toward him, weapon drawn and aimed, shouting at him almost in a panic.

With practiced ease, he kept his painted face half-turned toward the wall, in the shadows. He cut himself off from the pain of the knife wound, the blade still jutting from him. Ignoring the pain was simple for him, a sideshow trick he had picked up years earlier, like so many others. But nobody else knew that.

He stumbled, quite purposely, and bent over, clutching at his bleeding gut, hiding his face.

"Where is he? Where were *you*? We got everybody out!" the cop shouted, looking everywhere but at the killer.

"Bathroom," he groaned in response, as if that were all the explanation that was needed.

"Damn it!" the cop snapped.

The gun was now aimed over the killer's head, into the shadows of the stairs beyond. The officer was about to move past him. The killer slid the knife easily from his own flesh, then sprang up in a single motion, thrusting the blade with both hands up under the officer's chin, burying it to its hilt.

The cop went down. But even as he fell, the killer grasped his right wrist and stole his gun.

Then he ran. There were two other cops inside the theater and as he moved at them, clutching his bleeding stomach, they hesitated at the sight of the wound. Only for a second. He shot the first one in the head, blowing gray matter and shards of skull across the stage. The second got off a single shot before taking two in the chest. A Kevlar vest saved his life, but he went down hard, dropping his weapon.

He thundered down the steps to the stage and ran for the back door, slowed only a little by his wound. For only a moment, he paused to retrieve another dead officer's gun.

With a pistol in either hand, he kicked out through the rear door of the theater.

It was far from the first time Jenna had been attacked, but in so many ways it was the worst. This guy, this freak, just seemed so inhuman and somehow alien, that when he had first confronted her, before she could react, before she could even cry out, she had frozen for just a moment. Not even a moment. An eye-blink, no more. But in that space between heartbeats, she had felt a kind of eerie, shuddering terror that was unlike anything she had ever felt before. It was as though she had been tainted.

But then she had sprayed him, and he had shouted in pain and run. As she caught her breath and watched him flee, with full knowledge that the police had been observing every move, relief flooded through her. The paint would do it. There would be no escaping for him this time.

Yet that taint, the feeling that she had been soiled in some way by his monstrous touch, remained.

Danny had reached her only seconds after the chameleon had taken off, running. Flannery was right behind him with an entire coterie of officers, both uniformed and plainclothes. The lion's share, however, went in silent pursuit of the killer. The shouts of the cops around her made Jenna feel safe, but she knew they were just as much for the chameleon's benefit as her own. That was part of the plan. Make him feel like he had a way out, an opening. Meanwhile the net was closing in.

While the killer ran, and the police moved to encircle him, Danny held Jenna in his arms.

"I'm all right," she told him yet again. "What's happening?"

Joe Flannery had been the one to tell them. The killer had run to the small theater just around the corner, two buildings away. The police had him cornered, front and back.

But then the radio squawked and someone was shouting that he'd gone back inside the theater. Both Danny and Flannery had offered up an array of colorful curses, then glanced at Jenna.

"I'm fine," she snapped. "Just get him."

"Let's back 'em up!" Danny called to the handful of other police officers who remained at the scene of her attack.

They moved as one, rushing across the parking lot behind Coleman Auditorium, and Jenna followed.

"Why are you going this way?" Jenna asked, frowning. "The theater's around the front."

"We want the back. They've got plenty of men in front, but there's a back door. He'll try that, if he can."

It felt oddly thrilling and yet safe to Jenna to be marching at a fast clip across the pavement with so many armed men and women, and noble ones at that. In her secret heart, she also reveled in the knowledge that they would catch him now and when they did it would be because of her. Her ideas, her intuitions, her research.

The bastard.

The words came almost unbidden to her mind. More bitter than she would have imagined, in spite of everything, as though they welled up from a place even deeper than that secret spot in her heart. The depths of her soul. The animal in her blood. In that moment the two things were identical. Though she would never admit it, not to Hunter and Yoshiko, not to Danny, and not even to Slick, she wanted desperately for them to shoot the chameleon, to know that he was dead and it was really over.

The murders, the chaos, the hatred on campus, all of it had been his doing. Worse, Jenna felt keenly that she had lost Damon, and she blamed the chameleon for it. It wasn't about race, what was happening between her and her boyfriend. She knew it. But she was not fool enough to think that the stress of it all had not contributed.

This was a monster, this killer. She had come across others, but none that disturbed her, that unnerved her like this one.

The police ran up behind the theater. Their weapons were drawn. Several cars, blue lights spinning, pulled up to the edge of the lot and bumped up over the grass to roll to a stop not far from the rear exit of the place.

Danny was eight or ten paces ahead of Jenna, but suddenly he stopped and turned to face her. He frowned and trotted over to her, service pistol aimed at the grass.

"You've done enough. I should've sent you home with a uniform, but this is all coming down too fast," he said. Then he called out to Sergeant Bellamy, a blond woman Jenna had met many times. "Claire! Get Jenna out of here."

"I'm not going," Jenna heard herself say, surprised at the steel in her own voice. "I'm in this, Danny. I'm not going to get in the way. I won't take another step."

He spat some angry words under his breath but did not argue. Instead he pointed to a patrol car. "Take cover, then. Do not get any closer than that vehicle." Danny gave Bellamy a hard look. "Stay with her."

"You got it, Detective," the sergeant said.

Then Danny turned and ran toward the other cops who were moving toward the rear door. Joe Flannery, with his scruff of three-day growth and beer belly, was right in front. Jenna was surprised at that, but then realized she should not have been. Flannery could be a real jerk, but that did not mean he wasn't a good and courageous cop.

"Come on, Jenna," Bellamy said, taking hold of her arm.

They began to hurry toward the patrol car when a series of muffled thumps came from within the theater.

"Shots fired!" Bellamy called out.

"Danny!" Jenna turned to go after him, but the sergeant grabbed her arm and hauled her in back of the patrol car to take cover.

When Jenna looked up over the car she saw that Danny and the others were falling back a respectful distance as well. They had not gotten twenty feet when the back door burst open and the killer appeared. His features were Asian, or Indian, she could not be sure, but the streak of white was across his face. There were other clues to his identity as well.

He held a pistol in each hand.

"Guns!" Jenna shouted on instinct, and found herself calling out in unison with Bellamy and several other officers.

Too late to help the young Latino in uniform who was closest to the back door. He was the first to be shot, and the bullet tore away the left side of his face, spun him around and dropped him to the ground like he was a toppled scarecrow.

Bullets flew. As though he had completely lost control, the killer's pigment seemed to flow. His skin color changed from light to dark and back again. His face changed, and she realized that his features must be returning to normal, to his real face. A face she had never seen.

His guns roared.

Several other cops were hit even as they started to return fire, shooting at the chameleon.

Jenna caught his eye. She stared at him, there in the sickly glare thrown by the parking lot lights, and he saw her. It was only a single instant of recognition, and then it was followed by another. For once he had seen her, his expression turned even more savage and he began to swing his arms over to aim both guns at her, a pair of smoking barrels pointing her way.

She *felt* the bullets tearing through the air toward her and he had not even fired at her yet.

Gunshots rang out. Fifteen feet in front of the patrol car where Jenna stood, Danny Mariano and Joe Flannery stood side by side and fired at the chameleon.

Somebody hit him. The bullet punched through his shoulder and spun him around. A second hit him in the back and knocked him down. He shifted once, there on the ground, trying to get up. Then he collapsed and was still.

The reaction was instantaneous. Cops swarmed in from the parking lot and from around the front of the theater. Others who had pursued the chameleon into the theater from the front came out the back with guns drawn. They all had their guns drawn.

Jenna had never seen so many guns.

Police radios barked all around. Officers shouted to one another and to faceless authorities on their radios. Blue and red lights swirled from atop patrol cars and not far off an ambulance siren could be heard. Danny and Joe Flannery were among the group of cops that moved in on the unmoving killer. They had their arms out straight before them, rigid with tension and wariness, gun barrels aimed at the man whose blood was steaming on the frozen ground.

"Nailed the SOB," Sergeant Bellamy said quietly.

Jenna glanced at her, frowning. It would have been nice if she felt half as confident, but she did not. Her instinct should have been to go to Danny, confirm he was all right, let him know she was okay, and then go home. Go home and sleep and try to forget the long, disturbing nightmare she had been through. But either there was something wrong with her instincts or she had been shaken so badly that a man barely dead was already haunting her.

A feeling came over her, so familiar and yet so obscenely troublesome. Her lips and tongue tingled with the urge to speak, to say something, to form words that her brain had not yet supplied to them. Her mind churned with a ghost of a thought that she was unable to express. Every fiber of her being crackled with the knowledge that there was danger here, and yet her rational mind took in all the police officers surrounding her and told her instincts to shut up.

With all those guns pointing at the chameleon, and all that blood on the ground already, Jenna should not have been so afraid when Joe Flannery knelt by the killer's still form. The Cambridge cop reached out and grabbed the man's wrist, felt for a pulse. He held on for what seemed to Jenna an inordinately long time. Then Flannery dropped the man's arm, and his expression made it clear.

The chameleon was dead.

Finally Jenna allowed herself a sigh of relief. Her danger-radar was still squawking but starting to subside. The corpse was facedown on the ground and a couple of uniforms moved in to roll him over. Jenna stood on tiptoe, peering across the frozen grass, trying to see the killer's face. Even with so many flashlights on him, she could not make out his features. But she could see the color of his skin. Not white. Not very dark, though.

Her gaze went quickly to Danny. He seemed surprised as he glanced over at her.

"Jules Barros," he called, a frown creasing his forehead.

Jenna's mouth opened in a small O of surprise and though she was aware of how silly it must have made her look it took several moments of focus to erase the expression. Jules Barros, main mouthpiece for the Coalition for Racial Diversity, the man who had become the central figure in the racial strife on campus, as a huge percentage of the student body looked to him for leadership.

"Barros," Sergeant Bellamy said. She turned to Jenna, her blond hair strobed with blue from the lights of the patrol car, breath pluming in the cold air. "Isn't that?—"

"Yeah," Jenna interrupted.

"I don't get it," Bellamy said. "Do you think he did all this to make himself the center of attention? Just for the power?"

Jenna had an idea that there was much more to it than that. A guy growing up with the condition Barros had, not to mention with whatever other racial tensions existed for him, it was possible that skin color, race in general, had become anathema to him. He hated all races with equal fervor. That last, at least, she felt certain of. But why he did it, really?

"Guess we'll never know," she said, both to Bellamy and to Danny, who was too far away to hear her, but who would see the confounded expression on her face and understand.

And he did.

Detective Mariano shook his head as he turned back toward the corpse. Already several of the uniformed cops had moved off to begin taping off the crime scene. Jenna knew that Slick would be called, and that he would most certainly scold her for taking such grave risks.

Slick. He wouldn't have the trouble getting close to the corpse this time that he had had the first time they thought Jules Barros—she had been thinking of him as the chameleon—was dead. There had been snow then, but it all had melted off now, before growing much colder again tonight. Slick would be able to get close enough.

Jenna swallowed hard. Pulse. Flannery had checked Barros's pulse but nothing else. The guy had been shot twice, but still.

All along there had been words on the tip of her tongue. Now they were ready to come out, loud and clear, exorcising the annoying little demon that had been gnawing at the back of her mind. Jenna called out to Danny and he turned toward her. Even as he did, though, Jenna looked past him, at Joe Flannery, who stood only a few feet from the corpse of the killer and smoked a cigarette, joking with Mike Cardiff in that old-boy network way.

"Make sure he's dead!" she shouted to Danny.

He looked thoughtful for a second, then turned to stare at the corpse. Beside Jenna, Sergeant Bellamy laughed.

"He pulled one over on us before, Jenna," the

woman said. "But he's got two bullets in him now. You saw him go down."

But Danny did not brush her off so easily.

"How?" Detective Mariano called back.

It sounded like a stupid question, but it was far from that. If the man had no pulse, no other life signs, how were they supposed to know if he was really dead or not?

"Just watch him closely until Slick gets here," she called back, self-conscious now, because at least a dozen nearby officers and detectives were staring at her.

"Oh, come on!" she heard one of them say with a snicker.

Which was when it happened, just as the tiny voice in her head and the enormous dread in her heart had feared it would.

"Danny!" Jenna shouted in alarm.

Others were shouting as well, but not at Danny. They were shouting at Joe Flannery, who had a cigarette in his gun hand when Jules Barros rose up, clothes soaked in blood and streaked with white paint, stripped the aging detective's gun from its holster and then shot him in the back of the head.

Flannery went down amidst screams of fury and horror. Barros kept firing and managed to shoot Cardiff once in the chest before every one of the cops on the scene let loose. Jules Barros's body did an obscene, macabre dance as the bullets tore through him, and yet he managed to stay on his feet as they drove him back four or five steps. Bullets shattered bone, tore flesh, sent blood spraying against the wall of the theater. Finally, just short of the rear door, he went down.

Jenna was surprised to find herself crying, not for Barros, but out of pure horror. Sergeant Bellamy had fired her service weapon until it was empty, and Jenna wondered if she had paid much attention to the three other cops who were in her field of fire. Fortunately, none of them, including Danny, had been hit.

"Make sure he's dead?" Bellamy shouted suddenly. She opened the patrol car door, reached in, and popped a shotgun off its rack. "I'll make sure he's goddamned dead!"

"Claire, what are you doing?" Danny shouted at her as she marched toward them, toward the dead man, across the frozen grass.

"I'm making sure he's dead!" she screamed at him, right up in his face.

For Sergeant Bellamy, and many of the officers on the scene, Jenna realized that a line had been crossed between possible and impossible. To her it was science, pure and simple. Weird, sure, but real and true. To them . . . it simply could not be. Jules Barros was dead. Whatever he had managed to survive before, cutting out the pain and slowing his pulse and respiration to almost nothing, that was one thing. But the chameleon was little more than roadkill now. Torn flesh and bone barely recognizable as human.

Jenna thought that was both ironic and appropriate.

She could have told the spooked cops that Barros was dead. Danny must have known it, too. But the

CHRISTOPHER GOLDEN

anger and guilt and awe over what had just happened made them all stay silent as Bellamy stalked over to the bullet-ravaged corpse of a killer, leveled a shotgun at his chest, and fired both barrels.

The blasts echoed across the Somerset campus.

Then, quiet.

252

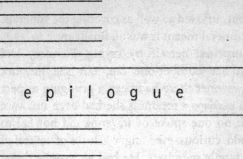

On a pristine morning, under a crystal blue sky, Detective Sergeant Joe Flannery was buried in his hometown of Everett, Massachusetts. His family was there, of course, and the Cambridge Police Department gave him a send-off complete with the kind of pomp and circumstance that would have had the gruff old cop muttering with annoyance had he been in attendance rather than the subject of the services. It was a solemn service, with full honors, flags flying, and hundreds of police officers from all over the state, a sea of blue uniforms.

Joe Flannery was the last of four police officers killed by Jules Barros to be buried, and the only detective among them. It was a tragedy that echoed from Somerset, through Beacon Hill in Boston, and across Massachusetts.

Even the media kept a respectful distance. They had spent days interviewing the officers who had been wounded but survived as well as covering the funerals. Flannery's funeral meant it was all finally over.

Jenna surprised herself by crying. Flannery had never been her number-one fan, nor she his, but despite his manner there had been a grudging respect there, even perhaps a fondness she had been unaware of. Though no one spoke of it, Jenna did not fail to catch the odd, curious, even angry glances of several of Flannery's family members. He had an ex-wife there, but it was the deceased's two grown children, both in their late twenties or so, whose expressions bothered Jenna the most.

The chameleon had been a Somerset P.D. case. The department had called upon other local police forces for backup, but none of them had to go. Flannery had been willing to make the trek, make the extra effort, because Jenna Blake had put herself in the way of danger and Flannery had not wanted to see anything bad happen to her.

So every time one of his family glanced at her oddly—even though she knew it might well be her imagination—Jenna could not help but think *it's my fault. He's dead because of me.* The worst part was that, in a sense, it was true. Not that she had that kind of control over anyone. Flannery was a grown-up. He knew what he was doing, and it was his job, and he might have helped out on the case no matter who the bait was. But that did not change the circumstances.

The only thing that helped Jenna weather those odd looks and her own feelings of guilt was the certainty that Jules Barros would still be at large, still be killing.

The fallout from that night had been immediate. Her mother was furious with her but instead of rushing up to Somerset to take her to dinner or out shopping to have it out and work at Jenna's conscience like a dentist on a root canal, once April Blake was certain her daughter was all right and there would be no additional Missions Impossible for the time being, she did not call Jenna for days out of absolute fury.

Fury and helplessness. When they finally spoke, that very morning, April revealed that yes, she was angry, but more than that, she was horrified by the thought of what might have happened. The idea that the first couple of times Jenna had been in danger might not have been a fluke, that this sort of thing might happen again, filled her with despair.

Jenna promised it would never happen again, but they both knew she was lying, that she would put herself in danger if she thought it was necessary. Not that she was in any rush to do that, but they both knew. They knew. In those days when, instead of fussing over her, April had let her be, Jenna had understood that, at last, her mother considered her an adult.

She was far from certain how to feel about that.

When Flannery's funeral was over, Danny and Audrey walked over to meet Jenna and Slick as they all went back to their cars. Audrey grimaced as she walked, favoring one side, so that even if Jenna had not been aware of her hospitalization it would have been obvious that she had been injured. There was a little something extra in the grimace as well, and Jenna knew right off what it was: self-loathing. Danny had once revealed how completely Audrey hated weakness, particularly in herself. She had fought so hard to reach the level she had in her career, a fight made more difficult by her race and gender, that she hated showing any sort of vulnerability at all.

In that way, it occurred to Jenna, Audrey was not unlike Slick.

It came as no surprise, then, that when the detectives approached, Slick did not ask how Audrey was faring. Jenna took his lead. They all said their hellos, passed a few words about Flannery, and then Audrey looked at Jenna with uncommon tenderness.

"How are things on campus?" she asked.

"Still very tense," Jenna replied. "A lot of bad feeling is still out there. And the Frank Abernathys of the world don't go away when a killer is caught. SAAL is claiming the killer would have been caught sooner if you guys hadn't focused so much on race."

Danny scoffed. "Like the racial element of the case wasn't important? It was all about race."

"Revisionist history," Audrey told him. "Pretty much what I expected."

"It's going to take a while for it to all go away, but I really think it will," Jenna said. "It may be next semester, after a long summer break, before things really start to feel right again, but we'll get there. Nobody can live like this forever."

Audrey's expression hardened. "I wish that were true."

"It's cold out here," Danny put in. "Not to mention maybe not the best place in the world to catch up. Why don't we go have a coffee, maybe someplace with fewer dead people?"

They all agreed, but Slick suggested they go back to Somerset first. If he needed to rush off in a hurry he did not want to leave Jenna stranded or dependent upon Danny and Audrey for a ride. Jenna had ridden over with the M.E., and he drove her back as well. She knew that the only reason he agreed to coffee was for her sake. It was a lot of trouble for him to get in and out of the van just for a moment of socialization, but he did it without balking at all.

In the van on the way to Paula's Bakery Café, they were silent for quite a while. Jenna figured Danny and Audrey were already there, given that they both drove too fast. Slick took his time. He never rushed anything, in fact.

"How are you?" he finally asked, when they were crossing into Somerset.

Jenna smiled warily. "You've asked me that about ten times in the last three days."

He kept his eyes on the road, but he did not smile. "This time I want you to tell the truth. How are you?"

Her smile faltered. "I've been better," she confessed. A lock seemed to open somewhere in her and a torrent of emotions and words came out. She told him about her feelings of guilt, and about her mother, and a lot of other things besides. By the time they were parking near Paula's, Jenna glanced over at him and started to laugh.

"What's funny?" he demanded.

"This," she said. "I just . . . I guess you weren't expecting such a thorough answer, huh?"

He put the van in Park, then turned to her and reached out for her hand. She let him take it, though she was surprised by the tenderness of the act.

Slick studied her eyes. "You are not responsible for Joe Flannery's death, Detective Cardiff's being wounded, or anything else that happened."

"I know that," Jenna started.

"Jenna," Slick said, voice hard and clear. He stared at her. "You are not responsible."

She swallowed and caught her breath. Closed her eyes and nodded. When he squeezed her hand again, she opened them and saw that he looked angry.

"From now on, though, you clear your plans with me before suggesting them to the police. I would never have approved of you playing bait if I had been prepared."

Jenna balked. "It wasn't part of my job. I don't understand why I need to—"

"Because if you don't you won't have a job," he told her firmly.

She could see that he meant it. And also that he cared very deeply.

"All right," Jenna agreed.

When the van was all locked up and Slick was propelling himself along the sidewalk to Paula's beside Jenna, he paused to give her that grave look once more.

"By the way," he said, "you're also not responsible for what happened with Damon. It isn't easy to do what you're doing and keep a relationship, but sometimes I wonder if that isn't half an excuse. It isn't ever easy, really."

"How did you know?" Jenna asked, surprised that

he would have realized or even noticed that anything had happened between herself and Damon.

Slick frowned. "I'm neither blind nor deaf, Jenna."

Then he preceded her into the café, and Jenna found herself, miraculously, laughing softly. "No. That's for sure," she said to his back, though not really loud enough for him to hear.

Damon had come by only once in the days since the bloody climax of the chameleon case. The morning after it all happened, when the police were still putting it all together and even Jenna was writing a report for Slick to attach to his own, there had been a knock on the door. From her desk, Jenna had turned to look up at Yoshiko, who sat reading on the top bunk.

Somehow, both of them knew who it was. Perhaps they had become used to his knock. Either that, Jenna had thought later, or it was one of those weird psychic moments people get from time to time.

When she opened the door and saw Damon standing there, hands in his pockets, concern plain on his face, she felt her love for him rise up within her again. Angry as she had been at him, she was only sad.

"Hey," she had said softly.

"Just wanted to make sure you were all right," he said, shrugging as though he felt the need to apologize for looking after her.

"I'm fine," Jenna replied.

For nearly a minute they looked at each other and searched for some way to put their feelings into words. When that minute had elapsed, they took another one.

"I guess I'll see you later," Damon had finally said.

All Jenna had been able to muster at the time was "yeah." Just "yeah," and she hated herself for it.

After that, they saw each other in the corridor or the stairs from time to time, and exchanged nothing more than greetings. Damon was still angry with her, and hurting from all the pain that had gone around like some kind of virus. Jenna still thought he had been completely over the line . . . but she wanted a chance to start again, to pull it all back.

When Damon came to the door again, the day after Flannery's funeral, she was very glad that Yoshiko was not there. Once again, the expression on his face spoke his feelings with great eloquence.

"Can I come in?" he asked, eyes steady, meeting her gaze.

Jenna nodded and stepped back. Damon came into the room and wandered over to her desk. He picked up a serpentine-shaped brain teaser, a puzzle made of a hundred tiny shapes of various colors, and fiddled with it a moment.

"Damon."

He turned.

"Jenna, listen, I've turned this over in my head a million times," he began. "I really do care about you—"

She held up a hand. "Stop." Her gaze drifted and as hard as she tried to force herself to focus, to look at him, she could not. She wondered if she was simply not as brave as he was.

"Just tell me one thing," she asked, voice low and tight. She had known it was coming, but that did not make it easier. Not at all. "I know better now than to think that race isn't important. I was naive before. Probably still am. Maybe it's just human nature, maybe it's just society and how screwed up everything is. But race is an issue. Sometimes it's a problem. I guess what I want to know is, was it *our* problem?"

Damon began to shake his head before she was even finished. "No," he said adamantly. "No, Jenna—"

"Because with all we've had to deal with the past couple of weeks, if you said it was a problem for you, I would understand. Really, I would. I just have to know. I . . . care for you, Damon. A lot. The color of your skin never mattered to me."

"But Barros made it matter, Jenna," Damon said flatly. "You don't care. There are plenty who do."

Jenna grew angry. "So what? I don't care about what anybody else thinks!"

"Neither do I," Damon said firmly. "It wasn't easy. It wouldn't have been easy. But this? What's happening with us? It isn't about race. I swear to God it isn't. I'm selfish. I know that. But I guess I just need someone to whom I'm more of a priority. Someone I don't have to be afraid for all the time. You're miles away, Jenna. You're out in the real world already and the rest of us are back here just getting an education between parties. I guess some of that is part of this, too. You've got a whole other world out there that doesn't include me."

Jenna allowed herself the tiniest laugh, but there was no smile to go with it. She shook her head. "God, you really are selfish."

Damon nodded in agreement. "No doubt."

Finally she met his gaze. "You're not going to start dodging me now, are you?"

He smiled. That beautiful, arrogant, charming smile that she had noticed the very first time they had bumped into each other in the corridor.

"J, come on," Damon said. "I live down the hall. My friends are your friends. Even if I wanted to dodge you, which I do not, I couldn't do it."

Before she could talk herself out of it, she went to him and slid her arms around him. Damon held her tightly and kissed her on the top of the head and Jenna bit her lip and forced herself not to cry. Damon was not the only selfish one. Valentine's Day was coming up, and so was her birthday, and she could not help thinking how they would hurt without him.

With a deep sigh she pushed him away. "All right, get out of here," she said, only half teasing, and shoved him toward the door.

She would be all right. Jenna promised herself that. She had loved Damon, but not for very long, after all. It would hurt, but it was not as if she had not felt it coming. Part of her was very relieved that it had finally happened, if she allowed herself to feel that sensation. Things had gone sour between them very fast, and she thought it was better that it should be over rather than drag on.

After Damon had gone, his words still echoed in her mind. *It isn't about race*, he had promised. But the more she thought about it, the more she became convinced that they would never know that for sure.

*   *   *

All that changed less than three weeks later. It was a Tuesday, and warm enough that a lot of students were sitting out on the library roof, reading and studying. Still winter, certainly, but a tempting hint of spring not far off. Jenna had been reading Raymond Chandler, *The Big Sleep*, and had looked up to see Damon walking along the path behind Brunswick Chapel.

He had his arm around Caitlin Janssen and they were laughing together.

A bitter thought flashed across her mind. *I guess it really wasn't about race.* She closed her eyes and swallowed hard as a shiver went through her, and suddenly she learned a difficult truth. She had wanted it to be about race. Ugly as it was, that would have made it easier to take; it would have been something out of her control.

Jenna lifted the book to hide her face but could no longer read the words. She wondered if the people around her had noticed; if they could tell she had a broken heart.

Turn the page for
a preview of
the next
Body of Evidence thriller

BURNING BONES

Available February 2001

If looks could kill.

That was the phrase that jumped into Laura Depuy's head when she saw Alan Nash hustling along the sidewalk toward her, twenty-seven minutes late by her watch. She glared daggers that would have dropped him in his tracks . . . if looks could kill. Laura liked Alan, she truly did. But she was a stickler for punctuality, and it frustrated her endlessly that he simply could not seem to arrive anywhere less than fifteen minutes late. Fifteen. That was actually on time for Alan. It seemed like very little when she thought about it, but when twenty, thirty, or even forty minutes late was more common, it became a lot less tolerable.

To Laura, it represented a lack of respect and consideration. Alan did not understand how much she resented the implication that her time was somehow less valuable than his.

If looks could kill.

It was a Friday night, the first week of March, and though the days had started getting longer, and spring was tantalizingly close, it was still winter in New England. After dark there was never any mistake about that. It was cold. Laura shivered as she stood in front of DePasquale Brothers, a faded little Italian restaurant on a back street in Somerset, where she and Alan had dinner at least once every couple of months, mainly out of Alan's nostalgia. Laura didn't think much of the place, honestly. The decor was tacky, and the food was just okay, but Alan and his father had gone there all the time when he was a boy. Alan, Sr., was dead now, so Laura was fairly good-natured about these regular visits to DePasquale's. It meant a lot to her boyfriend.

The one she wanted to kill at the moment.

She shivered as a party of seven parked across the street and hurried toward the restaurant's front door, barely beating Alan to the restaurant. They went in, only to be added to the list of those waiting to be seated inside. The place was not *that* good, but it was a neighborhood favorite, had been there forever, and on Friday nights, at least, it was busy.

Like tonight.

"Hey, babe. Sorry I'm late," Alan said quickly as he reached her. He slipped his arms around her and held her close, kissing her forehead.

Laura stood stiffly, unsmiling. Alan released her and stood back to regard her carefully.

"Come on, Laura. Don't be that way. I got held up at the office. I had a closing today, and it ran long."

"You *always* have a closing," she said bitterly. "And it *always* runs long."

"Look, the real estate market—"

"Is hot right now," she finished for him. "And who knows how long things will stay like this, and you're a real estate lawyer, and you've got to take advantage of the market while you can, and on and on."

He gazed at her sullenly. Several moments passed before he spoke again. "What do you want me to say?"

"I don't want you to say anything, Alan," she

snapped. "I want you to do something. I want you to be *on time* for a change. Apparently that's too much to ask, but it's what I want."

Alan winced. "Don't you think you're overreacting just a little?"

Laura gaped at him, astounded at the depths of his tactlessness. She shuddered again, but now it was with anger rather than cold. A dozen responses came to mind, including two that would have ended their relationship on the spot. Despite her anger, that was not what she wanted. Alan was a decent, kind man, handsome and well-educated and funny when he wanted to be. He wore little round glasses that somehow matched his small mouth perfectly, and his hair was perpetually trimmed much too short, as if he believed being a lawyer required it. His absentmindedness could sometimes be charming. But the lateness, it was just so . . .

"Do you have any idea how rude you can be?" she sputtered, shaking her head. "I have been waiting here for you for three quarters of an hour. You're half an hour late. Our reservation has long since been given away. Add to that the fact that it's cold out here, in case you hadn't noticed, and that this is not necessarily where I would choose for us to go out to eat on a Friday night. Then throw in your general attitude, and that innocent, who-me façade of ignorance you work so hard to cultivate—at least I hope to God that's it, 'cause I would hate it if you were actually as dismissive of my part in this relationship and as totally lacking in courtesy as you appear to be. Add that all up, Alan, with the fact that you do this all the time, and then tell me if you think I'm overreacting."

Eyes wide, Alan stared at her dumbfounded, then blinked a few times, as if someone had just popped an extra bright camera flash in front of his face.

"I thought you liked to eat here," he said, a tiny bit of whine in his voice.

"Oh, for God's sake, Alan!" Laura cried, throwing up her hands.

Alan laughed and reached for her. "No, no, I'm kidding. Really."

"Not funny," Laura told him firmly.

"I really am sorry," he said, his voice low. He reached out and grabbed her hands and held them gently. "You're right, of course. You always are. I'm an ass sometimes and I know it. And yeah, sometimes I don't think about how annoying and inconvenient it is for you when I'm late. *Mea culpa*. Punish me as you see fit."

Laura looked at him, seething with anger.

"But I love you, Laura. I do, and all I can do is promise that I'll be more aware and more considerate. I swear I'll make it up to you. Starting right now. Want to go somewhere else? Capitol Grill? Il Bacio? You name it."

Though she still wanted to make him suffer, he was so earnest in his apology that Laura could not stop a tiny smile from tugging at the corners of her mouth. She rolled her eyes.

"Next time I will *not* wait. Are we clear on that? I will be gone."

"Clear as crystal. Waterford crystal."

With a sigh, she relented. "We can stay here. I know it's special to you. But I will take a rain check on *both* the Capitol Grill and Il Bacio, and I don't care how many closings you have, I want you to schedule a long weekend in April so we can go to New Orleans."

Alan grinned. "Done."

"Good," she said, and nodded once, sharply. "Now go in there and pull some strings and get us a table pronto, 'cause I'm starving."

He looked at her tenderly, then stepped close to kiss her lightly on the lips. "I love you, Laura."

"Hungry," she replied coolly. Then she smiled. "I love you too."

Alan opened the door to DePasquale Brothers and stepped into the little foyer. A party of four was just leaving, and in the narrow space they had to jockey around one another. Alan bumped into one of the women, apologized, and then bumped a man as he backed up. He smiled sheepishly, and the expression only endeared him further to Laura.

She stood aside, holding the door open for the people who were leaving. Then she looked back into the foyer.

Alan was staring at her in alarm, as though he had just thought of something catastrophic. He spoke her name, but his voice had died and there was only a whisper left. For just a moment she feared he might be having a heart attack of some kind. There was panic in his eyes, and he stared at her as though he thought she might be able to do something to help him.

Then Alan burst into flame.

All at once, fire engulfed his body. His clothes and hair blazed even more brightly than the rest of him, but Laura could see that his skin was burning too.

Blistering. The flames covered him in shimmering waves.

Alan was screaming.

Laura realized that she was screaming too.

The people on the sidewalk and inside the restaurant were shouting in alarm and horror. A waiter thought quickly enough to run for the nearest fire extinguisher.

Alan fell to the ground and thrashed about, trying to put out the flames. His skin started to blacken, and after a moment, his thrashing slowed to shocking convulsions.

By the time the waiter arrived and doused the flames with chemical foam, Alan was dead.

Laura kept screaming.

Look for the next
Body of Evidence **thriller**
BURNING BONES
by Christopher Golden and Rick Hautala
Available from Pocket Pulse
February 2001

about the author

CHRISTOPHER GOLDEN is the award-winning, *L.A. Times*–best-selling author of such novels as *Strangewood*, *Straight on 'til Morning*, and the three-volume *Shadow Saga*. His other works include *Hellboy: The Lost Army* and the *Body of Evidence* series of teen thrillers (including *Thief of Hearts* and *Soul Survivor*), which is currently being developed for television by Viacom.

He has also written or cowritten a great many books, both novels and nonfiction, based on the popular TV series *Buffy the Vampire Slayer* and the world's number one comic book, *X-Men*.

Golden's comic-book work includes *Batman: Realworlds*, *Wolverine/Punisher: Revelation*; stints on *The Crow*, *Spider-Man Unlimited*, *Buffy the Vampire Slayer*, and *Batman Chronicles*; and the ongoing monthly *Angel* series, tying into the *Buffy* television spin-off.

As a pop culture journalist, he was the editor of the Bram Stoker Award–winning book of criticism, *CUT!: Horror Writers on Horror Film*, and coauthor of both *Buffy the Vampire Slayer: The Monster Book* and *The Stephen King Universe*.

ABOUT THE AUTHOR

Golden was born and raised in Massachusetts, where he still lives with his family. He graduated from Tufts University. He is currently at work on *Prowlers*, a new horror series for Pocket Books. There are more than three million copies of his books in print. Please visit him at www.christophergolden.com.

. . . A GIRL BORN
WITHOUT THE FEAR GENE

FEARLESS™

A SERIES BY
FRANCINE PASCAL

FROM POCKET PULSE
PUBLISHED BY POCKET BOOKS

3029

Buffy the Vampire Slayer™

SPIKE AND DRU:
PRETTY MAIDS ALL IN A ROW

The year is 1940.

In exchange for a powerful jewel, Spike and Drusilla agree to kill the current Slayer—and all those targeted to succeed her. If they succeed with their plans of bloodlust and power, it could mean the end of the Chosen One—*all* of the Chosen Ones—forever....

A *Buffy* hardcover
by Christopher Golden

Available from Pocket Books